They rounded a bend in the path, and Fraser pulled Claire behind a tree. She stood on the hump of roots, which put her almost at eye level with him. She leaned against the tree and waited to see what he would do.

He drew her into his arms and held her close, their bodies intimately aligned. Everything inside her seemed to thicken, while her heartbeat escalated. She felt quivery with anticipation, and so hungry for him she had to force herself to wait and let him take the lead.

His hands were caressing the sides of her neck now, while he trailed kisses over her face, whispering endearments, and telling her how much he missed her; how much he thought about the time they had made love.

He unbuttoned her dress, and his hand cupped her breast and lifted it so it was exposed. Her body, reacting to him, his nearness and his words, was running ahead of her, not heeding her reminders to be reserved.

Also by ELAINE COFFMAN

THE HIGHLANDER
THE ITALIAN
THE FIFTH DAUGHTER
THE BRIDE OF BLACK DOUGLAS

ELAINE
COFFMAN
LET ME BE YOUR
HERO

MIRA®

ISBN 0-7783-2092-8

LET ME BE YOUR HERO

www.MIRABooks.com

Printed in U.S.A.

For Enrique Iglesias

Your children are not your children.
They are the sons and daughters of Life's longing
for itself.
They come through you but not from you,
And though they are with you, yet they belong
not to you.
You may give them your love but not
your thoughts. For they have their
own thoughts.
You may house their bodies but not their souls,
For their souls dwell
in the house of tomorrow,
which you cannot visit, not even in
your dreams.
You may strive to be like them, but seek
not to make them like you.
For life goes not backward nor tarries
with yesterday.
You are the bows from which your children
as living arrows are sent forth.
The archer sees the mark upon the path of the
infinite, and He bends you with His might,
that His arrows may go swift and far.
Let your bending in the archer's hand
be for gladness;
For even as He loves the arrow that flies,
so He loves also the bow that is stable.

—Kahlil Gibran (1883–1931)
Lebanese-American mystic,
painter and poet
The Prophet "On Children" (1923)

One

Lennox Castle, Inchmurrin Island
Loch Lomond, Scotland
In the year of our Lord, 1741

It is said that the people of Scotland are molded by the landscape.

If that be true, then the four daughters of Alasdair, Lord Errick, 18th Earl of Errick and Mains, would be as tranquil and quiet as the slow, smooth running waters of the River Leven, whose very name comes from the Gaelic word *llevyn,* meaning slow.

But that was not the way of it.

In truth, when one thought of the earl's four young daughters, it did not evoke an image of the placid, meandering rivers or the sweet-natured and gentle hills at the southern end of the bonnie shores of Loch Lomond. Rather, they called to mind more high-spirited, descriptive Gaelic locution; that of the rugged glens and mountains of the northern end of the loch that gave birth to the tumultuous waterfalls and raging hill burns, so oft poetically described.

"Where a wild stream, with headlong shock,
Comes brawling down its bed of rock."

The earl's daughters considered it fortunate that, in 1390, Duncan, the 14th Earl, abandoned Balloch Castle on the Leven River in favor of a new stronghold on Inchmurrin Island, not only to escape the plague, but also because he considered it more secure against attack. Little did he know that almost four hundred years later, his gladsome descendants would delight in his choice of an island in the southern end of Loch Lomond—or mind you, that he chose the best and largest—as the place to build Lennox Castle.

And that is how it came to be that Lord Errick and his family happened to reside within the fortified walls of their stronghold, secluded in the beauty of a beloved, remote island called Inchmurrin.

Besides his daughters, Claire, fifteen; Kenna, fourteen; Greer, thirteen; and the youngest, ten-year-old Briana, the earl was also father to three sons: nineteen-year-old Breac, seventeen-year-old Ronaln, and Kendrew, age twelve. In a time when treachery, murder and plots abounded, the earl's children passed a happy childhood within the confining bounds of Inchmurrin, protected and loved by their father, the powerful earl and chief of the ancient Celtic Clan Lennox.

As they grew older, the earl's eldest sons, Breac and Ronaln, began to leave the island to accompany their father as he groomed his heir, Breac, Master of Lennox, to follow him as the 19th Earl of Errick and Mains, and prepared Ronaln to be the man he was meant to be.

As for the earl's daughters, they were safely co-

cooned in the embrace of the lovely island, where they were free to explore the three-quarter-by-two-mile island, end to end, to their hearts' content—all under the watchful eye of their governess, Aggie Buchanan, and Dermot MacFarlane, who always accompanied them.

And speaking of the earl's daughters, they were, at this very moment, fighting their way through a dense growth of rhododendrons that grew near the remains of a seventh-century monastery founded by the tutelary saint of Paisley, St. Murrin, which was where the island got its name.

A light breeze stirred. Light filtered through the trees nearby. A stag drinking at the lake's edge lifted his head, water dripping from his muzzle. He sniffed the breeze searching for a scent before he turned to climb the bank. When he reached the highest vantage point, he stamped his foot and breathed heavily through flared nostrils.

The stag stamped again, and snorted as he lowered his head to swing his antlers, as if trying to meet some unknown challenge.

Leaves rustled. A twig snapped.

From somewhere within the dappled shadows of the woods laughter rang out, as if the rhododendrons themselves shook with the voice of joy.

Three young girls emerged, as if driven by a March wind. Wearing identical green capes, they ran out of the forest and stopped. One by one, they pushed their hoods back, and the sun drew fire from hair in varying shades of red.

Briana, the youngest, put her hands to her hips, in the same manner as Aggie often did, and called out, "Claire? Claire Lennox, are ye deaf?"

"No," a voice called back. "My hair is caught in the rhododendrons."

"We told ye not to be pushing yer hood back," Kenna said.

"Faith! I am as trussed as the knight what rode the hippogriff behind Atlantes!" Claire called back.

This was followed by such a racket coming from the thicket that Greer glared at her sisters and called out, "Claire, will ye be needin' some help?"

Leaves rustled. "Oof! Ouch! I willna have a hair on me haid if this keeps up. Ooch...! Aah... There! I ken I have it now, thank ye kindly."

The leaves parted, and Claire Lennox stepped into the clearing, her dress torn in half a dozen places, while a good portion of the rhododendron bush dangled from the long tendrils of her bright red hair.

Claire had barely joined her sisters when Aggie and Dermot came around the bend in the path, followed by three brindly gray deerhounds, Lord Duffus, MacTavish, and Maddy. The dogs caught the scent of the deer and broke into a run.

The stag was an old one, and wise, for instead of running he turned and leaped into the lake and began to swim toward the western shore. The dogs followed until Dermot called them back.

The dogs returned, and Lord Duffus, who so loved Claire, stopped next to her and sat down. He watched her with a soft look in his dark brown eyes. She smiled and spoke endearingly to him, then put a hand on his flat head and began to scratch her way back to his ears. She could not help smiling at his almost euphoric expression. Was there ever a dog who could turn ear-scratching into a mystical experience, or display a look of such enraptured bliss? Aah, ecstasy. There must be nothing like it.

While Claire was attending to Duffus's need for attention, Aggie had been observing Claire with a critical eye. "Och! Ye are a fright," she said. " 'Tis glad I am that yer father is away, with him wanting ye to become a lady 'n all. Have ye forgotten what I said to ye, and how a lass must think o' herself as a flower? Ye with yer fair skin and red hair—'tis yer mother's Celtic bluid showing, ye ken, and ye must have a care for yer complexion." She stepped back and looked Claire over, as if wanting to make certain she did not miss something. "Tsk-tsk-tsk… 'Tis no fine example ye be setting for yer sisters. To think that such affected tricks should flourish in the earl's eldest daughter. Why, just look at ye. How am I to teach ye the refinements when ye look like ye have been wallowing with the pigs? What have ye been into, lass?"

Claire was rubbing her head. "The rhododendrons held me fast. I have left half o' my hair with the tree."

Aggie began to pick the twigs and leaves out of Claire's hair. "Weel, if it is half o' yer hair, and ye have this much left, then I ken ye had too much to begin with," she said.

Dermot, a man of few words, had been silently observing them. "Are ye hurt, lass?"

"No, my head throbs, but 'tis nothing mortal, ye ken." Claire lifted her skirts to observe the damage to her blue gown. "It would seem my gown has seen the worst o' it."

"Ye should take the path and not be going through the rhododendrons like a heathen. Ye are yer father's eldest daughter, and although ye should see to the setting of a fine example for yer sisters, ye dinna. Mrs. Buchanan was right, I ken, to tell ye to be mindful ye are a lady. Have a thought for yer age, lass, for ye willna be finding yersel' a husband cavorting about like that."

Claire saw the scowling black line of his bushy brows, but the fine blue eyes beneath were alive with amusement. She ignored the former and focused on the latter, and gave him an exaggerated curtsy. "I thank ye kindly for yer advice, Dermot MacFarlane, but I dinna believe I will encounter the likes o' my husband-to-be here on Inchmurrin Island, riding down the path on a white steed, himself looking as fine as the flowers he brings me, while on his way to pay me court."

"Och! If not by land, then perhaps by sea," Dermot said. His smile faded as he looked beyond her.

Following his gaze, Claire saw a boat with three men rowing toward the island, and they were no Lennoxes. Her expression turned thunderous. "Now, who do ye think that would be, looking proud as peacocks and rowing themselves over to Inchmurrin like they were on the receiving end o' an invitation?"

Dermot looked amused. "I ken it would be Grahams, judging from the look o' them and their plaids."

"Grahams?" Aggie said. "Why, they have not been to these parts in a good many years. Why do ye suppose they would be coming here to pay us a visit, after all this time?"

"I ken it could have something to do with the fact that the earl has not been here since his father died and he became Lord Monleigh. Mayhap he thought it time to pay a visit to Grahamstone Castle, to see how things fare with his own eyes, instead of the eyes o' his retainers."

Claire lifted her chin proudly and spoke with an authorative tone. "And where do ye think they are going?"

"To Lennox Castle would be my guess, unless I make our presence here known." With that said, Dermot made his way down to the water's edge.

The Grahams noticed him straightaway, and one of the men in the boat waved.

Dermot waved back, and the boat veered toward him.

Overhead a goshawk screamed, and Claire brought her hand up to shield the sun from her eyes as she followed the hawk until it disappeared over the tops of the trees. Curious now, she watched the boat approach, and as it drew closer, she could make out the faces of the three men on board.

She remembered having seen Jamie Graham once, before he became Lord Monleigh. As Aggie said, it had been many years since the last time any member of the earl's family showed his face in Stirlingshire. She remembered he had come with his father, but she had been about Briana's age and did not have much memory for anything beyond that.

She decided the man who waved was Monleigh, and wondered who the other two were. Grahams, she was certain, but whether they were brothers or clansmen remained to be seen.

Several times now, her eye had been drawn to one of them in particular. It was the obvious handsomeness of the one sitting in the back that snagged her attention, and she seemed unable to free herself from it. Even from where she stood, she could tell he was older than her fifteen years, but not by more than five years or so. His hair was as black as a kettle, and at times, the sun struck it in a way that made it glint with fiery flashes of light. She found herself hoping that his eyes were not black, or even brown, but blue...as beautifully blue as the deepest waters in the loch.

She stood next to Aggie, with her sisters scattered about, each of them seemingly content to watch Dermot wade out and grab a hold on the boat, while the three men inside dropped over the side and into the water.

Kenna came to stand on the other side of Claire. "They must be Lord Monleigh's brothers," she whispered, "I see a likeness between them. They are all handsome-featured, but I like the one in the middle."

Dear Kenna, with her newly emerging interest in a man's features. Claire felt a stab of pity that their beautiful mother could not be here to see the maturing of her daughters. She gave a glance in Briana's direction, and when her gaze rested upon the bright strawberry hues of her curly reddish-blond hair, she felt an aching tenderness for this sister who never knew the soft gentle touch of their mother, who died three days after Briana was born.

"Tell me, Claire," Kenna asked, "which one of the brothers do ye favor?"

Claire tried to imagine what their mother would have said. "Dinna get yer heart all fettered. Ye have plenty o' time, and the lads are numerous."

"Does that mean ye are no interested in *any* o' them?"

"Not in the least." Claire kept the braw, dark-headed one in her line of vision. She knew it was a bit brazen of her, but sometimes boldness was called for.

"But, Claire…"

"Kenna, ye are too young to talk about men and such."

Kenna's eyes narrowed. "Such? What mean ye by such?"

Claire shrugged, suddenly aware that she was wading in deep water, and it was getting deeper. "Men... and the things what go with them."

"What things are ye speaking aboot?"

"Romantic things."

"Och, ye mean kissing and such?"

"Kenna Lennox, if our father heard ye say that, ye would be in a heap o' trouble, ye ken?"

"Aye, but he no is here and I ken ye willna tell him."

"I will if ye dinna stop."

"I canna exactly ignore what is obvious, now can I?"

"Weel, then ye can focus on the knowledge that they didna come here to pay us court, and they willna be here long enough for ye to charm them."

Kenna sighed. "Aye, but och! 'Tis such a pleasant feeling to gaze upon such a bonny face. I wonder what his name is? Do ye remember the names of Lord Monleigh's brothers?"

"No, Jamie was the only name I recall, but we will learn who they are soon enough."

Two

Take me to you, imprison me, for I,
Except you enthrall me, never shall be free,
Nor ever chaste, except you ravish me.

John Donne (c. 1572-1631),
English divine and metaphysical poet.
Last lines of *Holy Sonnets,* no. 14

Claire and Kenna watched as the men pulled the boat ashore. Claire shuddered at the sound of the hull scraping on the rocks, but she did not take her gaze from the figure of the tall, braw one in the back. As he waded to shore, she saw the flex of muscle beneath the wet trews.

He was pleasing to the eye, and a fine example of a man in his prime. He was well dressed, in a white linen shirt and trews, with the red Graham plaid that was worn by the Great Marquis of Montrose in the seventeenth century, when he was sent to the gallows. The other two men wore the blue Graham Menteith.

Dermot conversed with the men for a few minutes. Claire knew him well enough to know he not only approved of the Grahams, but that he also liked them, which was not a common occurrence with Dermot, who was reputed to be as particular as Duffus when choosing those he favored.

Claire's heart began to pound when the men laughed and started toward the women. As the eldest daughter, Claire would be introduced first. Her palms began to sweat, something that had never happened to her before, but then, never could she remember her heart beating so fast at the mere nearness of a man.

Hout! If she didna feel like a genteel lady—that is until she remembered her torn dress and the bits from her encounter with the rhododendron thicket still lodged in her hair.

She knew that in the absence of her father and brothers, she was expected to welcome the Grahams with kind regard, as her family's representative. She well knew the Grahams were an ancient clan of much consequence, that went all the way back to Gramus, a Caledonian chief, who fought to repel the Romans. She oft heard her father tell stories of their military prowess, and how they were known as "the gallant Grahams." Their strength and valor in battle was legendary, and many a fine leader died fighting beside Robert the Bruce and William Wallace.

Jamie, Lord Monleigh, was an important earl in the tradition of his ancestors. He was held in high regard, having earned the respect of his peers, his clan and the lower classes as well. His opinion was sought, his judgment sound, his treatment of others known to be honest and fair. Most important, the Grahams and Lennoxes had long been friends and allies, to the point that many of the members of each clan shared the same blood.

"Claire," Dermot said, "do ye remember Lord Monleigh from the time he was here a few years past?"

She noticed that although he carried himself proudly, Monleigh's eyes were kind, and that did much to put her at ease. "Aye, I do remember, although his lordship has grown considerably taller since that time. I dinna expect ye will remember me, Lord Monleigh, but on the behalf of my father, I welcome ye and yer men to Inchmurrin and Lennox Castle."

"Lady Claire, I thank ye for yer gracious welcome. And ye are incorrect about my memory. I remember quite well my first sight of ye. How could I not remember, when I witnessed how ye so capably punched the sheriff's son in the eye for hitting yer sister and pushing her into the mud."

Everyone laughed, and Claire instantly felt a burst of heat upon her face. That was followed, she knew, by an explosion of color across her cheeks, as fiery and red as her hair. Lord above, she would never forget that incident, but she had forgotten it happened on that day, so long ago, when the Grahams were at Inchmurrin.

She also remembered her father's stern scolding, and the subsequent punishment of being unable to ride her pony for one month. Once that was handed down, she heard her father say, "On the other hand, I dinna remember ever seeing anyone, man or lad, taking such a well-aimed punch and executing it with a more perfect delivery. Mayhap ye should have been a lad, Claire. Young Lachlan will have a black eye that he will no be able to hide. I fear ye have made an enemy for life, lass, for he will never forgive ye for the fact that it was a lass what bested him."

"And I am two years younger that him," she boasted, with much pride in her voice.

"Fine words butter no scones, Claire. I will not have ye putting on the plaid of a braggart. Now, come here and give me a kiss and then off with ye."

The memory faded away, along with the warmth of her face, when Claire looked at him.

Monleigh was smiling. He asked Dermot if he had witnessed the punch.

Dermot nodded. "Oh, aye, I saw the moment she caught young Lachlan on the side of the cheek with her fist, and it slid right into his eye."

Monleigh was laughing when he turned to his brothers. "The puir laddie went down in a heap. By the time we got there, his eyes were glazed and his arms limp."

"Ye mean he was knocked unconscious?" the one with the bluest, heavenly eyes asked.

"Aye, he was no' doon verra long, ye ken, but long enough that there was no mistake but what the wee lassie was capable o' defending herself and those she sought to protect."

"Tell me, has Lachlan Sinclair forgiven ye for the punch?" Monleigh asked, his eyes dancing with humorous indulgence.

"No, he swore a vow of retribution, and although he has not yet collected, I ken he ha' no' forgotten aboot it."

Monleigh then apologized for not introducing his brothers, and corrected the oversight immediately. "May I present my brothers..."

Claire barely heard the name Niall, but when he introduced her to Fraser Graham, Claire regretted to the bottom of her heart that she had punched Lachlan Sinclair in the eye, and she swore on her mother's grave, that from this day forward, she would strive to be more ladylike, then added a short amendment. *At least when Lord Fraser is nearby...*

They talked on for some time, the brothers interacting with Claire and her sisters, and then Claire invited them to stay for dinner.

Monleigh seemed pleased. "Thank ye for yer kind invitation. We had plans to go straight to Grahamstone Castle once we left here, so we would arrive before nightfall. However, such an invitation is difficult to turn down. What are a few miles ridden in the dark? What say ye, brothers?"

"I am quite fond of midnight rides," Niall said.

"A modest price to pay," Fraser said, "in exchange for a few hours of good conversation, in the company of such lovely lasses."

"Do ye think," Kenna asked after the men walked off, "that in our times it could happen that a man would be so besotted over a lass that he would kidnap her, like they did in bygone times?"

"Are ye daft?" Claire asked. "Faith! Where do ye get yer ideas, Kenna?"

"From the same place ye get yers, Claire."

"Weel, I dinna sit around dreaming aboot nonsense."

"'Tisn't nonsense. I ken it could happen."

"All right...fine...think it then, and have it yer way."

"Ye dinna have to get mad aboot it."

"I am not mad. I dinna understand what has come over ye all of a sudden. Ye were fine this morning, and now ye are spouting nonsensical. Why would a man want to kidnap ye, when he could just as easily ask ye to marry him."

Kenna was suddenly very quiet.

"Weel now, has the cat run awa' with yer tongue? Dinna ye have an answer?"

Kenna shrugged. "Not today, but I ken I will ha' one tomorrow."

Lennox Castle was built on a natural rocky outcrop on the southwest point of the island. A defensive ditch ran along the east side, which faced inland. It was a position that afforded both security and an effective way to control the coming and going of boats.

It was not as beautiful as some later-constructed castles, for it was a fortalice, a fortress built for protection and defense, and not intended to be pleasing to the eye. Yet, there was a certain charm to it—a certain romantic atmosphere it possessed—with its small tower, the keep, grounds, orchards and the beauty of the small island, and the enchantment of the lake surrounding it.

The castle itself consisted of three floors, hewn of native stone, three to four feet thick, castellated, and topped in the usual manner by a parapet. On the first floor, the kitchen and staff dining hall lay to one side of the tower, and to one side the cellars, laundry, the armory, and a narrow, steep stairway that led down to the dungeon. The rest included rooms devoted to castle maintenance and service. On the opposite side of the tower were the large dining hall and a library that also served as the earl's study. From the main hall, a beautifully arched door opened into the courtyard.

There were two staircases that led to the upper floors: the second floor housing the family living quarters and the solar; the upper floor for those who worked in the earl's employ.

All of the windows on the upper floors were like doorways to the tranquil and picturesque world beyond the island, and gave no hint to the savage and brutal events that had taken the lives of several Earls of Lennox, and members of their clan.

Aggie and Greer left shortly after the introductions so Aggie could alert the cooks that there would be guests for dinner. Claire, Kenna and Briana were going to take the familiar path back to the castle, while Dermot accompanied the Grahams in the boat.

With a backdrop of bright green meadow and the darker foliage of the thicket, the three lasses stood on the white pebbled shore, where the loch's gentle billows washed against the rocks with soft liquid sounds that mimicked the sound of the sea. They watched Dermot and the Grahams push the boat into deeper water and then climb inside, and much to Claire's delight, she noticed Fraser Graham's movements were as graceful as a sea otter's. She sighed, never taking her gaze from his person for even a second.

There must have been something desirous in that sigh, for Kenna immediately looked at her through two very suspicious eyes. "I thought ye said ye were no' interested in men and such."

Claire did not say anything.

"Claire, I heard ye say ye were no' interested in the least."

"What is the point ye are making, Kenna?"

"Ye scolded me for looking and speaking about their being so pleasing to the eye and all."

"Aye."

"Weel, now ye are doing the same thing, when ye said ye were no interested. Now, what say ye?"

"Mayhap I lied."

"That is so like ye, Claire. It is what I find most infuriating aboot ye."

"What? That I spoke the truth?"

"Aye, ye always stop me when I am nigh into an argument with ye, and then I have no way to let the steam off the kettle."

"All I said was, I lied."

"Aye, and how will I be finding myself a way to argue aboot that? I canna chastise ye for lying since ye have already admitted it."

"Ye will think of something, I ken. Come now, we must start back if we are to arrive afore them."

They started up the path, Claire going first and Kenna falling in behind her, the angry thrust to her chin saying she was still searching for a way to let the steam off the kettle.

At one point the path dipped where the trees thinned, and they caught a glimpse of the boat as it went around the rocky promontory that rose out of the deeper water. Wild roses and honeysuckle climbed the rocks to tangle with the flowers and ferns that grew in the crack. To the side where a small inlet lay, the water was smooth and still—it reflected like a mirror, the beauty of the island hanging over it.

From a short distance away came the sound of laughter, which cut through the silence like a crackle of static, and Claire felt a sudden stab of loneliness that she did not quite understand. Her father and brothers left for Stirling two days ago and were due home on the morrow, so she should suffer no loneliness for them in such a short absence.

Yet it was such an odd sensation that she thought about it for a while—until she decided it was really more a feeling of loneliness, mixed with an odd sort of longing. That was followed by a horrible thought that suddenly occurred to her. Losh! What if she was having a glimpse into her future? And what if that meant she would go to her grave, a shriveled, innocent old maid?

The thought was so horrifying to her she immediately pushed it aside, said a quick prayer and thought upon something more pleasant—dark hair, and the bluest eyes that ever graced a bonny face.

Aye, she did not know the cause of these strange and new feelings, but she had a strong feeling as to the cure.

Fraser Graham had caught her eye, but she feared it would never go beyond that, for he and his brothers would stay for a time at Grahamstone Castle, and then they would return to Monleigh Castle, on a promontory that met the North Sea. So very far away.

If only there was a way to keep Fraser and his brothers nearby, then perhaps there would be time enough for them to be together, and to become, each to the other, too dear.

Three

O, then, I see Queen Mab hath been with you.
She is the fairies' midwife...
And in this state she gallops night by night
Through lovers' brains, and then
they dream of love.

William Shakespeare (1564-1616), English
poet and playwright.
Romeo and Juliet (1595), act 1, scene 4

A fine meal was served, but no one paid much attention, for the best part of the evening was the friends they shared it with.

They were all settling into the wine and verbal exchange that follows dinner, when Claire heard a commotion in the outer rooms and wondered what the noise was about. That is, until she heard a booming laugh.

No one laughed like her father, and it was a pity, for Lord Errick had the most marvelous, magical laugh, and when anyone heard it, they knew immediately they were missing some wonderful part of life and wanted to participate.

His laugh was infectious and so endearing to her, for it brought back the memory of her childhood when she would go into the library and interrupt his work, and he would laugh and put her on his knee. He would tell her the story of how laughter came into the world, and how the first laugh was the sound of Adam's joy when his first child was born, and how the laugh traveled across the room, until it bounced against the wall and shattered into millions of pieces. And when he heard the sound, God sent the angels to gather up all the pieces, and they gave one to each new child that was born, so there would always be joy and laughter in the world.

To Claire, that endearing laugh meant her father and her three brothers had returned from Stirling—a day earlier than she expected them. The commotion grew louder, and louder still, until the door to the great hall swung open and Alasdair, Lord Errick, walked into the hall. His captivating presence filled the room, for the sight of him in his dark green jacket with the pewter buttons, the black boots and heavy silver spurs was awe-inspiring and demanding of respect.

She smiled at the sight of her handsome, ginger-haired brothers, Breac, Ronaln and Kendrew, and was soon joined by her sisters when she went to greet them. Soon the Lennox men were surrounded by the four loving females in the family, who joyfully welcomed them home.

After many hugs and welcoming kisses, Alasdair greeted his guests, with two daughters tucked under each arm. "God's love, Monleigh, had I known ye were coming I would have postponed my trip to Stirling. How long have ye been here?"

"We only arrived earlier in the day," Jamie said. " 'Tis good to see ye, Lord Errick. Do ye remember my brothers, Fraser and Niall?"

He released his daughters. "Och, of course I remember, although they were not quite so tall the last time I saw them." Then to Monleigh he said, "Please, call me Alasdair like yer father did. I was present the night ye were born, and we prefer to dispense with the formalities here."

Jamie grinned. "Aye, we do the same at home, so it would please me greatly to have ye call me Jamie." Alasdair greeted each of them with a few comments and a warm slap on the back, but when he greeted Fraser, he said, "God's blood, Fraser, ye have the look of ye father about ye, and a strong resemblance it is, too. 'Twas like walking into the hall and seeing him here. I ken ye ha' been told that before."

"Aye, I have heard it a time or two, but it is something that I never tire of hearing."

"Dermot," Alasdair said, "will ye tell someone to bring us some ale." He turned to his sons. "Please sit doon, my laddies, and we will have some conversation with our ale."

Once they were all seated, Alasdair said, "Losh, but 'tis good to be home. I ken if I had my way, I would never set foot off the island. Whenever I return home, all the woes of the world seem to disappear the moment I step off the boat. There is always so much turmoil in Stirling."

"I take it you went on business and not pleasure," Jamie said, his tone saying he had been there himself, denoting he understood the feeling perfectly.

"Aye, it was the worst kind of business...the kinfolk

kind," Alasdair said. "Ye do remember my brother, William?"

"Aye, I was sorry to hear he died. Two years ago, was it?"

"Three. He left a widow, Isobel, who has been a thorn in my side since the day William died."

"Isobel...she was married before, was she not?" Fraser asked.

"Aye, she was the wife of Sir David McLennan. They had a son, Giles."

"I dinna know her personally, but I have heard her name bandied about," Jamie said. "She is keeping company with Lord Walter Ramsay, I believe."

"Oh, aye, she latched onto him almost immediately. Thick as thieves, they are. They barely had time to remove my brother's body afore Lord Walter moved into Finlay Castle. William left Finlay to her, along with a sizable inheritance, only that doesna seem to be enough to satisfy her voracious appetite for worldly goods."

"Ye mean she is after money?" Niall asked.

"Aye, my money, and plenty of it. She hired herself a lawyer and was asking for half of everything I owned. She claimed I was no' entitled to my father's entire estate."

"On what grounds?" Fraser asked. "I am sure your father's title was properly entailed and ye, being the eldest son, were entitled to it."

Before Alasdair could answer, Jamie laughed and gave Fraser a teasing elbow to the ribs. "Fraser has studied law in Edinburgh for the past two years, so he will naturally focus on the legalities."

"'Tis my only fault," Fraser said, "and my focus is

what saved ye enough coin to do the renovations on Grahamstone Castle, so dinna be too hard on my wee bit o' legal knowledge."

"'Tis true, I canna deny that," Jamie said. "'Tis not the sound o' me complaining that ye hear."

Fraser's face grew intent. "Tell us more about yer troubles with Isobel Lennox. What did she present as evidence?"

"'Twas no *prima facie* case, according to my lawyer."

"What is that?" Claire asked.

"It is a judicial case in which the evidence is sufficient for a judgment, unless it is disproved," Fraser said. He then asked Alasdair, "What did she present as evidence?"

"The only bit o' supporting evidence she had was a legal document supposedly signed by my brother, outlining how it was my father's wish that I share the things not specifically entailed with the title equally with him once he became of age. It also said that there was originally a document signed by our father attesting to the fact, but it had been destroyed...presumably by me."

"Your brother signed such a document?" Jamie asked. "I knew William to be a man of honor, and find it hard to believe he would do such."

"He didna," Alasdair said. "The document was proved to be a forgery...a verra good forgery, but thankfully it ended the suit."

"And Isobel?" Fraser asked. "Have they brought charges against her for lying and forgery?"

"No, and I dinna think they will, since she is claiming she didna ken the document was forged. She said she found it in William's papers after he died, but there was no reason for William to have such a document. He had plenty of money and lands, but Isobel was never one to be satisfied with what she had for verra long. She was always pushing William to buy bigger castles, so she could live like a queen," Alasdair said, then he reached for the cup of ale offered to him.

Everyone was silent while ale was served around the table to all the men, save Kendrew, who had watered wine with his sisters.

After a few minutes, Niall put his cup down. "Avarice is a demon that once it has ye under its control, it is verra hard to ever extract yerself from," he said.

"Aye," Jamie said, "for every one of us who works to make an honest coin, there are dozens who fantasize about the inventive ways to take it from us."

Alasdair nodded. "Isobel rather likes being in its clutches, I wager. Needless to say, she has gone through all of the money William left her. She has sold three castles, and has only two left. She is starting to feel the pinch of shoes that her big feet have outgrown."

"So, the case is settled then?" Breac asked.

Alasdair nodded. "Aye, unless she fantasizes aboot it some more."

Fraser gave Alasdair a sympathetic look. "I wish I could tell ye I think ye have heard the last of her, but people of that ilk tend not to realize when to quit. She will be back, as soon as she regroups and comes up with another plan."

"I suspected as much. She was very contrite today."

"But that was because she was in the presence of others," Breac said. "For when we rode off, I saw the way she looked at ye, Father...as if she wished ye dead."

Alasdair ruffled Breac's Celtic-red hair. "Wouldna do her a bit o' good, though, would it...since ye are my heir?"

"I dinna trust her, either," Ronaln said. "She is evil. Whenever she walks past, I expect to see the leaves on the trees wither."

Somewhere in the castle, someone must have opened a door, for a draft of wind was sucked down the chimney and a cool current of wind swept into the room. Claire shivered and was about to comment when it suddenly ceased, and everything settled back to the way it was before.

"Weel, that was a bit queerish," Claire said.

"Aye," Breac said, "makes ye think Auld Cloutie didna like us speaking o' his disciple Isobel so disrespectfully."

Auld Cloutie... At the mention of the Devil, Claire felt prickles of fear dance across her skin. The words played over in her head. She knew Breac had referred to Isobel as the Devil's disciple in jest, and she prayed it was not the clock striking thirteen.

"The Devil can have Isobel and Lord Walter, too," Ronaln said. "And he can have Giles along with them."

"Tell me again, who is Giles?" Niall asked.

"'Tis Isobel's son by her first marriage," Breac said. "We are about the same age."

"Except Breac is a muckle more bonny," Ronaln said, and everyone laughed.

Claire settled back and listened to the conversation

once more, but her thoughts were on Fraser. It pleased her to know that he had noticed her, for he did glance in her direction enough that even Kenna noticed, and began to nudge Claire with her knee each time Fraser's gaze wandered her way.

Claire could not deny she was drawn to his unashamed good looks, and she watched him whenever she could. Neither could she refute she had studied him since he arrived. He fascinated her, and she liked the feeling she got when she watched him. Even better was the feeling she got when he watched her. Smitten as she was at the very first sight of him, she was pleased to see it was not only her, for he did seem to be mindful of her as well. She wished she had a name for this peculiar aching she felt in her chest.

Jamie's gaze moved across the opposite side of the table, where Claire and her sisters were seated. "Lord above, Alasdair, 'tis a comely lot o' daughters ye have, and all o' them proudly displaying their Celtic bluid. Every one o' them has some shade o' red hair." He let his gaze move over Alasdair's sons and added, "And that includes yer sons, too."

"Aye, and they have the temper to go along with it," he said, and everyone laughed, including Claire.

Jamie was still smiling when he said, "Ye ken yer daughters are of an age now when all the laddies aboot are going to come calling at yer door, and then yer troubles will begin. Ha' ye betrothed any o' them?"

"Nay, I promised their mother I would not do that, and vowed I would try to let each o' them follow the dictates o' her heart."

"Weel now," Niall said, "that is a bit unheard of, but 'tis not something I find displeasing."

"And what about the three o' ye?" Alasdair asked, "not to mention those rapscallion brothers of yours… Calum, Bran and Tavish…"

"Dinna forget Arabella, Father," Claire said.

Alasdaire winked at Claire. "Och, lass, how could I forget fair Arabella. What of the Grahams?" he asked. "Any weddings I didna hear aboot?"

"Nary a one," Niall said.

"No betrothals, either?"

"None," Fraser said.

"Weel, Jamie my lad, it is time fer ye to think about taking a wife, to secure yer title, is it not?"

"Aye, and I have been thinking aboot it, but I canna seem to make myself get beyond that point. 'Tis devilishly difficult to do, ye ken, to pick just one."

Claire lowered her head and rolled her eyes. From across the table came a muffled laugh. She raised her head and looked at the proud countenance of the man sitting across from her, and saw a teasing light was dancing in Fraser Graham's eyes. She gave him a cross look and focused her attention on his brother, which appeared to amuse him even more.

Claire stifled a yawn. "I am tired," she announced, and felt the kick on her leg from Kenna, but she ignored it. "I think I shall go above stairs, if you will permit me to say good-night."

Jamie and his brothers stood. "We have stayed overlong, due to enjoying ourselves so much, but we've a long ride tonight."

"Ye are welcome to roll out yer plaids here," Alasdair said.

"Thank ye kindly," Jamie said, "but we are expected tonight, and if we dinna arrive I am sure they will have a patrol out looking for us. Before we take our leave, I would like to invite ye and yer sons over to Grahamstone tomorrow. There will be a meeting of several of the peers who live around Fintry. We are meeting to discuss the sudden increase in cattle raids. Have ye had a problem with it?"

"Aye, and the raids seem to be coming closer together. Mayhap I will bring Breac and Ronaln with me. 'Tis something we all have an interest in."

After saying good-night, the men walked outside. Claire's sisters all went above stairs, but Claire waited to tell her father good-night. She was wandering aimlessly around the hall when she noticed Fraser had left his gloves sitting on the end of the table. She snatched them up and ran across the hall. She threw back the door and ran—right up against Fraser.

"Oof!" It was all she could manage before Fraser's arms went around her, which put her nose no more than an inch from one of the pewter buttons on his jacket. When she looked up, he grinned down at her.

Oh, he was a fine-looking one, he was, and she had a feeling women went after him like salmon after a shiny hook. She knew she should chide herself for having such shameless thoughts about him, but the will to do so was not there.

"'Tis not ladylike to run in the hall," he remarked, "but I canna say I am sorry ye did, for if ye hadna, then I wouldna be holding a fire-haired lass with eyes o' greenish-gold in my arms. 'Tis not a bad feeling. Pity ye are so young."

"I am not *so* young. I am fifteen. And ye dinna look so verra old yerself. So, will ye be telling me yer age? Or are ye so ancient ye canna remember?"

"I have four more years than ye, Lady Claire...and soon to be five."

"Then ye have no business calling me young. I am a woman full grown."

"No need to tell me that, lass. 'Twas one o' the first things I noticed aboot ye."

Claire had been waiting for his retort, only now she found herself completely distracted by his closeness. His chin was square and proud, his cheekbones high, his face tanned enough to make his blue eyes so very, very blue.

She had already judged him to be a gentle man, but standing so close to him, with his arms around her, she realized there was nothing about him that was soft and gentle now, for he was tall, powerful and handsomely dark-haired, with a fine edge to him that could turn ruthless and dangerous when called upon. Several times tonight he had demonstrated he had a mind that was as quick and sharp as a razor's edge.

"Where were ye going in such a hurry, lass? We' ye rushing to give me a farewell kiss?" he asked, amused.

"I would sooner kiss a pig's liver," she said. "Ye ken I had no such thought, and ye are a devilish brute for saying such."

"Aye, and ye have a devilish temper to go with it, so we are a matched pair, you and I."

"I wouldna be matched with the likes of ye, Fraser Graham, for all the gold in King Solomon's mines."

"I could easily prove ye wrong on that account," he said. He grinned cheerfully and said, "Och, 'tis a false face ye put on now, lass, for ye kept yer gaze on me a goodly part o' the evening, and while I find it pleasing, it doesna please me to think ye are the kind who willna own up to it."

"Ye did a muckle amount o' looking yerself," she said.

"Aye, but I own up to it. 'Tis not so strange that a man would find it pleasurable to gaze upon a lass as bonnie as ye, for ye are a beautiful woman, Lady Claire Lennox, and ye have no' seen the last o' me."

"'Tis folly to think I will be watching the loch pining for a sight o' ye or yer boat," she replied, looking disinterested.

"Ye will learn soon enough that I am not overly fond of resisting temptation, lass."

He kissed her suddenly, quick and hard, but long enough that she felt the warmth of his tongue and the urge to put her arms around him and kiss him back, but he released her with a laugh. "'Tis sorry I am that I dinna have time to do that a wee bit longer, but that will have to hold ye until next time, when I will finish it properly."

Her mouth dropped open in a sort of speechless wonderment. She was stunned, searching for something to say. "I only wanted to return yer gloves to ye," she said, and thrust them toward him.

His hand cupped her chin and lifted her face, and the look he gave her was powerful and too overwhelming to resist. When he released her, she was trembling inside.

"My lass," he said, and then he was gone.

She ran to the door and crossed the yard, then hurried down to where the boat and his brothers waited. She went to stand by her father, and his arm came around her. Secure and protected within her father's embrace, she watched Fraser give the boat a mighty push, and then he jumped inside.

Together, she and her father watched the boat move toward the opposite shore, and she felt the power of Fraser Graham reaching out to her, even after darkness swallowed the sight of him.

Four

Ye Highlands and ye Lawlands,
O where hae ye been?
They hae slain the Earl of Murray,
And hae laid him on the green.

He was a braw gallant,
And he rid at the ring;
And the bonny Earl of Murray,
O he might hae been a king!

O lang will his Lady
Look owre the Castle Downe,
Ere she see the Earl of Murray
Come sounding through the town!

"The Bonny Earl of Murray,"
Anonymous

Only Kendrew was in the great hall when Claire came below stairs the next morning. She stopped when she saw the near-empty room and asked, "Where is everyone?"

"Did ye forget, Claire? Lord Monleigh invited them

to come to Grahamstone today. They left early. Father said to tell ye goodbye. He said ye shouldna wait up for them, because it will be late when they return."

"Did Breac and Ronaln accompany him?"

"Aye, and eager to go, too, they were."

"Did anyone else go with them?"

"Aye, Duncan and Hugh." He studied her face. "Ye look troubled, Claire. Are ye faring well?"

"Aye, I am faring well, but I am distressed that they left afore I awoke. I wanted to tell them goodbye."

"Then ye should have gotten up earlier."

"Aye," she said, and wandered off to the kitchen to get a cup of tea, puzzled over the strange emptiness she felt inside.

The sun dropped behind the walls of the keep. Long shadows stretched over the figures of the Grahams as they made their last farewells to Alasdair, his sons and the two clansmen who accompanied them.

"Ye are certain ye do not wish to stay the night?" Jamie asked. "Think it not better to leave early tomorrow?"

"Nay," Alasdair said, and swung into his saddle. "'Twill be pleasant riding in the cool o' the evening, and we will be home before dawn."

"Godspeed ye, then," Jamie said, and he stood with his brothers and watched the Lennox men wheel their horses and ride at a canter through the gate. Once they were on the other side, they broke into a gallop, and the gates of Grahamstone Castle closed behind them.

Alasdair and his small party of five rode away from Grahamstone Castle and into the deepening shadows of the approaching night. He saw the moon rising, a silver orb, that seemed to balance magically on the tops of the hills in the distance. He thought of the miles that lay between him and the shores of Loch Lomond, and wondered if Claire would prove faithful to his request that she not wait up for them, and with a smile and a shake of his head, he surmised that probably she would not.

She was so like her mother, loving, devoted, faithful, with a quick wit and an even quicker temper. She was both a blessing to remind him so much of the woman he loved, and a curse to remind him of the love that he lost.

He put his spurs to his horse, and under the bright light of the full moon, he and his sons and clansmen rode through the empty streets of a small town. When they passed through the outskirts on the other side, they rode noisily over a wooden bridge, hooves pounding the dry wood beneath them.

The moonlight guided them along the narrow track on the other side. Once, he thought he heard the sound of horses coming behind them, but when he checked his horse and told the others to "listen," there was no sound, save the rushing water of the burn they had just crossed.

They continued on their way until the tall, spiked tops of the trees announced the woods were just ahead. The track curved around the slope of a hill and disappeared into the dark, huddling trees.

Once they entered the forest, they rode only a short way when they were suddenly overtaken by a warlike horde of at least three dozen men. Wielding drawn swords and hurling curses with furious voices, they sprang upon Lord Errick and his unsuspecting party.

At first the Lennox party was stunned, but when the attackers closed around them, swords drawn, they had no choice but to meet their challengers. The ensuing ring of the Lennox swords being drawn echoed through the trees, but by the time Alasdair drew first blood, with a stroke that cut deeply into the shoulder of his opponent, he knew they were outnumbered, hemmed in and surrounded. The reality of it only made him fight with a renewed energy, but soon he knew their fate was certain, and they would all be cut down like trees.

There, among the crannies of the rocks and whispering leaves of the trees, they struck against the enemy, beneath the cold, impersonal glimmer of stars overhead. The air rang with the clang of metal and the guttural utterances that followed a well placed cut from a sword. The smell of blood was strong; the smell of death even stronger.

He searched desperately for his sons, and saw Ronaln's red head and was renewed to know his middle son still stood. Beyond him, Breac fought like the Highlanders of old, fierce and quick, defending himself with nimble agility against man after man who rushed him. Weapons flashing in the moonlight, Alasdair hacked his way through the diminishing ranks of the enemy in an effort to reach his sons, for he knew they would soon tire. When Ronaln was close enough that the earl could reach out and touch him, he saw the thrust of an enemy sword aim at him. Before Alasdair could move, he saw his son run through, until the bloody point exited his back.

"Nooooo," Alasdair cried, and reached for Ronaln before his son's slumping body fell from his horse.

Someone from behind him took aim, and Alasdair felt a blinding pain as the sword cut deep into his shoulder and his own sword fell from his useless hand.

His horse reared as the swing that nearly severed Alasdair's arm also sliced into the flank of his mount. Alasdair fell, and landed near the place where his son's lifeless body lay. With his good arm, he grabbed Ronaln's sword and turned, frantically searching for Breac, and found him just in time to see the slicing arc of the sword that completely severed Breac's head.

"Kill me!" Alasdair shouted, and rose to his feet. Holding his sword firmly, he attacked, cutting his way through man after man, barely feeling the wounds he collected, until at last, he was set upon.

"Do not kill him," one of them said. "The honor goes to Lord Walter."

"And an honor it will be."

Alasdair, bleeding mortally, felt his life ebbing away with each heartbeat. "Lord Walter," he whispered, the sound faint and papery. "I curse ye in the name of the Father, and the Son, and the Holy Ghost. May yer days be numbered, and may yer death bring ye thrice the suffering ye bequeathed to my sons and me."

"'Tis what I would expect of ye, Alasdair. Ye always were so verra brave. 'Tis a pity ye didna accept the forgery as real," he said, "and now, to save yer wealth, ye have lost yer sons."

"Ye willna get away with this."

"Correction. I have already gotten away with it. A few dead cows have been scattered about, and since ye and yer party were on yer way home after a meeting regarding the theft of cattle, it will seem perfectly clear that ye came upon a party o' cattle thieves and found yerselves outnumbered. Of course, yer name will be glorified and stories will circulate about the bravery of yer party, and the tragic deaths of ye and yer sons. The tragedy will spread when a few miserable cattle thieves will forfeit their lives in retribution, but in the end, no one will ever come close to imagining the truth. So, ye see, it is as I said—I have already gotten away with it."

"Ye will pay for what ye have done this day."

Lord Walter and his men laughed. "Aye, and ye think yer daughters will do the job ye and yer sons could not do? Do ye see Lady Claire taking up the sword and running me through? Surely 'tis not yer twelve-year-old heir that ye expect to avenge his father's death. Aahh, I can see by yer face that ye are concerned for your young heir, who will be, in a short matter of minutes, the new Earl of Errick and Mains. 'Tis a pity it has to end this way, but tonight ye will die, Lord Errick, and before ye draw yer last breath, ye will know that at this very moment, Isobel is on her way to London to seek the right of the new earl's ward, which will hand her control of him until he reaches his majority, and that of yer castles, yer land and yer daughters."

"Kendrew willna be young and under yer thumb forever," Alasdair said.

"Alas, I hate to tell ye this, coming as it is on the heels of the other misfortunes ye have suffered this day, but unfortunately, Kendrew willna reach his age of majority. 'Tis a pity that he will have to join ye and yer sons, for we have other plans for yer title."

"Ye canna gain control of the title, even if ye do

murder Kendrew, for in the event of his death, the title will pass to one o' my daughters."

"Aye, and yer daughters, I think, will be much more malleable by the time they reach their age of majority."

"My daughters will never bend to yer will. Never."

"Weel, ye willna know the answer to that, but ye will know this. Before the month is out, I will be sleeping in yer bed."

"Ye may sleep there, but ye willna die there. Be forewarned. Ye will make a mistake, and when ye do, ye will be hunted down like the dog that ye are. The only pleasure I will see this day is to know I will soon be with my sons, and that ye will, ere long, suffer a far worse fate, and that afterward, ye will burn eternally in hell."

Lord Walter turned to one of the men. "Put his son's head on a pike, and let the high and mighty Earl of Errick and Mains have, as his last sight, what his greed has wrought for him this night."

"Finish me," Alasdair said, and turned his head away from the display of Breac's head as it was thrust in his face. "End it now, ye spineless bastard."

"With pleasure."

Alasdair never felt the blow that ended his life.

Five

Cruel with guilt, and daring with despair,
The midnight murderer bursts the faithless bar;
Invades the sacred hour of silent rest
And leaves, unseen, a dagger in your breast.

Samuel Johnson (1709-84),
English author, lexicographer.
London

Claire was in the solar with Aggie and her sisters. As they had been doing for the past three years, they worked over their embroidery frames, diligently completing an embroidered tapestry that depicted scenes from the history of Scotland, much in the same manner as the Bayeux Tapestry, although theirs was on a much smaller scale.

"Ye would think that Father would send word if he decided to remain at Grahamstone Castle until today," Kenna said.

"Aye," Claire agreed, "ye would think so, for he surely does ken how we will worry aboot them."

Greer looked nervously around the solar, then

sighed deeply. "It is midafternoon. Ye would think they would be home by now."

"I hope nothing has happened," Briana said.

The needle jabbed into Claire's finger, and she turned angrily toward Briana. "Dinna say something like that...not ever! Do ye ken? Never, ever let me even think ye could harbor such a horrible thought."

Tears welled in Briana's eyes. "I didna mean anything bad, Claire. Truly."

Claire did not say anything. She sucked the blood from her finger and picked up her needle when she noticed a drop of blood had fallen on the tapestry she was working on. It was a replica of Lennox Castle, and the blood dropped in front of the door.

At the sound of her indrawn breath, her sisters all looked up and stared at her anxiously.

"What ails ye, child?" Aggie asked. "Yer as pale as milk."

Kenna left her seat and went to Claire's side. "Claire, dinna ye feel well?" She was about to say more when she saw the drop of blood. Her hands flew to her mouth, as if she wanted to stop the words that cried out to be said.

Briana started crying, and Greer looked helplessly from Claire and Kenna, to Aggie.

"My lambs, dinna fash yerselves so. 'Tis naught but the stomach flutters, brought on when ye let yer fears get the best o' ye."

In the midst of this most trying of moments, Dermot walked into the room. "The Earl of Monleigh and his brothers would like to see all of ye in the library."

Claire's heart seemed to stop beating at that moment. No one, not even Lord Monleigh, had to tell her why the Grahams were here. She knew the moment she saw Dermot's face that her worst fears were now true. *Oh, Father, what have ye done? Where are ye? What has happened to ye and my brothers? Please, God, dinna let them be harmed. Ye have blessed Heaven with our mother, dinna leave us with no one.*

She stood calmly, yet with weak knees and an even weaker constitution. She did not want to be strong right now. She wanted to run, crying and screaming below stairs, but she could not. No matter her fear, no matter her grief; she was her father's daughter. She would not cry; she would not lose her composure. Yet, there was nothing her iron will could do to prevent her heart from crying out, *Let it not be true. Please let it not be true...*

Her voice trembled, then grew stronger with each word she spoke. "Our father and brothers have accompanied Lord Monleigh, have they not?"

With an agonized look and a broken voice, Dermot said, "Aye, Lady Claire, yer loved ones...they have come home."

She turned to her sisters. "Wait here."

"We want to go down with ye," Kenna said.

Claire's eyes flashed fire when she flicked a quick glance at Aggie, who was already moving to where the three of them stood. She spoke softly and put her arms around Kenna's and Greer's shoulders, while Briana clutched Aggie tightly around the waist. "I will remain here with yer sisters, Lady Claire. Ye go and see to the rest o' yer family."

Dermot waited until Claire passed, then followed her from the room. No word was spoken, for words could offer no comfort any more than they could change what waited for Claire below stairs.

When she reached the library, Claire paused a moment to take a deep breath. Ye are a Lennox, she reminded herself, and ye will get through this. She released the breath she held, lifted her chin with all the pride of family her father had instilled within her, and stepped inside the silent room where the Grahams waited.

She was greeted by the grave faces of Lord Monleigh, Fraser and Niall. "Where are they?" she asked. "And who did the despicable deed?"

Jamie came to her. "Do ye wish to sit doon?"

Claire shook her head. "I want to see them."

Fraser moved to stand next to Jamie and spoke with heartrending gentleness that bespoke great pain. He searched Claire's face and started to speak.

When her lips trembled, he took her in his arms with a comforting embrace. "Oh, lass, one look at yer face is enough to tear the heart oot o' the strongest man."

She pressed her face against his fine wool jacket, as if she got close enough to him, some of his strength would flow into her. He stroked her hair and spoke soft, gentling words audible only to her.

It was so quiet that she could hear the great clock ticking all the way from the gallery. After some time, he pulled back enough to get his hand under her chin. He lifted her face and looked into her eyes. "Are ye certain ye want to do this? Ye have the right to do as ye wish, ye ken, and we are not telling ye that ye canna, but ye must remember if ye choose to see with yer own eyes what the night hath wrought, it will be something ye will see over and over again for the rest of yer life. Ye will always remember them the way they looked the last time ye saw them. Would it not be better if ye remember them the way they were the night before, when we were all gathered in the hall—loving family and the dearest of friends?"

Claire could maintain her composure. She could stifle the sobs and screams that wanted to tear at her throat. But the tears that rolled silently down her face, she could not manage, for they had a power all their own. "I ken yer words are to soften the agony and to spare me the reality of what happened, but they are my flesh and bluid, and I canna leave them alone, and I canna leave what must be done to someone else. My sisters and I will prepare their bodies. I will need someone to ride to kirk and inform the minister."

"I have already dispatched one o' my clansmen to bring the minister," Jamie said.

Claire turned and put her hand on Dermot's arm. "Dearest Dermot, it pains my heart to ask this o' ye, but will ye see to the coffins? I ken my father would have asked this of ye, if it had been my sisters an' myself instead of them."

Dermot nodded and left the room without saying a word. He did not mean to be disrespectful by not giving her a verbal reply. Claire understood it was not rudeness. He simply could not find the words that lay buried beneath the weight of so much sorrow.

She put her hand to her head and tried to sort through the vague order of thoughts jumbled in her brain. She put her hand on Jamie's arm and asked, "Where are they?"

"In the great hall," Lord Monleigh replied.

She took a step toward the door and paused, long

enough to ask, "Fraser, would ye be kind enough to give me yer arm?"

Fraser complied, and she slipped her arm through his.

She had made the journey between the library and the great hall many times since the days when she first learned to walk. Never had it taken so much time to traverse the short distance as it did at this moment in time. She tried to take preparatory measures by telling herself she was about to see something more horrible than anything her gaze had ever touched, although she knew no amount of self-counsel could soften the blow she was about to receive.

Her father's glorious reddish-gold beard was the first thing she saw upon entering the great hall. She stopped just inside the doorway, feeling as if she had only this moment awakened from a long, long sleep. Benumbed, and with trembling hands, Claire tightened the hand that held on to Fraser's arm so tightly, not aware that her fingers were digging into the fabric of his jacket.

How agonizing to see the bodies of the three beloved members of her family lying so still upon the table where they had laughed and dined only two nights ago. She turned to Fraser. "Why is the cloth over Breac's body?"

"Do not ask, so I willna have to answer ye. Some things are better left unsaid."

"It matters naught whether ye tell me or I remove the cloth and see for myself. My sisters and I shall prepare their bodies. We will have to see what you have sought to hide at some point."

"He was beheaded, Claire. We hoped to spare ye this."

Her bottom lip trembled and she caught it between her teeth—pain was preferable to any display of weakness. Anger, born of fear, gripped her heart. "Breac was not spared. Why should we be?"

She swallowed back the tears. They were dead. Whatever pain and horror they suffered, it was finished. They would suffer no more the pain and indignities men inflict upon one another. Nothing would bring them back any more than she could change the manner in which they were taken from her.

She would have chosen another way for it to happen—to die in your sleep seemed a peaceful way. It was not their way. Not one of them would have chosen it. They died defending themselves, against what, she knew not. The only thing she could do was to bear up under this in a manner befitting her family and her clan. Yet, she could not ignore the cold fingers of fear that skimmed lightly down her spine. What will happen now, she wondered, when her brother Kendrew inherited the title, too young and unprepared to bear being mantled under the weight of certain responsibility.

She put her hand to her head. She felt faint. Nausea churned her stomach.

Later, she would wish she had listened to Fraser, for if she had not seen the dreadful reality, perhaps she could have convinced herself that it was not true. Nothing, absolutely nothing, could have prepared her for the sight of her father, Alasdair, and her two eldest brothers, Breac and Ronaln, their bloody bodies laid out in the great hall, their beautiful eyes closed forever.

"I would like to see them now," she said softly.

"Ye are certain?"

"Aye, but will ye stay with me?"

"Aye, I will stay with ye, Claire. For as long as ye wish."

She gazed upon the beloved face of her father, unable to believe the laughing giant of a man who rode off with her brothers two days ago had come home for the last time; his face a deathly pallor, the eyes that always looked at her with love, closed, and the lips that told her stories of the Scotland of old, silenced forever.

She touched the deep slash across his forehead. The blood was cold and crusted. She did not try to staunch the flow of tears that gushed forth when she saw the deep gash in his shoulder and the badly mangled arm that was hardly connected to the rest of his body.

She leaned forward and kissed his cold lips. She brushed the hair back from his face. "I am sorry, Father. Sorry that I was not born a boy, so that I might avenge yer deaths. Sorry that I didna wake in time to see ye off. Sorry I am a weakling now, who tries to pretend she is strong. Sorry that I not have the knowledge to give to Kendrew to help him to stand in yer shoes at his tender age. I take my only comfort in the knowledge that ye are with our mother and that she will be alone no more."

She started to move to her brothers when she thought she felt her father's hand grip her arm. She saw the sadness and grief in his eyes, and when his lips moved, she heard naught, but the words formed in her mind.

Be strong, Claire....

She was frozen in a crystal of silence as anguish

gripped her throat and tears fell from her face. She wanted to tear her clothing and take up arms against those who did this cowardly deed. She waited to hear more from him, but the hand released her and the crystal of silence shattered. She could hear the wails of her sisters coming from the solar above.

She did not mention to Fraser what happened, or what she thought happened, for she knew it was only her distraught imagination doing its best to bolster her flagging courage, yet it was also the exact thing her father would have said to her: *Be strong, Claire....* It did not matter if it was real, or not real, for it did not have to be one or the other, for her to find comfort in them.

Ronaln's handsome face was marred not. She found it odd that it disturbed her more than her father's face, with the story of what he suffered written there. Ronaln's face spoke naught, for he was only sleeping. It was not until she saw the circle of blood upon his chest that she realized he had been cowardly killed with a blade through his back. "*A fhleasgaich oig is ceanalta,*" she whispered in Gaelic. *Oh, lad, so young and gentle...*

It was not until she stopped beside the cloth that covered Breac's body that she doubted herself. *Can I do this? Can I see the horror of that which my father fought to shield from his daughters? Will I be able to endure this, or will I go the way of weakened constitution, and faint? God, help me. Grant me courage. Make me strong.*

She reached for the cloth, but Fraser's hand closed gently over her wrist. "Are ye certain this is the way ye wish it to be, Claire? Once ye have done it, ye willna ever forget what ye saw."

"It is not what I wish, but what I must do," she said.

He released her hand and stayed by her side. She drew the cloth back and gasped at the sight of his head lying where it should be, with the bloodied and bruised evidence of his dreadful death, so painful for her to see. The purple, swollen neck, crusted with blood, seemed to cry out to be joined once again to the bloodied stump from which it had been split asunder.

His hair was as it had always been, thick, beautiful and brown, spiced with ginger-red. She touched his hair. It was silky and cold. It was somehow fitting that today the mournful words in her heart came not in Scots, but in Gaelic, *"Fhiranleadain thlath," lad of lovely hair.*

She could not staunch the flow of tears that seemed cursed to flow eternally, and splash one after the other upon her outstretched hand.

Unable to move, she felt like one awakened from an opium dream, disoriented and unable to make a choice. As if he understood, Fraser captured her by the wrist and pulled her away, and after he drew the cloth over Breac's body, he walked her from the room.

"I am dying inside, Fraser, where ye canna see. I bleed from a thousand wounds inside me. Can ye no see what I feel? Will it always be on the inside? I want this pain gone from me, and yet it stays. How can I let it oot?"

"There is no fast and simple way to healing. We all take different roads, but the distance we must travel is the same. Ye have no choice. Ye must make the journey, but ye will not have to go it alone. I am with ye, Claire, for as long as ye have need o' me, I am with ye."

Six

I should like to know who has been carried off, except poor dear me—I have been more ravished myself than anybody since the Trojan War.

Lord Byron (1788-1824), English poet.
Letter, October 29, 1819, answering accusations of debauchery (published in *Byron's Letters and Journals*, vol. 6, ed. by Leslie A. Marchand, 1976)

Lord Monleigh and his brothers remained on Inchmurrin Island during the terrible days that followed. By the second week after the funeral, Claire, her brother and her sisters realized they had accepted them as part of the family.

Out of their tragedy, Kendrew, the youngest and only surviving male of the Lennox family, became the Earl of Errick and Mains. Claire was concerned for him, for Kendrew was only twelve, and too young to bear the weight of such a title.

She was grateful to have the Grahams there. It was especially good for Kendrew to have Lord Monleigh there to encourage him. He spent hours with Kendrew, teaching him the clansmen he could entrust various jobs to, as well as those to keep at a distance. He told him to rely on Claire's judgment and the experience of Dermot, whom his father trusted with his most prized possession, his children.

Day by day, Claire saw Kendrew's confidence return, albeit by slow degrees. Her sisters, too, although saddened and given to moments of tears and despair, were also able to laugh when they all gathered in the evening and spoke of their fondest remembrances, but Claire was not doing as well. Attentively, she listened to the tales of love and humor related by her siblings, and those contributed by the Grahams. Upon occasion, she could relate a special moment of her own.

The similarity ended there for, unlike the others, Claire did not laugh, nor could she cry. She still carried her grief inside, and in spite of Fraser's encouraging her to cry and let the pain out, she could not.

Earlier that morning, Jamie left for Edinburgh, where he would meet with his lawyer to start the necessary proceedings to seek the guardianship of Lord Errick's children. Niall rode with Jamie in the boat across the lake, but instead of accompanying him to Edinburgh, he rode to Grahamstone Castle, to attend to things there until Jamie returned.

Fraser remained at Inchmurrin, temporarily assuming the role of Lord Errick, daily carrying out the tasks and chores as Alasdair would have done, with Kendrew tucked beneath his wing.

"What do ye think it means to be an earl?" Kendrew asked, when they were taking a break from going over papers in the library.

Fraser stopped and looked across the loch, where Ben Lomond stood with his humped shoulders, solitary and alone. "Take a look at Ben Lomond," he said. "When ye are young, ye are crowded together in a range of mountains, but when ye become an earl, ye are like old Ben Lomond, standing all by himself, solitary and alone."

Fraser could see the concern in the grave expression on the boy's young face. He ruffled Kendrew's rosy hair. "'Tis a chore and a duty to be an earl, 'tis true. I am not worried that ye canna handle it, however."

Kendrew stopped to pick up a few pebbles along the shore, where the gentle waves of the loch seemed in no hurry to reach their destination. He pitched several in the water. "Lord Monleigh said I shall learn responsibility, and it was something as big as the word."

"Aye, he was right. I remember the first thing my father said to me on the subject. 'Fraser, he said—' and here Fraser did his best to imitate the stern, gruff voice of his father '—ye must remember ye are responsible for decisions ye make in regards to situations ye are not responsible for.' "

Kendrew kicked a rock and pointed to a red shank that flew overhead, the identifying white edge to the wings easy to see in the sunlight.

"Noisy birds," Fraser said, and enjoyed Kendrew's responsive laugh. Kendrew was a gentle-hearted lad, and one he hated to see burdened with the duty of his inheritance. "Do ye understand the difference between duty and responsibility?"

"Duty is the task and responsibility is taking the

blame if ye do yer duty wrong, or the praise if ye do it well. I hope I always do it well," he said, "for I dinna like to be wrong."

"'Tis a paradox, for no one likes to be wrong, and no one can be right all the time. Each thing ye do, every choice ye make, will be like a shadow that follows ye throughout yer life."

"I dinna understand what ye mean."

Fraser studied the freckles on Kendrew's Celtic nose. "Weel, Lord Errick, I have given ye a bite of the 'food for thought,' but it is up to ye to swallow it, or spit it oot."

Kendrew was quiet for a while, and Fraser asked him if he was troubled about anything.

"When I was little, it didna matter if I was wrong. Now that I am the earl, I am told I must expect that sometimes I will be wrong. I want to be a man like my father. I want to be strong. I dinna want to be wrong. Not ever."

"Weel, ye must realize that being right or wrong is not a judgment of yer manhood. Ye will be wrong, for no man can be right all the time, ye ken, but when ye are a man, ye realize ye will be wrong on occasion, and it willna crush yer spirit to accept that. In the end ye can only perform yer duty to the best o' yer ability, and then ye must have the wit to leave the rest to God."

When they arrived back at the castle, Fraser sent Kendrew off with Dermot to enjoy being a twelve-year-old boy who enjoyed fishing with a longtime friend.

Once he was gone, Fraser turned his thoughts to Claire. There was no doubt in his mind; he was in love with her. The frustrating part of it was, he knew this was not the time to pay her court, when her heart was broken with grief and her emotions nowhere near normal. As a friend, he did not want to take advantage of her time of sorrow. As a man, he wanted her in all the ways a man wants a woman, and it was becoming damnably difficult for him to keep his hands off of her.

He loved her. He desired her, and thought of little other than making love to her. He wanted to do the honorable thing and ask her to marry him, but she would need, and be expected by her clan, to observe her year of mourning.

Could he wait a year to bed her?

Not if she did not help him to keep his distance, for God help him, when it came to Claire, his constitution was weak. He hoped the occasion never presented itself, for he did not know if he would be able to resist her if he ever found her willing.

He could only pray that God would not let such a temptation present itself, yet when he did just that, he dreamed later that God had answered his request with the same words he had spoken to Kendrew. "Ye must remember ye are responsible for decisions ye make in regards to situations ye are not responsible for."

It must have been the week for dreams, for two nights later Claire dreamed her father spoke to her, as he did that day in the great hall, when it seemed so real to hear him say, "Be strong, Claire...."

The dream was disturbing and it awakened her. She did not understand why it upset her, or why it made her cry. Whatever it was, once she started, she could not seem to stop. Distraught, and in need of someone to offer her the sort of comfort and understanding she had given to her siblings, she left her room and went to find Fraser.

The castle was dark, and she decided Fraser had already retired to his room, when she noticed a sliver of light coming from under the library door. She opened it and saw him sitting in her father's leather chair, drinking a glass of brandy.

He was obviously surprised to see her. "Claire, what are ye doing here at this time o' night, in yer sleeping gown?"

Claire looked down. He was right. It was her sleeping gown, and she did not much care one way or the other who saw her in it. She was hurting inside, and that seemed to be all she could handle at the present time.

She crossed the room, the tears still falling down her face, and stopped in front of him.

"Claire, this is not a good idea. Ye canna come in here dressed as ye are and expect me to pretend ye are dressed for kirk. Go back to yer room."

"I canna. I had a dream aboot my father. I feel like everything inside me is broken. Can ye no see I dinna want to be alone? I want to be with ye, Fraser. I canna go back." She put her hands over her face as the tears came in a gushing torrent, and sobs racked her body. She could not help it, and nothing she tried had any effect as far as stopping it. If anything, she only cried more.

"Hell and brimstone," he said, and she felt his arms, warm and steady and reassuring as they pulled her toward him, and the next thing she knew, she was sitting on his lap with her arms around his neck, and doing her best to soak his entire shirtfront.

At least that is what he said, and when she sobbed out that she was "S-s-sorry," he said, "Dinna fret so, Claire. It will dry as soon ye do."

That only made her cry harder.

With his chin resting on her head, he rubbed her back, making big, lazy circles while she cried until there was not a surplus drop of water left in her body. That was when the hiccups came.

She felt the way Fraser's body shook when he laughed softly, and planted a kiss on top of her head. She tightened her arms around his neck and said, "I love ye, Fraser Graham."

He stood, with her still in his arms. It was not the declaration of love she hoped for, but then, it was no negative response to her statement, either.

He started across the room and she asked, "Where are we going?"

"We are going to take ye up to yer room and put ye in yer bed, and then I am going to my room and try the impossible…to go to sleep after what ye have put me through."

"Will ye stay wi' me, Fraser?"

"No."

"I want to be with ye. It matters naught if ye are in my room, or if I go to yer room…as long as ye are with me."

"Claire, ye dinna ken what ye are asking."

"Aye, I ken verra weel what I am asking, Fraser. I am asking ye to stay with me tonight. I dinna want to be alone. I want to lie beside ye, Fraser, because I find comfort when I am near ye."

"Ye canna ask that of me. If I stayed with ye, Claire, yer reputation would be destroyed, and no man of the caliber ye deserve would be interested in asking for yer hand, no matter how wealthy ye were."

"I care naught for what anyone thinks."

"Ye may not care now, but ye will care tomorrow, or the next day, or the next."

She did not say anything more. She nestled her face against his neck while he carried her from the library and up the stairs to her room. She did not say anything when her put her in the bed and drew the covers over her, or when he kissed her forehead in a fatherly manner and left the room quietly.

She was feeling the sting of his rejection, and she tried to go to sleep, but she kept seeing her father and her brothers lying on the table in the great hall, and once, when she dozed off, she dreamed Breac's head was lost and separated from his body, and it came to her and pleaded for her help.

She awoke crying. After what seemed a long, long time, and no relief came, she left her bed and went to Fraser's room.

She stopped outside the door and listened, but no sound came from inside. She put her hand on the doorknob and began to turn it slowly. When she heard it click, she pushed the door open—barely wide enough for her to slip through. Once inside, she closed the door and crossed the room in her bare feet. When she reached the side of the bed opposite the side where Fraser slept, she drew back the covers and climbed quietly into the bed.

His breathing was deep and even, and she knew he was asleep. She closed her eyes and lay as still as a mouse, waiting for sleep to come.

It did not.

She scooted closer to Fraser and froze when her hand touched his bare back. Her fingers inched lower…and then lower…and still she touched nothing but warm, smooth skin. She swallowed—a sound that seemed terribly loud to her own ears, but Fraser stirred not.

Her mouth was dry. Her heart pounded as if it were about to fly right out of her chest. Her curiosity got the better of her, and soon her fingers were on the move again. They inched downward until she knew the firmly rounded skin she touched was his buttocks, and then her eyes grew enormous with the reality of her discovery.

Fraser Graham did not wear a stitch when he slept.

She pulled her hand back and closed her eyes again, but it was not sleep that came to her, but thoughts… thoughts about the way his skin felt under her hand… thoughts about the power she sensed when she touched the firm mounds of his buttocks…thoughts about why he slept with nary a thread touching his body.

Why would he do such a thing?

Mayhap he liked it, she thought. Mayhap it felt good to sleep without nothing on. Mayhap *she* should try it.

She slowly inched her sleeping gown upward, then lifted her buttocks and pulled it up to her shoulders, which was the point when removing it became a wee bit more complicated.

At last, she finally had the gown off and she dropped it to the floor next to her. She stretched, feeling the smooth sheets against her naked flesh. It felt strange, but nice. She turned on her side, with her back facing Fraser's back. She closed her eyes and at some point she drifted off to sleep.

Some time later, when Fraser turned over, he touched something. He froze and lay perfectly still. He touched it again. He did not need to touch it a third time to know what he had in his hand was a breast.

A naked breast, at that.

His hand dropped lower...and lower...and lower still...

Damn ye, Claire, he thought. She was not wearing anything, and mighty good it felt, too.

At that point, Claire awakened and turned toward him.

Fraser groaned.

Claire's eyes opened. "Dinna say it," she said. "I ken ye are going to be angry with me."

"What in the name of the patron saint of yer choice are ye doing in my bed with yer clothes off?"

"I wanted to be with ye, and when I discovered ye had nothing on, I wanted to be like ye. I wanted to see what it felt like."

"Put your gown on and go back to *your* room and *your* own bed."

Her arms went around his neck. "Make love to me, Fraser. Make me feel something besides pain and sorrow. I want ye and I feel like I am burning inside for ye."

"Claire, I canna... God help me, I want to, but I canna. 'Tis not yer heart speaking, but yer grief."

"Ye are wrong, Fraser. 'Tis my heart, and 'tis my body that I offer ye. Teach me...show me what to do, so I..."

She did not get to finish, for Fraser cut her off when he said, "Damn ye, Claire. Damn us both."

His mouth was suddenly on hers, coaxing her with a kiss, telling of his feeling for her as it was full of desire. He knew she had not lain with a man before, and he did not want her first time to be painful or frightening for her. He did his best to temper the raging fire of need and desire that burned inside him, but even in that, Claire gave him no quarter. When he pulled back to pace himself, she became the aggressor, and to know it came naturally to her, and not from experience, pushed him beyond what he could endure.

His body took over, leaving his honorable thoughts tumbled in the dust of his mind. His desire matched hers in a primitive need to mate, but only with her. He could feel her body quiver beneath his. He inhaled the sweet fragrance of roses in her hair. He tasted the honey of her mouth again and again, and then kissed his way down, across the smooth flatness of her belly, until he found the place he searched for.

She sucked in her breath and whispered "No, Fraser" when he kissed her, but he did not stop, and a moment later, she opened to him and he heard her soft panting, breathless whispers. "I never knew… Oh… Oh, Fraser, ye are touching my soul and I want to flow outward the way a river joins itself to the sea."

She began to pant and writhe beneath the tutelage of his tongue, and he brought her to the edge then pulled back, and then brought her to the edge again. He muffled her panting cry with a kiss at the moment her body exploded, and then he drove himself into her.

He felt the barrier give way and he went mindless when he realized he was where he'd wanted to be since that day he first saw her standing on the shore, looking toward their boat with her regal bearing and an angry expression cast toward the intruders who dared approach her island.

If she felt a pain at all she did not show it, for she began to move beneath him, matching him, driving him forward with her frank honesty and sexual descriptions of how she felt, and the way she told him what she liked and how she liked it.

Spent, he rolled to his side and held her close to him. He dozed off, only to awaken some time later to realize Claire was doing some investigating of her own. She had her hand around him and he was warming up to the idea with every beat of his heart, which sent blood plummeting to that part of him that intrigued her.

"Ye are like magic here, and ye do magical things to me with it." And then, although he could not believe it himself, she took him in her mouth, and for the first time in his life, Fraser Graham had a woman do what he had done to countless women before. She drove him wild, taking him to the edge, time and again, and pulling back at the right moment to keep him on the edge of a very narrow precipice.

She was completely in control and he was in complete agony, wanting...needing her to finish what she started, until he reached the point where he was ready to take her in order to relieve the torture, when she brought him to the edge again, and instead of pulling back this time, she pulled him into a twisting torrent along with her.

When it was over, he realized there was a difference between making love and being loved, just as there was a difference between making love to a woman you loved, and making love to a woman.

"I love ye, Fraser," she said, and closed her eyes.

"Ye better, Claire, for ye are mine, and I have no intention o' letting ye go."

Seven

In the fell clutch of circumstance,
I have not winced nor cried aloud;
Under the bludgeonings of chance
My head is bloody, but unbowed.

William Ernest Henley (1849-1903),
British writer.
Echoes "Invictus.
In Memoriam R.T.H.B." (1888)

Jamie returned from Edinburgh with disappointing news.

"It was a wasted trip," he said. "It was already too late by the time I arrived, although I still canna understand how it could have happened so quickly," he said.

"What mean ye, it was too late?" Fraser asked.

At the moment, they were the only two in the library. Jamie was half sitting, half leaning against the corner of the desk.

Fraser was pacing slowly about the room with a serious look on his face.

"It seems someone else had already been granted the ward before I arrived."

"I find that hard to believe," Fraser said. "Were they given right of marriage as well?"

Jamie shook his head. "Fortunately, no. Only the ward was granted."

"Did ye find out the name o' who it was?"

"Och, aye, I found out all right. How do ye like the sound o' Isobel Lennox and Lord Walter Ramsay as guardians? Or better yet, how do ye think Alasdair would have felt if he knew this would happen? He never cared for Isobel, ye ken."

"I heard he blamed her for his brother's death," Fraser said, "although I never knew exactly what the circumstances were."

Jamie crossed his legs and leaned back. "He said William Lennox was healthy as a trout, and miserable living with Isobel and her son."

Fraser stopped pacing. "Ye mean he thought she might have had a hand with William's death?"

Jamie shrugged. "He never came out and said it, ye ken, but he did infer that was his feeling about it."

"What was the cause of his death?" Fraser asked.

Jamie thought about that for a moment. "Weel, I dinna ken the cause exactly. Seems I remember that he became ill and it worsened and then he died, but the doctors never knew what was wrong with him."

"So, where is Isobel's son now?" Fraser asked.

"Hmm," Jamie said. "I am no sure. Last I heard Giles was in Edinburgh, living well beyond his means, like his mother."

Fraser nodded. "I have heard the same about Isobel. Some say she has spent all of William's money already. That is probably why they needed the right to and withal to get the custody of Earl Kendrew during the time o' his ward."

Jamie nodded in agreement. "My fear is there willna be any money left by the time Claire reaches the age of majority when they will finally be free o' them."

"That must be why they wanted the right o' ward," Fraser said. "I am still puzzled as to how they managed to be granted the ward of Kendrew and Alasdair's daughters as quickly as they did. It must have come about by some type of political maneuvering and, unfortunately, we are dealing with the English crown. It is my guess that Isobel claimed it by right of kinship, seeing as how she is the widow of their father's brother, but I am at a loss as to how Lord Walter became involved."

Jamie withdrew a letter and unfolded it. "This was delivered to me today. It is from my lawyer. He pursued the matter a bit further and learned that the ward of Kendrew was granted to his aunt by marriage, Isobel Lennox, who then committed it to the care of Lord Walter Ramsay, of Inverness. So now we have confirmation that the two of them are in this together."

"How much time do we have before they take control o' Alasdair's children and his possessions?"

"Oh, they plan to move to Inchmurrin, and like many of their ilk have done in the past, I ken they will live like royalty on the inheritance of Alasdair's children, and by the time Claire reaches her majority, there willna be much of the fortune left."

"I do not like this," Fraser said.

"Neither do I, but unless ye have privy to the ear o' the King of England and hold sway with his opinions, we have no choice but to return to Grahamstone once the greedy pair arrive."

"This will no be easy for them to accept," Fraser said, "especially since we know how they all feel about Isobel and Lord Walter."

"I agree, but 'tis out of our hands now. All we can do is break the news to them as gently as we can. Do ye want to be the ogre what tells them, or shall I?"

"Perhaps we should do it together," Fraser said. "That way we can be a double-headed ogre."

And in the end, that is what they felt like.

Claire took it hardest of all, for she was the eldest and the one most capable of understanding what it meant, knowing the kind of people they would be dealing with, since Claire had said on numerous occasions that she did not like Isobel or Lord Walter. Although, Fraser felt, if he were to be honest, he did not know if that opinion was born of Claire's own preferences or because she knew her father cared not a whit for either of them. And Claire was ever her father's daughter.

Jamie and Fraser remained for almost a week before Isobel Lennox, the widow of the children's uncle, William Lennox, arrived with her paramour, Lord Walter Ramsay, at Inchmurrin Island.

The moment they entered the castle and discovered Fraser Graham and Lord Monleigh were there, Isobel wasted no time in producing the parchment documents attesting to the ward of Kendrew and his sisters being granted to her.

Since they arrived with all their baggage, ready to assume the roles they coveted, the pair moved in immediately. This left Fraser and Jamie with little choice. They had to leave.

"I wish ye could stay with us," Kendrew told Fraser.

"I wish so, too, but we have to obey the law," Fraser said.

It was a tearful parting, although Fraser and Jamie both did everything they could to make the transition go smoothly. Fortunately, and much to their surprise, both Isobel and Lord Walter were surprisingly kind-hearted toward the children.

"I canna thank ye enough, Lord Monleigh, for all ye did since the tragic news that orphaned these dearest o' children. 'Tis a blessing to know they have had yer guidance and protection until we could arrive. I do hope ye will find time to pay them a visit."

"Perhaps we will stop by on our return to Monleigh Castle, in order that we might say goodbye," Lord Monleigh replied.

"Oh, ye havena moved to Grahamstone Castle permanently?"

"No, we only came for a time to oversee some renovations, and to meet with the retainers and such. We will return home within the coming month."

"Please do stop and tell the children goodbye," Isobel said. "Ye are always welcome."

"Thank ye," Lord Monleigh said. "And now, if ye will excuse me, I will find my brother, so we can be on our way."

Fraser walked with Claire and the dogs, for he wanted to tell her he was leaving when they were alone.

"I wish ye could stay."

"Ye know it is not possible."

"Then I wish I could go with ye."

"Ye are needed here, Claire, and ye know it. Just

as I know ye wouldna leave yer brother and sisters. Not at a time like this."

"Aye, it is something I must do, ye ken, but I do not have to like it."

She stopped and he put his arms around her, content to hold her against him, while trying to imprint as much of her in his mind as he could, so he would have that much of her, at least, to hold on to in the months they would be apart.

Fraser knew it would be months, and not more than a year, for as soon as her year of mourning was up, he intended to marry her.

Their time together was too short, for Fraser saw Jamie coming down the track, and he knew the time to leave had arrived. He kissed her one last time, branding her with the passion and love he felt for her and, when it ended, he discovered how very difficult it was to leave her and walk away.

"I will write ye, lass."

She smiled weakly. "And I will write ye back, Fraser Graham."

While Jamie waited a discreet distance away, Fraser found he was not as strong as he thought. "One last kiss," he said, and drew her into his arms. "I love ye, Claire."

She started to cry then, but only for a moment before she got control of herself. "'Tis sorry I am that ye had to see me in a moment o' weakness. I love ye, Fraser, and it kills me inside to say farewell, but I have to stay strong, and I ken I will see ye again. I dinna want to come to the boat. I will stay here, in the spot where I first laid eyes on ye, and like I watched ye sail into my life, I will watch ye sail oot o' it."

"It willna be forever, lass."

She watched him walk up the track to join his brother, MacTavish and Maddy loping ahead of them. She gave Lord Duffus a pat. "Ye are always with me, are ye not?"

Duffus thumped his tail and raised a cloud of dust, then followed Claire down to the spot where she would wait for the boat.

When it came, she waved and kept on waving until the boat was absorbed into the bright reflection of the sun upon the loch. She wiped the tears drying on her cheeks and smiled at the look of sad understanding she saw in the eyes of her beloved dog.

"Come on, Lord Duffus, let us go home and see how we fare facing our future."

Claire fully expected Isobel to be as wicked as the Countess of Seaforth who had poor Coinneach Odhar, the Brahan Seer, pitched alive into a barrel of boiling tar. Yet, when Claire returned to the house, Isobel came to greet her warmly.

"My dear niece, it grieves me that I did not hear about yer loss right away. Had I known, I would have rushed to yer side immediately. I ken I canna take the place of your dear father, but I will strive to be a friend, and a loving aunt."

She took Claire by the hand. "Come, your sisters and I are going through some beautiful fabrics that I bought in Paris. They are of the latest colors and prints. I want each of ye to choose a fabric ye favor, an' we will have a dress made of it."

"We canna have new dresses, unless they are black. Have ye forgotten, we are in mourning?"

Isobel looked at Claire's somber black gown and

smiled. "No, I have not forgotten that, dear. Hout! With so much black about, this place looks as cheerless as a winter day. However, by the time yer mourning period is over, I want ye to have new wardrobes. Therefore, I think we should start with making each of ye a new dress or two now, and we will add a dress, here and there, until we have ye suitably attired."

Claire agreed to join her sisters. There were dozens of fabrics spread all over the long table in the great hall, the likes of which Claire had never seen.

"Claire, look at the one I have chosen," Briana said, and held up a soft yellow muslin. "Aunt Isobel said the color would be perfect for my hair. Do ye think so?"

Claire smiled to see Briana's face so happy. "I think it will make ye the prettiest lass in kirk. The color is beautiful, and the muslin will make a lovely dress."

"Look at the one I like," Kenna said, and held up a dark green velvet. "I want a dress for the wintertime out of this. I feel the dark green color is especially good for red hair. What do ye think?"

"With yer hair and yer eyes, ye should have nothing but green, and how regal the velvet looks."

"Aye," Kenna said while she ran her hand over the softly napped velvet. "It will be a welcome change after so long in somber colors."

Claire looked for Greer and saw her at the end of the table. She wandered toward her, taking a few moments to stop whenever a fabric caught her eye. "Have ye decided on yer fabric?" she asked.

Greer sighed and spoke softly. "I like them all. This brown wool would be warm for wintertime." She put it down and picked up another choice. "This dark blue linen would make up nicely. And this—" Claire noticed the way Greer's eyes seemed to light up "—is so beautiful." She held up a pale green print. "I ken it is no' a sensible choice, since we seldom go to parties."

Claire smiled. Greer was the dearest, sweetest person God ever created. She was the kind who returned a compliment with a grander compliment, or wrote a thank-ye letter to someone who sent a thank-ye letter to her.

"Do ye want to know what I think?" Claire asked. "I think ye should get the one that makes ye the happiest. Even if ye choose the green print, ye will enjoy the wearing o' it, even if it is in yer room, or to walk the dogs. Ye should dress to please yerself, Greer, and hang all those fussy rules. Sometimes a luxury can do much more for yer spirit than a dozen necessities. It is how ye deal with it in yer heart."

Greer smiled. "Oh, thank ye, Claire. I wanted it, ye ken, but I was afraid it would be too vain to want something that was not practical."

Claire leaned close and whispered, "Ye have a trunkful of practical, though, do ye not?"

"Aye, and I shall have the green print." She hugged Claire.

As for Claire, she chose a thin wool twill in a deep purple, and white bobbin lace to edge the low-cut neck.

"Weel now, my lovelies," Isobel said. "Tomorrow I shall take all of ye to Stirling, where ye shall be measured, so the dressmaker can set to work. Then we will shop for bonnets and flowers and furbelows, too, and petticoats and satin ribbons and stockings the color of cream."

"We can do all o' that in one day?" Kenna asked.

"Oh, my dear, of course we can. We will stay at the Inn of Two Doves. I think three days and two nights should give us enough time. If not, we shall stay one more day."

"What about Kendrew?" Greer asked.

"Lord Walter is taking Kendrew to Glasgow. There is a horse auction and they shall buy Kendrew his own horse."

The girls all gasped. "A horse for Kendrew," Kenna said. "He has always wanted his own horse."

"Weel, now he shall have it."

That night, when Claire said prayers with Briana and kissed her good-night, Briana hugged her fiercely and said, "I think Isobel is the nicest person."

"I think it is nice to see ye happy, darling Briana. Now, go to sleep, we have a long day tomorrow."

True to her word, Isobel, Claire and her sisters all left for Stirling the following day, and in spite of Claire's hesitation to accept Isobel, she had to admit the trip was the most marvelous outing she and her sisters had ever taken. In the beginning, Claire was a wee bit embarrassed for they looked like a traveling troop of mourners, all wearing their black, save Briana, whom Isobel said would do better in dark gray, due to her younger age.

When she mentioned this, Isobel laughed. "Let me tell ye something. Ye can put a beautiful woman in a wolf pelt and her beauty will still be noticed. It isna what ye wear, but how ye wear it that counts. Besides, there is a certain attractiveness about a beauty in mourning that attracts the eye…especially the eye of a lad, ye ken?"

By the time they returned home three days later,

they had been measured for one black mourning dress, and a dress from the Parisian fabric, and the proper petticoats and undergarments. Isobel also purchased sleeping gowns and black stockings.

Once they were home, things settled into a normal routine, with Kendrew spending time on his Highland pony, and Claire and her sisters busy with their lessons from a new governess that was hired, although the girls were able to persuade Isobel not to let poor Aggie go.

"But she is hardly a tutor," Isobel said. "Yer education has been horribly neglected."

The girls and Kendrew all put up such a fuss, Isobel agreed to keep Aggie and the new governess, Miss Kathleen O'Malley, who was as Irish as her name.

From the day of their arrival, life as the Lennox siblings had known it began to change drastically, and although they were happy for so many of the changes, they were still grieving for the loss of their father and two brothers, and naturally given to moments of extreme sadness and tears. But as the days passed, the sad days grew less long, and more infrequent, as the pain of their loss lessened.

Claire's tendency not to trust Isobel also lessened, and gradually she began to trust her as much as her sisters did. She did not try to understand why it was that her father detested Isobel and Lord Walter so much. Instead, she focused on what her father had taught her, and that was to "accept people as they appear to be, until they show ye a different face."

Gradually, the summer warmth began to turn cooler as fall approached, and then the next thing she knew, it was October. When the first cold days came, Claire made certain that she thanked Isobel for her foresight in having nice warm woolen capes made for all of them.

Christmas came and went, and was followed by a great freeze that completely froze the waters of the loch from Balloch on the south end and as far north as Luss. From her window, Claire could see curling teams on the ice, and red-cheeked children playing, while dozens of people skated merrily on the ice. There were men with loaded sleds driving across the stubbled fields—where golden grain had waved in the summer breeze a few months before—to take advantage of the shortcut across the ice.

How different it all looked from summer, and it reminded her that change occurs everywhere, and not only in her life.

As the year progressed and spring returned, Claire celebrated her sixteenth birthday, along with many new things that were added to their lives, such as music lessons and art lessons, and a dancing master who taught them how to perform the latest dances. This also meant some new employees were brought on, and some of the older employees were let go. "All done so that ye might have the refinement ye have sorely lacked in the past," Isobel said.

Fraser continued to send letters to Claire and, in turn, Claire gave her replies to Dermot, so he could post them for her. It was not the same as having him close, but it did help her keep his memory close to her heart. Claire did not tell Isobel about her letters, not because she was trying to keep Fraser a secret, but because she did not want to share her letters with anyone, and she feared that Isobel might ask to read them.

In order to keep it secret, when Claire was in town, she requested that her letters be held, and that she would come for them the next time she returned. That way, she could send and receive her letters in complete privacy.

While Isobel was becoming an important center of the girls' lives, Lord Walter's main focus was Kendrew. This did not go unnoticed by Claire, who worried that Kendrew would be the one most affected by the loss they suffered. Claire still had her female connection in her sisters, but Kendrew lost all the male influence in his life at one time.

Claire was an honest person, and it troubled her that she had been so suspicious and distrusting of Isobel and Lord Walter, which she now understood came about because her father was always wary of the couple. One afternoon, she had the perfect opportunity to bring it up with Isobel.

She and Isobel were working on their embroidery in the solar, while her sisters finished their music lessons.

Isobel took a stitch, tied the knot and snipped the thread. As she threaded the needle again she glanced at Claire, who was frowning over an intricate stitch.

"My dear Claire, ye seem troubled today. Is anything amiss? Has something happened to upset ye? I hope ye ken that Lord Walter and I want so much to be a part of yer loving family. If, at any time, we err in our judgment or commit some other infraction, I do hope ye will address it." She laid her embroidery down. "Is there anything we have done that ye would like to discuss?"

Claire put her embroidery in her lap. "Aye, I have

been troubled of late, Aunt Isobel, but not for the reason ye speak of. 'Tis a guilty conscience what eats at me."

"A guilty conscience? Och, how could ye have a guilty conscience when ye are a tenderhearted lass with a loving spirit? I canna believe you could be guilty of anything that would cause ye to harbor such feelings."

"Your kindness, understanding and gentle guidance has contributed much toward the easing of our suffering. It has caused me to regret my hastiness in judging ye, and I wish to offer ye my apologies for being too stubborn to accept ye from the very first."

"I knew it was yer grief what held ye back, and I willna have ye punishing yerself over it. Think no more upon it. I have forgotten it, and so should ye."

Lord Walter continued to spend his time going over the accounts in the library, or making trips to inspect the various holdings that her father had owned, for none of it was located on Inchmurrin, which was too small an island to provide much space for anything larger than a family garden, and certainly no large herds of cattle could graze there. He also found more time to spend with Kendrew, who by this point had grown quite fond of him. There were times when Lord Walter would leave for a week at a time, to inspect another Lennox property, and each time he did it was obvious to all how much Kendrew missed him.

Claire was beginning to think she would never see Fraser again, when he wrote her that he was going to Edinburgh in three weeks time, with his brothers Calum and Tavish. He wrote of his longing to see her, and to feel the warmth of her sweet kisses. "I plan to come to Inchmurrin for several days once we arrive in Edinburgh."

Anticipation was good for one thing, in Claire's opinion, and that was to make time pass painfully slow. She did not know why she chose to do it, but she did not tell Isobel about Fraser's plans to visit until a few days before he was due to arrive.

"Fraser Graham is coming here for several days?" Isobel said. "I do not think that is a good idea, Claire. How will it look for a man to come to see ye specifically, and to reside in the same house as ye?"

"We willna be alone," Claire said, "and with three sisters and a brother like mine, I canna anticipate we will have any time alone."

"Why is he coming?"

"The Grahams were friends of my father before he married our mother, and they continued to be. The last time they were here, we all became very close friends with Lord Monleigh, Fraser and Niall."

"Weel," she said, "what is done is done, and we canna do anything aboot it now. However, in the future, do not be so lax in advising me of yer plans. There is a reason why a young woman yer age is placed under the guidance of an adult."

Eight

When a woman wants a man and lusts after him, the lover need not bother to conjure up opportunities, for she will find more in an hour than we men could think of in a century.

Pierre de Bourdeilles, Abbé de Brantôme (c. 1530-1614), French courtier, soldier, author. *The Lives of Gallant Ladies*, "First Essay" (1659)

He knew Claire must have seen his boat as it approached the island, for she was waiting for him on the dock.

When Fraser stepped off the boat, she came to him. "Welcome back to Inchmurrin, Fraser. We have missed ye sorely."

Fraser was speechless. She had matured, and was so breathtakingly beautiful that the words he had ready to say to her suddenly seemed inappropriate, and unworthy of such a woman.

Her smile alone would put a thousand candles to shame, for it seemed to light up the world, or at least that small part of it that he was occupying at the moment.

He could not believe his good fortune to have a woman such as Claire who loved him.

"Ye came," she said.

"Aye, do ye think I would allow anything to stop me from seeing ye? Ye are more beautiful than I remembered."

Dermot picked up Fraser's portmanteau, and Claire slipped her arm through his and walked with him down the path. "Welcome back to Inchmurrin. 'Tis good to have ye here."

"I am already wishing I could take ye with me when I leave. 'Tis not easy for me to be so far from ye."

"'Tis the same for me."

"How are your sisters?"

"They are adjusting better than I thought they would. Much to my surprise, Isobel and Lord Walter have proved themselves to be quite the grandest guardians."

"I will have to add my name to the list of surprised persons," Fraser said, "for I dinna trust either of them."

She put her hand on his arm. "Do not be critical and judgmental, especially when ye have no reason to be."

"Anything you ask," he said. "When will we have some time alone?" He saw the color rise to her cheeks and he wondered if her feelings for him had changed, or if she was simply shy, due to their long separation.

"It willna be a simple task to find a place or a time to be alone," she said. "The island is small and my sisters know every inch of it and, of course, there is no hiding from the dogs."

"We will find a few minutes alone, surely. How are ye at climbing trees?"

She gave him a look that was half surprise and half humor. "I canna believe ye said that."

"What do ye mean? How could I have said something wrong?"

She smiled and hugged his arm. "Not wrong at all, Fraser. To the contrary, it might prove to be the opposite. I had completely forgotten about it until you reminded me. When my sisters and I were much younger, we loved to climb the trees and watch the boats on the loch, and whenever one came toward the island, we would run to find someone to tell them."

"Like a sentry," he said, amused at her animated voice.

"Aye, like a sentry. But, one day we saw a boat and Kenna wanted to be the first one down, so she could be first to tell our father that a boat was coming. In her haste, she fell out of the tree. My father feared she had broken her back, but thankfully it wasna that bad, but she couldna climb trees for a long time."

"And that is all? That is all ye wanted to tell me?"

"No, of course not. At first we were forbidden to climb the trees anymore, but when Father saw how glum we were over losing our favorite pastime, he had a ladder built so we could climb it, and then they built us a little house in the tree. It had a door and three windows, so we could look in different directions on the loch. And the walls kept us from falling out."

Fraser laughed. "Claire Lennox, are ye suggesting that we climb a tree so we be alone, in a house built for fairies?"

"Fairies?"

"Aye, if ye and yer sisters were small, then the house must be a wee house, and in case ye have not noticed, I am not a short man."

"Weel, I think if ye truly want to be alone with me, ye will find a way to accomplish it."

Dermot was already holding the door open by the time they arrived. Once they entered, he followed them inside. Isobel and Lord Walter were waiting to greet Fraser.

"Welcome to Inchmurrin," Lord Walter said. "I trust your trip went well."

"Thank ye, Lord Walter. I canna complain about it. Nary a problem, for which I am thankful."

"Walter, do give me a chance to welcome our guest." Isobel took Fraser's arm. "We were so delighted to hear you were coming. Do come into the hall. The girls and Kendrew are most anxious to see ye. It will be a good place for us to visit until dinner is served. I trust ye brought yer appetite?"

"Never leave home without it," Fraser said.

Lord Walter gave Claire his arm and they followed Isobel and Fraser into the hall. Immediately, Fraser was bombarded with welcome greetings from Claire's sisters and Kendrew.

By the time dinner was served, Fraser found he enjoyed this time of interaction with Claire's family. Her sisters were of the age that he found utterly charming, and he had already decided Briana was going to be a heartbreaker for certain, for she was already a little coquette.

Fraser happened to ask them how they all liked living on an island.

"It is peaceful," Greer said. "And we have no wolves."

"I find it lonely," Claire said. "Yer friends rarely come to visit, because they dinna like to ride the boat over here."

"Weel," Briana said, "ye should find yersel' some other lonely people, and then ye willna have to be lonely anymore."

"There isna enough room to ride yer horses verra far," Kendrew said.

"And ye, Briana?" Fraser asked when she had not said anything. "Do ye find it lonely living on an island?"

"Aye, ye have to go ten miles to find a mosquito."

Listening to all the conversation, Fraser found himself amazed at Kendrew, and begrudgingly had to admit that Lord Walter had done much to pull him out of the cocoon of sadness he had surrounded himself with. All of them looked healthy and happy, to the point he was beginning to wonder if he had misjudged Isobel and Lord Walter.

When Claire came down for breakfast, she learned that Fraser had eaten earlier, and then went for a walk with Kendrew. When they returned, Claire began to fear she might never have even five minutes alone with him, for he was the center of everyone's attention and was literally being pulled in five different directions by her siblings. Aye, it was enjoyable to observe the way he interacted with them, but Claire could not hold the stab of jealousy that attacked her now and then.

At first she blamed her sisters and brother, and then she blamed Fraser, for it seemed to her that he could have ended it at any point and suggested he and Claire take a walk. She did not think that she might have done the same. Instead, since he did not choose to do so, she began to wonder if he had given up on the idea entirely.

She was about two shakes away from being quite cross with him when Fraser untangled himself from his admiring throng and came to take her hand and pull her to her feet.

"It is time I gave Claire some of the attention I have given all of ye," he said, and turned to Claire. "Would ye care to show me around yer island? I am not accustomed to being idle, or indoors for much o' the day. A walk would be nice aboot now. What say ye?"

Before Claire could answer, they were surrounded and heard a chorus of "We want to go with ye."

"Not this time," Isobel said. "I believe Fraser has earned his walk and a few minutes alone with Claire. After all, he didna come here to while away his hours with the five of ye, now did he?"

"Kendrew, I believe Lord Walter has need of ye down at the boat dock. He said ye were going to go to the mainland today to ride. Have ye forgotten?"

"Aye, Aunt Isobel, I forgot," Kendrew said, and hurried from the room.

"As for the rest of ye, I have something I want ye to help me with," Isobel said, while she gave Claire and Fraser a wave of her hand, which told them to take advantage of the moment to slip away.

Which they promptly did.

"Weel, I will have to say that surprised me," Fraser said. "And here I was thinking Isobel and Lord Walter were going to make it nigh impossible for us to have even one moment together."

"See? I told ye how nice they were. Now, dinna ye feel poorly for thinking the worst o' them?"

"I suppose I should," he said.

"Aye, ye should," she said, and cocked an eye at him. "Ye should, but I can tell that ye dinna."

They rounded a bend in the path, and Fraser pulled Claire behind a tree. She stood on the hump of roots, which put her almost at eye level with him. She leaned against the tree and waited to see what he would do.

He drew her into his arms, and backed against the tree as she was, when he held her close, their bodies were intimately aligned, and in her little black muslin dress, there was plenty of him to feel. Everything inside her seemed to thicken, while her heartbeat escalated. She felt quivery with anticipation, and so hungry for him, she had to force herself to wait and let him take the lead.

His hands were caressing the sides of her neck now, while he trailed kisses over her face, whispering endearments, and telling her how much he missed her; how much he thought about the time they made love.

"Ye smell like flowers and rain and sunshine all rolled together, and yer skin is softer than a rose petal." He unbuttoned her dress, and his hand cupped her breast and lifted it so it was exposed. Her body was reacting to him, his nearness and his words, running ahead of her, not heeding her reminders to be reserved.

His thumb moved back and forth over her nipple and she pressed her cheek against his dark head when he leaned down to take her into his mouth. The first tug on her breast sent wave after wave of desire throughout her body. She wanted him almost to the point of ripping her clothes off and pulling him down on top of her.

He brought his head up and covered her mouth with his, drawing her tongue into his mouth, then giving her the feel of his in return. She moaned and moved against him, and heard his breathing deepen, as she sensed a heightened sense of urgency pressing, pushing and driving him forward, as if some unknown had taken over. She felt his hand on her bare leg, and wondered how he got her gown up and his hand under her drawers without her knowing he had done so.

Then she felt his fingers touching her and her knees almost buckled beneath her. "Ye are ready, lass. Where? Where can we go?"

Her head was thrown back and she was breathing in short pants. It took a moment for her to speak, so overcome with wanting him as she was. "If ye dinna stop touching me like that, I willna be able to go anywhere, Fraser. Why do ye torture me so?"

"So I can ease yer suffering," he replied.

Still not trusting her voice, she took his hand and led him through the trees. They cut through a corner of the rhododendron thicket and climbed up a rocky embankment, until they reached an enormous tree with vines trailing down from its lofty branches. There was nothing around, save the woods behind them and the wide expanse of loch on three sides.

Claire stepped around the tree. The ladder was still there, although overgrown with vines. She hitched her skirts and started up, pushing vines aside as she went.

When she reached the landing, she was surprised to see the wooden floor had been swept clean by the wind, and the boards were still sturdy. She crawled forward and pulled herself up.

By the time Fraser reached the top, she already had

the door open and was inside looking around. There were a few leaves in the corner, but she was not certain that there might not be an insect or two hidden among them. She was wondering what to do when Fraser poked his head in and took her hand, drawing her back to the landing. She put her hand on the railing and looked up at him, a question in her raised brows.

He removed his jacket and laid it on the boards, and started to undress.

"Here?" she asked.

"Aye, I canna fit in that wee box. My elbows will be knocking the walls oot."

She smiled, and began undoing the rest of her buttons. She turned her dress to the wrong side and laid it near his jacket. By the time she finished, Fraser was as bare as a bone. She studied the magnificent body, the smooth, firm muscle, the flat contours of his stomach, and lower, until she smiled. He was her man, and he was truly ready for her.

She began to tug at the ribbons of her chemise. When it was off, she lay down, wearing nothing but her drawers.

He was beside her quickly, and his hands began to caress her, touching each breast and teasing it to heightened awareness, before he ran his flattened palm over her ribs and the flat planes of her stomach, and lower. Her heart began to hammer so furiously, she wondered if it possible to have a heart that beat until it flew right out of her chest. A thought suddenly popped into her head, and she wondered if she was being too easy and too brazen, or if she had fallen too quickly into such a comfortable feeling with him, and now he intended to see that she gave him what he brought her out here to receive.

Yet, if she were honest, she had to admit that it was the same reason she allowed him to bring her here, which made it seem that she wanted this as much as he. Since it seemed to her that they were even in desire, purpose and need, there was not much point in considering such thoughts beyond that.

She turned her head to give him her mouth, and he wasted no time in kissing her, but not the same hot, passionate kiss of a moment ago, but a languid, probing kiss that said he knew exactly what he was about, for it had her writhing beneath him—or was the cause the delicious things he was doing to her with his wandering hand?

She kissed him back, matching him thrust for thrust, wanting more of his hot tongue inside her mouth. He dug his fingers into her hair, and whispered erotic Gaelic phrases in her ear, of what he wanted to do to her, and what he wanted her to do to him. He told her how beautiful she was and how much he had wanted to do this since the moment he stepped off the boat, and saw her there waiting for him.

"That was when I knew I always wanted ye waiting for me when I came home. I love ye, Claire, and I want ye with me for the rest o' our lives. I ken this is yer time o' mourning, and ye canna think aboot things too clearly, but will ye think upon it during this time, and let me know if ye think ye might feel…"

"Fraser, will ye hurry up and ask me to marry ye so I can say yes, and then we can get back to what we came up here for?"

He suppressed his laugh against her throat, but she

felt the rumbling vibration of it and smiled. She was a fortunate lass to have found this wonderful man at a time when she needed him in her life the most. She was glad her father had known Fraser, and that he would have heartily approved of her marriage to him. She had some other thoughts, too, but when Fraser put his mind and his hands to it, he could be most persuasive with his distractions.

Those magic hands, they were everywhere, and he knew each place and how to touch her and how to make her want him with a deep, aching need that made her want to be closer, to open wider, to go wilder than she thought herself capable of, or that she had any previous knowledge of. And then she felt it, somewhere deep inside, she felt the first trembling of a far-reaching reaction that set off another reaction, which continued on and on. She was not prepared for such a raw awareness of intimacy that drew her into him and made her want to please him as much as he pleased her.

Slowly, consummately, she was being drugged by a lazy coil of tightening desire that pushed her forward, past caution, past inhibition, past everything save the need to couple with him, to feel his power, to hold him inside her until he cried out her name. Time and again, she thought she was at that point, only to have him leave her panting and writhing, almost pleading at the entrance to a new world of knowledge and passionate response, a world of sexual desire that yawned like temptation before her, calling…beckoning…*come in...come in....*

She feared she loved him too much, and wanted to give herself to him to the point that she could lose herself completely within him, and then realize too late that he had completely surrounded her, until she was his prisoner, bound as tightly to him as an indentured slave.

Out of the heated excitement that controlled her, his face began to come into focus over hers, and she wondered if she had fallen for a mortal man, or one of the mythological creatures that lured foolish young women to their doom.

She felt his palm slide between her legs, which put his thumb in a most delicious place. She moaned and lifted her hips against it. Something strange was happening, something was driving her without her knowledge or consent. How did she know to do what she was doing, how to move just so, and where did the faultless rhythm come from?

Everything was perfectly synchronized, from the right amount of pressure applied by his thumb, to the slow, curling coil of desire in her belly, and the measured pace of her hips moving in sequence with each panting breath, each exquisite moan, every wave of response that pulsed through her.

His lips replaced his hand, and at the first touch of his tongue, she cried out. Her body convulsed, again and again, until she begged him to end it, but he would not.

"Ye are not through, lass. Ye have more to give. I love the way ye move against me," he said, and drove her beyond insanity again with his mouth. She was sweating, her body was convulsing with rippling sensations of pleasure that came, one after the other, rolling, and rolling, endlessly in the search for a way to keep the moment going, faster, harder, longer, with a feeling that was as beautiful as it was full of power.

He moved over her and eased himself inside, and the exquisite torture of wanting him again gripped her once more, and she went with him to that place that only exists somewhere between pleasure and pain, and she loved the power of it, and she gave herself up to the primitive side of her, and completely erased all thought from her mind, which gave her body full control.

The next thing she knew, she was on top of him, still joined with him, and he guided her with his hands on her hips, and when she leaned forward, her breasts brushed his lips and he drew her nipple into his mouth, pulling, drawing, tasting her in rhythm with her hips grinding down upon him.

She sensed the change in him, and the power that took over and drove forward, out of control until she felt him flow into her, and shuddered as the waves of fulfillment tightened intensely around her, and her body jerked, again and again, until she leaned forward to lay her head on his chest, completely exhausted; delicately, beautifully, perfectly changed forever.

His hands were gentle with their caresses now, his words soothing, and she wished she could fall asleep right where she was, and stay there forever.

Part of that request was granted, and she closed her eyes. She entered a winding grotto, cool and deep, where the sun did not shine and the moon was asleep. Splashes of color, rainbows without end that curved and arched and met with a bend. And she drifted through mutations of color and bands of light, until the world turned dreamy, and she floated out of sight.

Nine

False face must hide what the false heart doth know.

William Shakespeare (1564-1616),
English poet and playwright.
Macbeth (1606), act 1, scene 7

Much to Claire's delight, Fraser began to spend more time at Grahamstone Castle so he could be near her, and he soon became a regular visitor to Inchmurrin.

At first he was treated with the same courtesy that had been extended to him in the beginning, but as time passed, the hospitality Isobel and Lord Walter showed toward Fraser cooled drastically. When it became obvious that he was paying court to Claire, there were obvious and outward signs of their disapproval, until one day, Lord Walter asked Fraser into the library.

"I would like to have a few words with ye," he said.

Fraser was a better judge of people than Lord Walter gave him credit for, and he had been waiting for this moment to come along.

He took a seat in a chair near the desk, and watched

Lord Walter pick up a silver letter opener, curious to know if he picked it up for a purpose other than to stab Fraser with it. Instead, Lord Walter seemed content to twirl it with his long, slim fingers.

"I would imagine ye have an idea why I asked ye to come here," he said.

"I have an idea, aye."

"Then ye must know that Isobel and I do not really approve of your courting Claire."

"It has become quite apparent of late, I ken."

"It is not that we dinna enjoy yer visits, or that we dislike ye, it is naught more than our desire to have what is best for Claire."

"I ken Claire is quite capable of making that decision for herself."

Lord Walter carefully ignored that and went on. "Claire is a very beautiful, very special young woman. Her breeding is impeccable. She could have, I daresay, any man she wanted, and there has already been many inquiries and interest in her."

Fraser leaned forward. "Lord Walter, why dinna ye come out and say what it is that ye are running around the bush aboot?"

His face was not one that gave any hint as to what he was thinking, so what was presented was a false show to mask the truth behind it. It was difficult to detect at first, which suggested it was something he must have perfected some time ago, after a great deal of practice. "We feel Claire is destined for a great marriage. We have talked aboot discussing her with some well-placed acquaintances of ours, who could prove helpful in arranging an invitation for her to go to court in London. If all proved favorable, then an engagement to foreign royalty would not be out of the question for her. I would like to think that ye would want what is best for her, and not put yer own personal interests before Claire's. Such an opportunity for her canna be overlooked."

"It is my understanding that ye and Isobel were granted the guardianship, but not with right of marriage," Fraser said. "Is that correct?"

"Aye, it is."

"Then Claire is free to marry whom she chooses. I would think you would want to give her the freedom to do just that, since it is her right."

"I think Claire would see the opportunity in this for her."

"Then why dinna ye ask Claire instead o' me? Although, I can tell ye what she would say. Claire would rather sup with the Devil than spend one night in England, court or no."

"Claire is an intelligent young woman. I am certain that when we lay it all oot for her, she will be more favorably inclined."

Fraser stood. "Then by all means, lay it oot, and ye can tell me how successful ye were when I return next week. Now, if ye will excuse me, Lady Claire awaits me, and I dinna like to keep my lass waiting."

Claire was waiting for him in the gallery, where the portraits of her ancestors watched their every move. She was sitting by a large carved chest in a chair that made her look even smaller than she was.

He hated to see her in her mourning clothes. The black drained all the color from her face, but worse, Claire was such a lively, animated person that part of her seemed lost when she put on black and assumed her role of chief mourner, since she was the eldest. Still, he could not begrudge her mourning the deaths of three members of her family. He would live with the black, because it was part of who she was.

She stood when she saw him approach. "What did he want with ye? Did he ask ye what yer intentions were, like an inquisitive father?"

"No, Claire, he didna. It was quite the opposite. He, in so many words, warned me away from ye."

Her face seemed to go slack with disbelief. "Surely ye misunderstood him."

"Sweet love o' mine, there was no way to misinterpret what he said. He has plans fer ye, Claire, and they dinna include me."

"What kind o' plans?"

"How would ye like to go to court, and live in London, and be betrothed to some Spanish prince, or mayhap an Italian count?"

She gasped, then seemed to think better of it. "Ye speak in jest, do ye not?"

"No, love, I am serious to the core of my being. It would seem the worm is about to turn, on both o' us."

"They canna force me to marry, can they?"

"No, they were not given the authority, for if they had that, they would have been given a right of marriage decree from the king along with being appointed yer guardians."

"What can we do?"

He took her by the hand and they went outside. Lord Duffus appeared almost immediately.

"Does that dog sit around the doorway all day, waiting for ye to step oot?"

"Mostly," she said, smiling beautifully up at him.

"Ye are not worrit that I will leave ye and marry some Italian with Bourbon blood, are ye?"

"No, I ken ye canna find a better man than the one ye have."

They walked along the track that took them down to the white pebbled shoreline, so they could walk along the loch. The water was smooth, the top glassy from the reflection. Overhead, birds cried out and made an occasional dive into the water.

They walked quite some time, without either of them saying anything. Once they reached an outcropping of rock, they sat down on a boulder.

"Have ye thought about what ye want to do?" he asked.

"I dinna ken what choices I have. I will tell Lord Walter and Isobel that I dinna wish to leave here, nor marry into a royal family. I am sure they will understand."

"I doubt it, but for yer sake, I hope they do as well."

"Why are ye so negative when it comes to them?"

"It is a feeling I have…one I have always had aboot them. I didna trust them afore they came here and I dinna trust them now."

"They have been more than kind to us."

"Aye, and it was for a reason, ye ken, although I dinna ken what that reason is, just now. But give them time and they will reveal themselves. 'Truth will come to light,' as Shakespeare said."

"I would rather ye not use that quote."

"Why?"

"Because the full quote is, 'Truth will come to light, murder cannot be hid long.'"

"Aye, it was not a good choice."

"So, tell me, Fraser, what is the way oot of this fray?"

"We marry right away."

She was speechless. He could tell she wanted to say something, but the words were not there. "This is a shock to ye, I ken, but it is the only way to prevent further meddling. As easily and as quickly as they got the right to yer ward, I think they could just as easily come up with a decree from the king ordering ye to appear at court. Once that happens, yer fate is sealed. Of course, I am not trying to force myself on ye, either. Ye are free to make up yer own mind. I have made ye the offer of marriage, born o' the love I bear ye, but I respect yer right to make yer own decisions. I willna ask ye again, so if ye are leaning toward a lifetime as my wife, ye best be saying so, Claire Lennox."

She put her arms around him and kissed him softly, and again, this time with more passion, before she whispered the words against his mouth, peppered with kisses. "I will marry ye, Fraser Graham, today" *kiss* "tomorrow" *kiss* "next week" *kiss* "whenever ye say."

"Ye ken, ye canna mention anything aboot this to anyone. I need to work this all oot and make the arrangements. I will send word to Jamie, and once he arrives we will pay a visit to our friend, the Earl of Argyll, since he seems to hold the reins to everything that goes on in this area, especially since yer father's death. With my brother and the Earl of Argyll standing for us, I dinna think we would have any problems with yer guardians, but to be cautious, I ken it would be best for us to keep our intent to marry a secret. Ye canna mention it, even to yer sisters. Agreed?"

"Aye, Captain—Fraser, the man I love with all my heart—Graham, I agree."

"My bonnie Claire, ye are a delight to my soul and a joy to my heart."

"Aye," she said, "that I am."

In the hours long before dawn, Dermot MacFarlane rowed silently across the loch to the western shore. Jamie and Fraser stepped out of the dark shadows and greeted him.

"All is arranged?" Dermot asked.

"Aye," Fraser replied. "And my lass?"

"She awaits ye. I have her things in the boat." He scanned the area along the shore, up to the line of trees. "Ye have come alone?"

"The Earl of Argyll has sent thirty men. They await us just beyond the trees, along with twenty Graham clansmen," Jamie said. "Ye have transportation ready, in case it is needed?"

"Aye. How many will ye be taking to Inchmurrin with ye?" asked Dermot.

"A dozen o' Argyll's men and an equal number o' Grahams," Fraser said. "At the first sign o' trouble, ye will signal them. Pray to God, we willna have need o' them."

"I dout ye will ha' any trouble from Lord Walter," Dermot said. "He no had the foresight to bring an armed guard with him. It would appear he was bit by the bug o' overconfidence, and he is not a man to rally to a cause unless he is certain it will go in his favor."

"Then let us move the men and retrieve yer lass," Jamie said.

* * *

The sun must have overslept this morning, Claire thought, for it seemed well past the hour of sunrise. There was only the faintest hint of tinted sky that formed behind the black silhouette of trees. The wind blew not, the birds were quiet, and her heartbeat was thunderously loud.

She stood at the window in her dark room and waited for enough light to enable her to see, at least beyond the end of her hand. Her breathing was unsteady, and her palms were damp. Nothing stirred, as if the entire world was enveloped in the same sense of urgency that gripped her.

She was worried for Dermot, Fraser and Jamie, and whomever they enlisted to help them. If it were Argyll, she was not too concerned, for Argyll was too powerful to touch, unless it was by the king's own hand.

The plight of her sisters was utmost on her mind. For their sake, she thought it was good that Fraser did not want her to inform her sisters of their plans. Their innocence of the matter should protect them from any hostile retaliation from Isobel or Lord Walter, although she did not think that was likely. They would be upset, of course, that she chose to marry in this manner, but they would adjust to it in time. Lord Walter was like a father to Kendrew, and Isobel was equally maternal to Claire and her sisters. In spite of Fraser's distrust of them, Claire thought their motives pure.

When the sky began to grow lighter, she had a sudden attack of panic. What if something went wrong? What if Fraser was not on his way for her, but detained, or suffering a change of heart? That was followed by a sense of loneliness, and then an acute longing for the presence of her father.

Somewhere in the shadows she thought she saw something, and she pressed her face closer to the pane of glass. Were they here now, waiting for enough light to show their presence? She doubted Argyll himself would be with them, but he might have sent one of his men to present Lord Walter with a letter bearing the duke's seal, or perhaps it was given over to the sheriff who would present it. Or perhaps Argyll did not wish to involve himself and only Fraser and Jamie waited in the shadows for the coming of first light.

The sky was lighter now, and she could see the waters of the loch. Once she thought she heard the sound of someone walking over the cobblestones in the courtyard, but when she listened, she did not hear it again. The smell of oats cooking in the kitchen reminded her that she had not eaten. It also reminded her that somewhere in the castle, Lord Walter was awake and dressed, unaware of the guests or the surprise that awaited him.

She saw a man, standing just outside the courtyard wall, and then he turned and walked away, but not before she saw that it was Dermot. He must have penned the dogs, for they were always trailing behind him at this time of morning, and that gave her some reassurance that all was going well, at least so far.

From the corner of her eye, she saw Fraser and Jamie approach, and she left her room to make the longest walk of her life, down to the arms of the man who awaited her.

Lord Walter was livid with anger, and it showed

from every angle of his bearing, before she even saw the rage on his face. When he saw her, he turned angrily. "And this is how ye repay our many kindnesses toward ye and yer brother and sisters?"

Fraser did not give Claire an opportunity to speak, for he stepped forward, blocking even Lord Walter's view of her. "The fault lies not with the lass, but with yer own stubbornness in regard to Lady Claire's right to marry, which ye were not granted along with the right of wardship."

"I was not trying to force her, but merely offered my counsel. Ye are interfering in family business that is none o' yer concern."

Lord Monleigh moved next to Fraser. "There is no need for dissention and argument. This step was necessary in order to prevent painful and unnecessary discussions concerning the differences between yer preferences for Lady Claire's husband and her own, in an attempt to pressure and influence her to turn against the man she has declared she wishes to marry. I trust ye willna interfere and necessitate the intervention of Argyll's troops, and those of my own clan."

"Take her," Lord Walter said. "If she prefers to marry ye, I wash my hands of any concern for her, her future, or trying to arrange a great and grand marriage for her." Without another word, he whirled around and returned to the house.

Fraser put his arm around her, and Claire turned to go with him. For a brief instant she glanced up at the castle and saw Isobel standing at the window, an expression of hateful intensity that went beyond hostility twisting the edges of her smile. Most frightening of all was the look of pure hate in her eyes, and then it was gone, and Claire walked away with Fraser, wondering if it was Isobel she saw or some malevolent spirit impersonating her.

Ten

Fate sits on these dark battlements, and frowns;
And as the portals open to receive me,
Her voice, in sullen echoes, through the courts,
Tells of a nameless deed

Ann Radcliffe (1764-1823), British novelist.
The Mysteries of Udolpho (1794)

A bride. The words hung in the back of her mind, almost overpowering the words being said.

With her arm through Fraser's, she bowed her head and spoke the words led by the minister.

Oor Faither in heiven, hallowt be thy name;
Thy Kingdom come; thy will be dune on the yird, as in heiven.
Gie us oor breid for this incomin day;
Forgie us the wrangs we hae wrocht, as we hae forgien the wrangs we hae dree'd and sey-us-na sairlie, but sauf us frae the Ill Ane.
An thine be the Kingdom, the Glory and the Pooer, noo an forivver.
Amen.

* * *

The wedding was a small one, held at Grahamstone Castle, with Claire, Fraser, Lord Monleigh, the Duke and Duchess of Argyll, and a few of the Graham clansmen present.

The duchess, a kind and thoughtful lady, brought a gown for Claire, a lovely violet silk, trimmed with Irish lace the color of cream.

It was the first gown that was not black that Claire had worn since the death of her father and brothers. "I thank ye, yer grace. "'Tis the most beautiful gown a bride could ever hope to own."

The duchess put her hand on Claire's. "It is a gift to honor this day. Ye are the daughter of a fine, honorable and just man and the bride of a fine, honorable and just man. My husband and I are proud to call them both friend. I ken yer father is pleased with ye, Claire, and with yer decision to marry a man he knew and approved of, and what happier occasion to end yer period o' mourning than the blessed occasion of yer marriage?"

They gathered for dinner after the wedding, and some lively Highland dancing afterward. Claire was too much in love to give much thought to Isobel and Lord Walter, or to care if they approved of her marriage to Fraser or not. She had no idea that the happiest day of her life would also be a turning point, which would be followed by a time of pain and sadness.

Jamie returned to Monleigh Castle, while Claire and Fraser remained at Grahamstone Castle for a few months. Claire made several attempts to have her brother and sisters visit her, but Isobel and Lord Walter refused to allow them to leave the island.

Isobel's letters were always kind. She would speak

of how much she missed Claire, "for ye are like a daughter to me. I do hope ye and Fraser will take it upon yerselves to return to Inchmurrin and live where ye were meant to live, at Lennox Castle. I know ye are upset we willna allow yer sisters to visit ye, but as long as we are responsible for them, we think it best to keep them with us."

It grieved Claire, and her sadness compelled Fraser to ask a question he did not want to ask. "Do ye want us to live at Lennox Castle with yer sisters? Would that make ye happy, love?"

Oh, of course she did, more than anything, yet she hesitated because she knew that it would not be good for Fraser. That left her torn between her love and loyalty to her siblings, and her love and loyalty to her husband.

In the midst of feeling trapped in the middle of a dilemma, a letter came. It was from Kenna.

Dearest Claire,

We are all so terribly lonely withoot ye, and we miss ye more than wirds can say. I ken ye are happy with yer new life, and I am sorry to write ye with tidings that arena glad. I am verra worrit about Kendrew. For the past several weeks he has been complaining o' puir health. And this week, he has taken to his bed.

He is frightfully thin, and his skin is dry and pale. His puir hair is falling oot. I dinna ken what to do. Isobel is so worrit. Doctors have seen him, but they canna find oot what is wrong.

If ye can find a way to come to Inchmurrin, I ken it might be guid for Kendrew to see ye.

Your loving sister,

Kenna

* * *

Claire gave the letter to Fraser. "Of course we will go, love. We will leave early in the morning. It willna take us overlong, and ye can see yer family afore ye go to bed tomorrow night."

She was surprised that Dermot was nowhere around when they arrived, and neither were her dogs. She thought they must be on the other side of the island, as she lifted her skirts and hurried across the cobblestone courtyard.

The moment she stepped inside Lennox Castle, it seemed dark and gloomy. The drapes were all closed, and the air musty and stale. She glanced at Fraser, who obviously noticed it as well. Before she went upstairs, Claire pulled back the draperies and opened several windows to let in the fresh air.

"I have the drapes closed because I thought it best for Kendrew," Isobel said. "The doctor said the damp air was not good for him."

Claire was startled, for she did not hear Isobel approach. "Oh, I see. Well, I shall close them, then."

"I hope ye have come home to stay," she said. "Welcome back, Fraser. Although ye didna leave here on the best o' terms, I hope we can put that behind us and focus on the common good."

"I think that is best for everyone concerned," Fraser replied.

Isobel smiled, not a warm, loving smile, but neither was it hostile. "Good. I shall have someone see to yer room."

Claire glanced toward the stairs. "Kendrew…is he…"

"He is in bed, and much too weak to leave it," she replied.

"And ye have no idea what ails him?" Claire asked.

"No, and neither do a handful of doctors. They all have their different theories and their treatments, but nothing has helped. He is progressively growing worse day by day. It is terribly painful to watch. I feel so useless. I do not know what else to do."

"I shall go to him," Claire said as she wiped the tears from her face.

Fraser took Claire's arm and the two of them went above stairs to Kendrew's room. Claire stopped outside the door. "If ye dinna mind, Fraser, will ye wait here and let me see him alone for a moment? He might be uncomfortable to talk o' his illness in front o' ye. Give me five minutes, and then ye can come in."

Fraser hugged her to him and kissed the top of her head. "I will wait here."

Claire stood on her toes and kissed him softly on the lips. "I love ye, Fraser, and I am glad I have ye beside me."

He cupped her cheek with his hand. "I love ye more."

She turned and quietly entered Kendrew's room, but her beautiful brother was not there. In his place was a terribly wasted creature, nothing more than a collection of bones covered by thin, pale skin that had a yellow cast. His once fair face was pitifully shrunken, with sunken cheekbones and hollow eyes. He had lost almost all of his hair. His fingernails were loose.

When he saw her, he turned his face to the wall. "I told them not to tell ye," he said, his voice dry and papery. "I didna want ye to see me like this, Claire. Please go. Do not look at me."

"Hush, ye silly goose. 'Tis yer sister ye be talking to, and I willna let ye push me away." She went to his bedside and sat beside him. She took his frail hand, and when he turned to look at her, she smiled and said, "I am home, laddie, and I willna let anything happen to ye. Ye are going to get well, ye ken."

Tears gathered in his eyes. "I willna get well, Claire. I am dying, and I dinna mind, not really. I have told God that I am ready to go. I am tired. I find myself longing to be with Breac and Ronaln. I want to see our father and, if I may, I should like to see our mother, too. I think the male line of the Lennoxes is cursed, and I am the last of the ancient Celtic earls. Mayhap the curse will lift when I die, and ye and our sisters will not suffer the same fate. I thank ye for coming, and I am glad I was able to see ye one last time afore I go."

Tears were rolling down Claire's face. He patted her hand weakly. "Ye were always a guid sister to me," he said, "even when I was no such a guid wee brother."

"Ye were always exactly what I wanted in a wee brother, and dinna ye forget that."

She saw a slight smile lift the corners of his mouth, and she felt Fraser's hand on her shoulder. So moved by Kendrew's condition, she had not heard Fraser enter the room.

"What would ye say, Kendrew, if I told ye any wish ye had would be granted," Fraser said. "What would ye wish for?"

"I would wish for a boat ride on the loch, for I long to see it."

"We shall take ye tomorrow, then," Claire said, and she saw the disappointment in his eyes.

"I dinna see what is wrong with going today. How aboot ye, Kendrew? Are ye up to a boat ride today?" Fraser asked.

"Aye, I ken today is the day I must go."

Fraser bundled him up in his bedding and carried him from his room.

Isobel was waiting at the bottom of the stairs. "Oh, dear, where are ye going with him?"

"For a ride around the loch in the boat," Fraser said.

"Do ye think that wise? I was told he should have peace and quiet. The outside air is bad for him. The doctor specifically said to keep him inside."

"We have done all o' that," Kendrew said, "and it hasna made me better. It willna hurt me, Aunt Isobel. I willna get better even if I stay inside. I asked to go. I want to see the loch."

Isobel turned and put her face in her hands, and spoke with a muffled voice, "All right. If that is what ye wish."

They carried him down to the dock, put him in the boat, and placed him so he leaned against Claire. That way she could keep her hands on his shoulders, in case he should be unable to hold himself in place.

Claire knew Kendrew was weak, but even so, he found the strength to make a few comments about how beautiful the lake was. He must have thanked Fraser for taking him at least three or four times. They arrived back at the dock at sunset, so Kendrew could see the sun go down.

She would never know where Fraser got the

strength of ten men to row the boat as far and as long as he did, and still find the added strength to carry Kendrew back to the castle and up to his room.

Lord Walter and her sisters arrived shortly after they put Kendrew to bed. After a brief reunion with them, Claire fed Kendrew a little soup and tried to get him to eat more, but he turned his head away. "I would like to sleep now. Thank ye both for the ride. I wanted to see the loch again."

God must have had a reason why no men would hold the earldom of Errick and Mains, for young though he was, Kendrew's time on earth was all too brief. He died two days after Claire and Fraser returned to Inchmurrin, and the last of the great Celtic Mormears of Levenax passed away with the death of Kendrew, Lord Errick, Earl of Errick and Mains.

Because he was loved by everyone, each person took his death terribly hard. Claire's sisters had not stopped crying. Claire felt as if everything vital inside her had died with him. Fraser tried to console them all, but he felt helpless.

Isobel and Lord Walter were both terribly distraught over Kendrew's death. Isobel blamed herself. "I should have found more doctors."

Lord Walter disagreed. "Ye did everything ye could for him…more than anyone. Ye nursed him, read to him and brought in at least six doctors. There was nothing more that ye could have done."

They commissioned an elaborate marker for his grave, in the form of an ancient Celtic cross. Several times Claire saw Isobel in Kendrew's room, crying as she packed his things away.

Strangely, when she told Fraser about it, he was unusually sarcastic. "Mayhap she was looking for coins he might have left in his pockets."

"That was especially cruel of ye, Fraser. What has come over ye?"

"Could be that the strain of all of this is getting to me as well as ye and yer sisters."

He was right. It was getting to everyone, and when they were not crying they were waspish with one another.

Claire could not understand why his death had to follow so soon after her brothers' and her father's, or why Kendrew had changed from a robust, laughing child into a pale and thin lad, whom her sisters said never laughed and seldom seemed to notice anything that went on around him.

"It was as if he found another realm where he preferred to exist," Kenna said.

Claire missed the presence of Dermot, and had yet to see her dogs. She went to Isobel and asked where they were.

"Gone."

"Gone? Gone where? Dermot has been here since afore I was born."

"I know that, but he was getting too old. He was especially upset over Kendrew and did not want to remain and see the end of the male line. Lord Walter arranged for him to live on one o' yer father's properties near Appledore."

"And my dogs?"

"The doctor thought we should be rid of them. He thought they might carry some disease that infected Kendrew. Ye know how impossible it was to keep them oot o' the house. Dermot said he would like to have them, so he took them with him. If ye want them back, I am sure Dermot will understand."

"I would like Lord Duffus," she said, but knowing that would have to wait.

Fraser was sitting in a chair by the fire when Claire came into the room. He looked up and saw the pale face, the look of sadness in her eyes.

"What ails ye, love?"

"Do ye think our family is cursed, that we are all going to follow my father and my brothers?" She dropped to her knees in front of him, and with tears streaming down her face, she asked him, "Will I be the next to die?"

Fraser took her in his arms and pulled her into his lap. "Ye are not cursed, and nothing will happen to ye. For as long as I have a breath in my body, I will protect ye, Claire Lennox."

In spite of Fraser's loving words, Claire could never completely dispel the lingering feeling that her family had fallen out of favor, or perhaps it was that God had turned his back on them completely. She could not shake the feeling that the rest of them were destined to die off, one by one.

Shortly after Kendrew's death, the title was settled upon Claire, who became suo jure, the Twelfth Countess of Errick and Mains. As the Countess of Errick and Mains in her own right, she inherited the earldom and all unentailed estates of the house of Lennox.

She was also heir presumptive to the reversion of lands in Caithness and Argyll, which were entailed, under her mother's will. Her mother's will also entailed to her twelve oxgangs of the Halls of Airth and Monyabroch in Dumfriesshire.

It was a mantle placed unexpectedly across her small shoulders, and one she felt ill prepared for. She felt displaced. The walls of Lennox Castle, always so comforting, offered her no welcome and no peace. She felt faceless, nameless and terribly alone. Even the grass beneath her feet had its place where it could grow and be nourished, but Claire could only ask, "Where is my place?"

Time and again, Fraser tried to convince her to let him take her to Grahamstone Castle, or Monleigh Castle, or to live in any one of a dozen other castles she now owned, but Claire refused to leave her sisters.

"Canna ye understand, Fraser? I left them once, and I wasna here when Kendrew took sick. I came home too late to help him."

"Then I will ask Isobel and Lord Walter if they will allow us to take yer sisters with us."

"All right, ask them."

Fraser left immediately and found Lord Walter in his usual haunt, the library.

"I am surprised ye would ask such a thing, Fraser. Ye ken all of the Lennoxes were placed under our care and, as their protector, I cannot allow them to be out from under my supervision."

"I would think their sister would be capable of their supervision. Our castles are better staffed than this one, and their opportunities greater since they would no' be isolated on this island."

"I thank ye for yer interest in our wards, but my answer is final on the subject. As long as we hold the wardship, the girls stay with us."

Fraser was saddened to have to report the grim

news to Claire. "I am sorry, but they have the law on their side."

He tried to encourage Claire to become more involved with the running of the estates, now that she was the Countess of Errick and Mains. "I will soon," she would say.

The weeks passed, and the strain on Fraser grew until he felt stretched thin. There was nothing of importance for him to do here. He could not convince Claire to leave without her sisters, and they could not leave without Isobel and Lord Walter's approval. And Fraser was going mad. He loved Claire, but staying here would destroy him. He could not feel like a man when he had no role.

One afternoon, out of total boredom, Fraser worked in the garden. Later that evening, when he was putting the tools away, he accidentally knocked a bottle off the shelf with the handle of the rake. He picked it up and started to place it on the shelf when he saw a label, the type used by an apothecary. It was marked Poison. He removed the lid and saw it contained a white powder. There was no particular smell.

He dropped the bottle in his pocket, and the next day he took the boat and went into town, and stopped at the apothecary. He handed the proprietor the bottle. "I was wondering if ye could tell me what was in the bottle," he said.

"Aye, I can tell ye, for 'tis one o' my own bottles. 'Tis rat poison...arsenic."

"Hmm, ye wouldna by chance ken who ye sold it to, would ye?"

"I write them down, ye ken, and I dinna sell too many bottles of arsenic." He opened a bound ledger and began running his finger up and down each page. "A week ago, Dr. MacNeill bought a bottle of potassium arsenite, which he uses to make Fowler's solution. Hugh Fraser purchased a bottle a month ago to poison rats. Isobel Lennox purchased a bottle a little over two months ago for the same purpose." He read out two more names and said, "That is all I have in this book. If ye be wantin' more names, I would have to get the other book in the back."

"I think that was enough. Thank ye."

The chemist nodded and closed the book.

Fraser inquired as to the location of Dr. MacNeill's office, but he was told Dr. MacNeill had gone to the Isle of Skye to see to his ill mother.

When Fraser arrived back at Inchmurrin, he replaced the bottle and told Claire about finding it.

"Weel, what is so strange aboot that? She probably used it to poison rats. What else would she do with it?"

"What if she gave it to Kendrew?"

Claire gasped and her hand flew up to her chest. "Auld Cloutie take ye, Fraser Graham! How can ye say such a thing when ye saw how Kendrew's death affected her and Lord Walter both? And what about the monument for his grave? Do ye think that normal behavior for a murderer?"

"I am saying Kendrew could have been poisoned. I heard once that arsenic poisoning can cause fingernails to fall off, and yer hair, too. Ye saw the way his nails were lifting and practically off. And his hair..."

"A lot of things could probably cause that when ye are sick enough. I refuse to believe something so vile about someone who has been nothing but kind to all of us. Isobel and Lord Walter have never done anything to deserve that kind of blame. Do not mention that to me again."

She was right. He had nothing to blame his suspicions on.

Later that night, when they were in their room, Claire came to him and put her arms around him. "I didna mean to sound angry with ye today, Fraser."

"I know."

She stood on her toes and kissed him. "Make love to me."

He put his arms around her, kissing her as he worked the buttons at the back of her dress and slipped it down past her shoulders. Her skin was soft and warm, and he lowered his head to kiss her throat, and then lower where the velvety drag of his tongue over her breasts brought the desired reaction, and he felt them harden to tight crowns. He groaned with a drugged feeling, heavy and filled with desire.

He pulled her to the bed with him and pushed the dress down further, past the smooth planes of her flat stomach over the juncture of her thighs until it fell to the floor. She stepped out of it and helped him remove her drawers before she lay down beside him. His hands caressed her while he tugged at her breasts with his mouth, his hand sliding down her firm legs, which parted slightly when he stroked her there. He placed his fingers on each side of her, and parted her gently until she was open to him completely. He covered her with his mouth, finding the point of her desire and touching it until she moaned, and spread her legs wider, allowing him to thrust into her deeply.

His mouth moved up to kiss her, again and again, while he stroked and touched her until she began to writhe beneath him as he found the rhythm. She called out his name, and began to move with it, faster and faster until she began to convulse and cry out, her body jerking as spasm after spasm washed over her.

She was not sated, however, for he could tell by the way she still moved, the loving strokes of her hand, the way she searched for his mouth so he could kiss her. Knowing she was still highly aroused and wanting him, he lowered his hand and touched her, until she opened her legs wide again, enabling him to stroke her until she was unbelievably ready. Still he did not stop, but kept stroking her until she began to pant and press against him, thrusting her hips wildly until she went over the edge, shattered and crying out his name again.

He lost count of how many times he brought her to this point, for his mind was saturated with the knowledge that he was right to marry her, for she was the only woman for him.

He released himself from his pants, covered her with his body and began to stroke himself against her until she was writhing beneath him again, continuing until he was dangerously close to losing control completely, then drove himself into her and felt his body jerk as powerfully as she had done only a moment ago.

He held her close and drifted off to sleep, thinking that everything would be so perfect for them, if he could only get her out of this place and off the island completely.

Over the next few days, Fraser began to suspect that all of the kindness Isobel and Lord Walter showed to Claire and her brother and sisters was nothing more than a paltry subterfuge. Was it possible they intended to do away with Kendrew from the beginning? It made sense. With Kendrew out of the way, Claire would inherit, since the title was designated to heirs male or female, and of course Isobel and Lord Walter knew that.

Only, what would be the motive? If they did away with Claire, one of her other sisters would inherit. They were too smart and cunning to believe they could do away with all Alasdair's children and get away with it.

If they did not wish Claire's death, why kill Kendrew? What would they stand to gain by this?

When he had no answers, he decided to look at the past for answers, instead of trying to foretell the future. Scotland's past was liberally sprinkled with similar stories where children, especially if they were wealthy heirs, were virtually forced to marry a designated person, in order for the unscrupulous guardians to gain control of their fortune. He thought of the Sutherland case, where the Earl of Sutherland and his wife were both poisoned by a relative. The heir to the title was their fifteen-year-old son, Alexander, who was forced to marry the thirty-two-year-old daughter of the guardian. After several miserable years, the young Alexander Sutherland was snatched out from under his guardian's nose by several friends, who helped him hide until he reached his majority. When he came of age, he divorced the woman.

The case had a great many similarities to the Lennoxes. Right now Fraser was interested primarily in the motive. When Isobel Sinclair poisoned the Earl of Sutherland and his wife, it was her plan to poison their son, Alexander, but he returned home late from hunting and was warned by his dying father not to touch any food, and not to drink anything. His father then sent him away to stay at a friend's home. Isobel Sinclair's own son, who stood next in line to inherit after Alexander, came home shortly after Alexander had departed, and being thirsty, he asked for something to drink. The help, not knowing the beverage was poisoned, gave him the poisoned drink and he died, a victim of his mother's treachery.

The interesting parallel here was, Isobel Lennox had a son by a previous marriage. Giles was three or four years older than Claire. Since he was no blood relation, he could not inherit, but he could marry Claire and consequently assume control of her wealth.

If that were true, then only one thing stood in the way, and that was Fraser. If their plan was to force a marriage between Claire and Isobel's son, Giles, then Fraser would have to be eliminated.

However, this was all speculation—a lot of supposition and no proof. Perhaps Claire was right. Perhaps he was wrongly accusing them. Either way, he had no choice but to wait things out awhile longer, to see where it went from here.

After all, how much worse could it get?

Eleven

Like one, that on a lonesome road
Doth walk in fear and dread,
And having once turned round walks on,
And turns no more his head;
Because he knows, a frightful fiend
Doth close behind him tread.

Samuel Taylor Coleridge (1772-1834),
British poet.
Lyrical Ballads
"The Rime of the Ancient Mariner" (1798)

In the waning hours of the day, just before gloaming, Claire wandered desultorily down the path on her customary walk. She noticed the brilliant colors she saw earlier were starting to look faded and somber. The sun still gave off a bright light, but it was filtered through a haze that lay like a cloud suspended in the atmosphere, obscuring everything below.

The waters of the loch were visible from the point where she stood near a copse. A mist was now settling along the length of the shoreline, hiding the various landmarks that lay behind it. She seemed thinner, and upon first glimpse, any passerby might have wondered what tragedy had occurred in the life of one so fair, to cause such melancholy.

From time to time, Claire would find herself on the brink of calling her dogs. Other times, she thought she heard them trampling about in the dense thicket. Once, she paused to listen, so certain she was that she heard the muffled sound of them running up the path behind her.

If there could be any consolation or comfort to the absence of her beloved dogs, it was in knowing they brought joy into what had to be Dermot's lonely life, now so separate and apart from the family he had come to love as his own.

She saw a boat approaching the island, and as it came closer, she saw a woman passenger and two pieces of baggage. It rounded the corner and vanished from sight. She continued on, curious now, to see who the woman was, and why she had chosen to visit Inchmurrin.

By the time Claire walked through the entrance that led to the castle, she saw the boat was already docked. A reed-slim woman, dressed all in white, stood to one side, while one of the men unloaded her two bags. He placed them on the dock next to her.

Claire was close enough that she could hear the clink of coins, and the rather husky tones of the woman's voice as she thanked them.

She did not follow the woman into the house, but dallied about outside for a while longer, before she went inside.

Isobel and the woman were talking in a manner that bespoke they were old friends. When Isobel saw

Claire, she said, "Claire, my dear, do come and meet my dearest friend in all the world, Carolina, the Countess of Stagwyth."

The Countess of Stagwyth… Claire could not have been more surprised or shocked if someone had slapped her in the face with a pig's liver. That a woman of such immoral character, and infamous notoriety, was visiting in her home was astonishing.

If the woman had not been such a great beauty, her name alone would have been staggering, for her notoriety had reached even the furthermost corners of Inchmurrin Island. Although she was the daughter of a Scottish baron, she was educated in England and chose to remain there. She had been married four times, to a duke, two earls and a count. Her past was as colorful as her face was beautiful. Reputed to have an addiction to gambling, she had openly admitted she once visited an opium den on a dare. The parties she threw were said to outrival and outspend those given by the king. To pay her gambling debts, she used her jewels, promises to sponsor daughters into society, and, if the man she borrowed from pleased her, then the pleasure of her own body.

She was exquisitely beautiful; her skin unbelievably white and free of blemish—a fact attested to by those in the know—including the Earl of Sharrington. It was the earl who confessed, "I have kissed every square inch of her voluptuous body, and know all her identifying marks." To prove he was the uncontested authority on the subject, he published a pamphlet with a drawing that identified the location and a description of those marks.

"Countess," Claire said. "Welcome to Inchmurrin. I trust ye had a pleasant journey."

"Excellent," she said. "Isobel did not tell me you were such a beauty. My, with your looks and coloring, you could be the toast of London. You must persuade your aunt to allow you to come visit me sometime."

"Claire is married," Isobel said.

"Oh, that won't matter, darling," the Countess said. "Actually, many men prefer married women, and there are some of us women who prefer married men. So, you see, love, it works out."

"Thank you for the invitation, Countess, but my work keeps me much too busy to travel."

"I forgot to tell you that my niece is the Countess of Errick and Mains in her own right, and the Chief of Clan Lennox, so she is quite involved," Isobel said.

"My...a countess *suo jure*. Congratulations."

"Thank ye," Claire said. "If ye will excuse me, I will check on my sisters. Have ye seen Fraser aboot?"

"Aye," Isobel said. "He went upstairs an hour or so ago."

Claire spent some time with her sisters, who were doing their lessons with Aggie, then she went to find Fraser.

She was surprised to find him lying across the bed asleep.

She sat down beside him. "Och! Dinna tell me ye have turned soft as a tattie on me," she said. "What are ye doing in bed so early?"

"I have a headache...a bad one. Even the sun is unbearable."

"Is it better now?"

"A wee bit better, but I think I will stay where I am for the rest o' the evening. I do not feel like coming down to dinner."

"If I brought ye some broth, could ye eat it?"

"No, I canna eat anything for a while."

"I will send for the doctor."

"No, it is only a headache. Tomorrow I will be fine."

"I would feel better having the doctor, Fraser. I care aboot ye, and your suffering is my suffering."

He squeezed her hand. "I dinna need a doctor. All I need is ye, Claire. I would like to sleep now."

"All right. I will check on ye later." She kissed his cheek and quietly left the room.

Dinner was two hours away, so Claire decided to use the time wisely, and headed for the library to work on the account books that needed updating daily. However, when she entered, Lord Walter was sitting at the desk. He looked up when she walked in.

"Did ye need to see me about something?" he asked.

"No, I wanted to look over the ledgers and review the accounts of the summer crops." She withdrew a piece of paper from her pocket. "I have some figures I need to add to my last accounting."

"Ye needn't worry yourself with such as that. I am quite capable of taking care of everything."

"Oh, I ken ye are most capable, Lord Walter, and I thank ye for yer help, but now that I am the countess it is my responsibility, and I want to start familiarizing myself with everything."

"There truly isna enough work for both of us."

"Weel, that should be good news for ye then, for ye willna have to spend yer days cooped up in here."

Lord Walter did not say anything, but he did not need to. The angry expression on his face and the venom-filled eyes said it well enough. It was a stand-off of sorts, with her holding her ground and saying nothing more, and Lord Walter giving her hateful looks, but at last he shuffled his papers and carried them from the room.

It was not much of a victory, but it was the first she could remember having as far as Lord Walter was concerned and, that alone, made it seem much larger than it actually was.

Claire worked until dinnertime, when she closed her ledgers and put them away. She went immediately to check on Fraser and found him sleeping soundly. She pushed the hair back from his face and kissed his forehead, then went down to dinner.

The next morning, Claire was happy to hear Fraser felt like eating a little oatmeal, which she personally made and carried up to him. She stayed while he ate. When he was almost finished, she said, "I wanted ye to accompany me on the trip to check on the crops being grown on the southeast side of the loch, but I dinna think that would be a wise idea. Ye look too pale, and it is obvious to me ye are as weak as a lamb." She removed the bowl of oatmeal and put it on the bedside table, then she placed her head on Fraser's chest. "I want ye to get well, Fraser. Ye are my life. I canna live withoot ye."

"Ye are everything to me, Claire." He kissed the top of her head. "I would like to go with ye, ye know that, but I think it is best if I stay here. I dinna think my stomach is up to a boat trip right now."

Claire stood and touched his face lovingly. "Get some rest, my love. I long to see some color back in yer cheeks."

"I will, if ye will take yer sisters with ye, so ye dinna have to go alone."

She smiled at him. "All right. I will tell them to blame ye for making them get up so early."

An hour later, Claire and her sisters were in the boat for the trip across the loch, where they would be met by some of the clansmen who would escort them on horseback to make the crop inspections.

Things went on like that for the next several days, until Fraser asked her what was wrong with her. "Ye hardly give me a nod o' recognition throughout the day," he said.

"For some reason, knocking the Countess down in order to get close enough to ye to say 'Good morning' doesna appeal to me." And with that Claire walked off, purposefully ignoring Fraser's calls to come back.

That night, as she had every night for the past week, she pretended to be asleep when Fraser came to bed.

The next day, Kenna mentioned how she had several times witnessed the Countess throwing herself at Fraser. "Have ye seen how she behaves around him?"

"Aye, I ha' seen more of her than I care to see. If she keeps this up, I will shove her dimpled arse in the loch."

"Do ye think she is always like that, or is she simply taken with Fraser?"

Claire frowned. "Listen, Kenna, ye could put a pair o' man's breeks on a flagpole and she would proposition it. In London she is known as a flamboyant adulteress whose name was linked frequently with sexual intrigue, while at the same time she was known as the darling of the ton. People admired her open manner, her sensuality, languishing looks and her ethereal nature."

Claire noticed the horrified expression on Kenna's face. "Dinna tell me ye havena heard of the Countess of Stagwyth."

"No, I havena heard anything. What about her?"

Claire went on to unload every morsel of gossip she had ever heard or read about the Countess. "It is said that every prominent artist has painted her portrait at least once, and it was reckoned that she had slept with each of them in exchange for the artist's fee, since she was known to say no money ever exchanged hands. She seems to prefer married men to single ones."

"Oh, dear," Kenna said. "That will never do. We need to be rid o' her."

"Aye, and I am contemplating shoving her in the loch."

"With yer luck, she would probably float," Kenna said.

"Aye," Claire agreed.

The next morning Fraser had another headache, so he remained in bed. After checking on him, Claire spent some time in the library, after she and Lord Walter had made arrangements that she would have the library in the morning and he would have it in the afternoon.

It was almost lunchtime when Isobel came in and asked if she had checked on Fraser of late.

"No, why? Is he worse?"

Isobel shrugged. "I dinna ken, I only know he has no' come down yet."

"All right. I will check on him."

Claire put her things away and went above stairs.

She put her hand on the doorknob and turned it, but the door was locked. She tried it again, then she knocked on the door. "Fraser?"

She heard a noise, then a thump, and footsteps coming toward the door. When it opened, Claire said, "I came to see how ye were feeling…" The rest of Claire's words jammed in her throat for, instead of Fraser, it was Carolina who opened the door—Carolina with the smeared color on her lips and the unfastened bodice of her dress, one nipple peeking through the lacing as if it had hastily been shoved in place. There were red marks on her neck and shoulders, the kind produced by heavy kissing and love bites.

"What are ye doing in my bedroom with my husband, with the door locked?"

"I came to check on him, since he did not come down this morning. I did not realize the door was locked. It must have happened accidentally."

"Even if ye didna lock it, what was yer reason for shutting the door?"

"I didn't shut it. The wind blew it shut."

That made a lot of sense, Claire thought. "On a windless day, with all the windows shut, the door blows shut? The only wind strong enough to do that, Countess, is coming from yer lying mouth. Stay away from my husband."

The Countess smiled and walked around Claire without saying a word.

Claire went into the room. Fraser appeared to be asleep. The bed was tumbled. Claire put her hand on the sheets. They were still warm. That was when she noticed a wet spot on the sheets. She doubled up her fist and hit Fraser in the middle of the back. He groaned and rolled onto his back. He put his hand to his head and squinted at her. "Claire…"

"Dinna say my name with the same foul mouth that has been kissing that hussy. Lying up here…pretending to be sick… I have to admit that is a clever way o' having yer paramour slip into bed with ye, but ye might wait at least until I'm away from home afore ye do it."

"I dinna ken what ye are talking aboot, Claire."

"I'm talking aboot coming up here to check on ye and finding the door closed, and when I knock, the Countess opens it with her dinners hanging out and her lips smeared, and there is a spot on the bed that looks suspiciously like a lovemaking spot. Now, ye tell me ye dinna ken what I am talking aboot."

"I never saw the Countess. I haven't said a word to her since yesterday. If she was in here, she was awfully quiet."

"Ye are as despicable as the Countess," Claire said. She left without another word.

She spent the rest of the day with her sisters, and later that evening, she asked them to help her move her things into another room. "Do ye not love Fraser anymore?" Briana asked.

"Ask me that tomorrow," Claire said.

The next day Fraser felt better, and when he came down and tried to talk to her, she threw the incident with the Countess in his face. "I am as innocent of any wrongdoing as I was yesterday, Claire. I swear it on my mother's grave."

"I wouldna believe ye if ye tossed in yer father's grave for good measure."

Claire spent that morning in the library, but she did

not accomplish much. She could not seem to concentrate, because she kept thinking about Fraser. How could he be intrigued by that conglomeration of mischief and sensuality, that queen of seductive posturing, with her sun-drenched curls and a perfect heart-shaped face? How could he be warmed by the fire in her eyes, or be dazzled by that ridiculous way she had of arching one brow when she flirted? Men were said to fall hopelessly in love when they gazed into eyes that burned with the fire of desire. Bah! If men were overcome by her gilded glory, her flaming fire or her dazzling tempestuousness then more the fools they, and Fraser Graham along with them.

Claire finally managed to finish her work and left the library. As she entered the gallery, she met Isobel coming down the stairs. "I was looking for ye," Isobel said.

Claire paused and said, "I was finishing some work in the library."

Isobel nodded. "I was on my way there to see if you were working," she said.

Claire glanced up the stairs. "Are my sisters up there?" she asked.

Isobel shook her head. "No, I saw them through the window a moment ago. They were in the orchard. Why dinna ye check there?"

Claire walked down the hall, and although daylight brightened the rooms she passed, the corridors were dark and shadowy, and everything about her seemed cold, sad and silent.

She left the house and walked across the courtyard and down the narrow pathway to the orchard. It was surrounded by a low rock wall, which Claire walked along until she came to the gate. She opened it and found herself confronting a perplexing sight. Looking past some three or fours rows into the orchard, she saw the back part of a woman's blue dress, the rest of the dress, along with the woman's identity hidden behind the trunk of a tree. On the other side of the trunk, the back of a man's black head was unmistakably that of Fraser's.

There was little doubt that he was busily occupied with some task, and while she imagined he was becoming quite proficient in undoing the Countess's lacings, she found it hard to believe they would do something so flagrant in the middle of the orchard in broad daylight, with a dozen or so clansmen working about the island.

While she was trying to decide if she should confront them, or toss both their cheating hides off the island, they finished whatever it was they were about, and the blue dress laughed. A moment later, Fraser and Carolina came around the tree, then Carolina turned and put her arms around Fraser's neck and kissed him on the mouth.

"I was so tense, and now I feel so relaxed. Although you took a long time to come, I was so happy to finally find my relief, I did not mind."

She turned and gave Claire a direct look and a cat-what-ate-the-cream smile, then daintily crossed the distance to the gate and walked toward the castle.

"Claire, what are ye doing in the orchard? Did you come to give me some help?"

She saw the pile of dead branches he or someone had pruned from the trees, but today, unlike the previous times she had seen the Countess with him in an embarrassing position, she was more hurt than angry.

With a shake of her head, she turned and fled down the path that led away from the castle.

Twelve

A new disease? I know not, new or old,
But it may well be called poor
mortals' plague:
For, like a pestilence, it doth infect
The houses of the brain ...
Till not a thought, or motion, in the mind,
Be free from the black poison of suspect.

Ben Jonson (1573-1637),
English dramatist, poet. Kitely, in
Every Man in His Humour, act 2, scene 3

When Fraser asked Claire what was wrong and she confronted him with what she saw in the orchard, he laughed.

Truly, if she could have gotten her hand around a sizable object, she would have crowned him with it. "I have heard all the lies I want to hear."

"I am sorry for laughing, but it is so unlike ye, Claire, to be so jealous, when there is naught to be jealous aboot. I had been working and left to fill my jar with water. When I came back, I found Carolina standing by the tree with her hair caught fast on a low-hanging branch. I helped free it for her. That is all there was to it."

"Ye forget I heard what she said. 'I was so tense, and now I feel so relaxed. Although you took a long time to come, I was so happy to finally find my relief, I did not mind.' "

He seemed puzzled for a moment, and then he gave her that grin that was always her undoing...except this time. Today, she was not moved.

"She said she had been standing there a long time, waiting and hoping someone would come by. She meant she was so happy to have her hair uncaught that she did not mind my taking so long to help her."

"Ye always have a plausible excuse, I will say that for ye."

He reached out and pulled her against him. "Claire, ye have naught to worry yer pretty head aboot. 'Tis ye that I love and ye that I want to spend my life with. Dinna let things like this come between us. I miss ye, and want ye back in my bed."

"Indeed? Then ye should invite the Countess back. She knows where it is, since she has been there before." She turned away before he could say another word.

Claire avoided Fraser completely for the next two days. On the third day he was ill again, only this time it was much worse than a simple headache. He could not keep any food down. His head ached fiercely, and his eyes were so sensitive to the light they had to close the drapes. By the second day, he was quite dehydrated, unable to keep anything down.

They sent for the doctor again. He examined Fraser and prescribed medication. "There are quite a few cases of the grippe going aboot and many of the symptoms are similar to yer husband's—fever, chills, muscular pain and prostration. Keep him quiet and in bed. Here are two bottles. The blue one should be taken in the morning. The brown bottle at night before he goes to sleep. Call me if he worsens."

The second day he did seem worse, but Isobel said it wasn't enough change that they should pull the doctor away from other needy patients. "Let us give the medication another day to work."

The next day, Claire thought Fraser was worse, but Isobel insisted he was not as feverish as the day before. "And he is sleeping better."

Claire had been sitting by his bed for two days, sleeping in the chair. That night, Isobel told her to go to bed. "Ye will be no good to him if ye canna keep yer eyes open. I will check on him from time to time during the night."

It did not take much persuasion, for Claire was barely able to maintain an upright position. She went to her room and lay down on the bed without turning back the covers or removing her dress and shoes. She was asleep almost immediately.

She did not know how long she slept, but she was awakened at some point by Isobel shaking her. Claire sat up and saw it was dark outside. "He is worse?"

"I think ye need to see this, Claire, although it pains me greatly to be the one to tell ye."

"See what?"

"It's Fraser and..."

Claire hurried around Isobel and went into Fraser's room. He was lying on his back with nothing on save a bit of sheet that covered part of one leg.

Lying on the bed next to him, naked and asleep with

her golden hair fanned around her, Carolina was lying on her side facing Fraser, with one leg thrown over his.

Claire turned to Isobel. "Get her oot o' here and off this island."

Claire was sick to her stomach and her heart was broken. This was the last insult she could tolerate. Simply getting rid of Carolina would not solve the problem. Claire realized that, apparently, she was not enough woman to hold her husband.

Lord Walter had two men waiting with the boat. Once the Countess of Stagwyth was dressed, her bags were carried down and Isobel walked her to where Lord Walter waited.

Claire stood at the window of her room and watched the notorious Countess climb into the boat, then she turned away and went to bed.

The next morning she realized she could no longer live with Fraser. If not the Countess, then someone else. Men who were womanizers never changed, they only changed women. She could see the years down the road for them, with a multitude of women coming and going, much in the same manner as the Countess.

She dressed and had a cup of tea, then she went to Fraser's room. Just before she reached it, Greer asked her to come into her room. Kenna was there, and said she and Greer wanted to talk to her.

"What about?" Claire asked.

"Fraser," Kenna said.

"Dinna try to defend him. It is too late for that."

"We are no' trying to defend him," Greer said.

Kenna took her hand. "Claire, Fraser's illness is starting out just like Kendrew's. It's not the grippe. It's whatever Kendrew had all over again. I'm afraid he will end up like our brother."

"Thank ye for sharing that, but it doesna matter what ails Fraser. I do not wish his death, certainly, but I do not intend to live with him anymore. I am going to Edinburgh tomorrow to hire a lawyer, then I shall divorce him on the grounds of adultery."

"Oh. Claire…" Greer said.

"Stay out o' this, Greer, and ye, too, Kenna. 'Tis none of yer affair."

The next morning, Claire packed a small bag, and after she dressed and had her coffee, she went to see Fraser. He was obviously better, for he was partially inclined with two pillows behind him.

"I am glad to see ye, Claire. I was beginning to think ye had abandoned me."

"I want a divorce, Fraser. I am leaving in a few minutes for Edinburgh. I sent one o' my men to Grahamstone Castle, alerting them o' yer illness, and then I requested they send someone after ye. I want ye gone by the time I return tomorrow."

His expression was a combination of shock, disbelief and confusion. "I do not understand. What is wrong with ye of late? Ye are no' the woman I married."

"That is the first truthful thing I have heard ye say, Fraser. I am not the same. I will never be the same as I was because ye have destroyed that person."

"How…what have I done but love ye, Claire? What we have…'tis something too good and too beautiful to toss it away. Ye canna mean to end it like this. Ye canna."

"It is too late for talk now. My mind is made up. I canna live with ye after all that has happened."

He seemed startled by everything, but she paid it no mind. "Tell me, then. Tell me what happened. What was so bad as to push ye to this?" He looked directly into her eyes with the kind of confidence she herself used when she was speaking honestly and frankly, but instead of crediting him with sincerity or honesty, she branded him a consummate actor, who knew all the words and movements to sound convincing.

Her mouth was trembling. "I am talking about finding the two o' ye in this bed, without a stitch on yer bodies. Not only that, but the Countess...she was holding ye, Fraser, like ye was a particular friend o' hers."

"Claire, stop and listen to me for a minute. I think all of this, from the Countess's visit to what ye say happened when ye found the Countess in my bed—I have no memory of any o' that. How could I? I was sick. Can ye no' understand how verra sick I was?"

"Yer sickness is mighty peculiar, Fraser, for it seems to come just when ye need it for yer alibi. Ye are sick one day and fine the next, and then ye go several days looking fit as can be then poof! There ye are sick again."

"I think someone...either Isobel or Lord Walter has been poisoning my food. I think they might have given me a dose and then skipped a dose or two. As soon as I am able, I want to pay a visit to the chemist and the doctor to see if my theory is possible."

"Is that the only excuse ye can find? Ye are always blaming Isobel and Lord Walter, when they have been nothing but kind to all o' us. Ye shame us, Fraser, with yer accusations hurled at two perfectly innocent people. Why canna ye accept the blame yerself, since that is where it belongs. Ye can go to the chemist and the doctor if ye like, but do not come back here. I dinna want to hear any more o' yer lies. I do not want to see ye again, ever."

"Claire, don't fall into their trap so easily. Canna ye no see that this is all part of a bigger plan to gain control of yer fortune?"

"By doing away with ye? How would that serve them?"

"Ye would be free to marry Giles."

She burst out laughing. "Giles? Ye have truly come up with a far-fetched one this time. Honestly, where does yer imagination find these preposterous ideas?"

"And do ye not think it a bit preposterous that I was too ill to move, yet would feel up to an amorous liaison, or that I would stoop so low as to brave a tryst under the same roof I shared with my wife and her sisters, and worse, to have it in the bed I share with ye?"

"I do not know ye anymore, Fraser, so I canna answer that question."

"Then I suppose there is nothing else to say, is there. Ye have obviously grown so far away from me that ye would believe anything Isobel tells ye to believe. I have come against a mountain I cannot climb. I still love ye, and probably I always will. Poor Claire, ye are incapable of understanding because ye love with yer head and not yer heart. Even now, after all that has transpired between us...the deception, the false accusations...the betrayal...the words filled with venom, ye are still too dear to me, for ye reside in the very core o' my being."

Claire was barely listening, but she heard enough to reply in a haughty tone, "If ye truly felt that way about me, ye never showed it. What was I to think? I find ye asleep with that hussy, the Countess of Stagwyth, and now ye act as if *ye* were the one who was humiliated and insulted."

"I want to ask ye one last thing. How did ye manage to accidentally catch me in such flagrant situations with the Countess?"

"Isobel..."

"Say no more. It is as I suspected. Ye have played right into their hands. I fear for ye, Claire, for ye are walking on a thawing lake, and I am the last thing standing between ye and falling through the ice. I worry for ye...even now I worry about what will happen to ye, for I ken ye will be forced to marry Giles, and hand over yer inheritance to him. If ye dinna, then ye may find yerself in the same situation as Kendrew. For I believe if they canna bend ye to their will, they will do away with ye, and try the same tactics on yer sisters until one o' ye does as they wish."

He got out of bed, weak and wobbly in the legs, and she had a stab of remorse for throwing him out of his bed in this condition, but it was not strong enough to make her change her mind.

"Do not confuse my respect for ye with cowardice, for cowardly, I am not. I committed no wrong. I was in bed because I was sick. As for proof of how and why the Countess came into my bed I have none, but ye ken I have my suspicions, as I told ye. What surprises me is that ye have none. Think upon it, Claire. Aside from what I suspect, I wish ye would tell me that if I am wrong, then what could Isobel hope to gain by destroying our marriage?"

"Perhaps she sees ye for the lying adulterer ye are

and hopes to free me from a lifetime o' such. But, that is done. I cannot talk aboot it anymore. I am too devastated. I feel as if I have been run through with a dirk and mortally wounded. I bleed from a dozen holes. At first, I wanted to die, not only from the betrayal and humiliation ye heaped upon me." She stopped for she knew this was pointless. They could keep talking like this for weeks. Someone had to end it. "None of this matters now. The time for talking is over."

Fraser was putting his clothes on. "As was the battle before it started. I would have gladly given my life for ye, but that was never a choice. Ye have been duped and ye chose to believe yer eyes instead of yer heart. Ye give me no recourse, for I am left with only one option and that is to give ye what you want, without a fight. Very well, I will be gone from here as soon as I have dressed."

She realized then…she thought he might… What? What did she think he would do? Grab her and ride off on a white charger? Suddenly she felt confused. She wanted to salvage her wounded pride and heal the hurt he had caused. But the part of being separate from him did not truly hit her until he said he would give her what she wanted and ride away. "Leave…just leave? And that is it?"

"Aye, it is over. I am done, and I shall not try again. I leave ye free and unfettered to get the divorce ye want so badly. As for me, it will not be so easily done. I told ye once I would love ye as long as there was snow on Ben Nevis. Ye may have your divorce. I will not challenge it, but it will take more than words scribbled on a piece of paper to cancel the vows and my pledge to ye."

She lifted her head proudly. "How different we view things, for there is no oath so binding as to hold me to ye."

His pride was still there, although it was humbled considerably. "I believe ye have made that point before...more than once."

"I did not come in here to ask ye to stay. It is finished between us. If ye crawled on yer hands and knees from here to Thurso and back, it would make no difference to me. Ye have played the part of the adulterer, and in my own home. Ye told me once that my mind was like a bed...never made up. This should surprise ye then, for I will never forgive ye for what ye have done, and my mind is solidly in agreement."

"Ye will not be able to shut yer eyes to the truth forever," he said. "The moment is bittersweet and it pains me to leave ye, and yet I hope that I never see yer sweet face again. How much better it would be if our paths never cross, but should it happen, I pray to God that the face I wear convinces ye that not a fig of affection for ye remains."

He pulled her against him, and her head went so easily against his chest. For a moment, she wanted to throw her arms around his neck and tell him that in her heart she did not believe him guilty of adultery, but she was shy to speak of it, and hesitant after all the things she had said. Childishly, she waited for him to take the lead as he had always done before, to be the strong one, the leader, and to do whatever it took to keep them together, for the world already seemed so dark and lonely and terrifying without him in it.

Still, she tried to muster the strength of will, if not to ask him to remain, at least to suggest they talk about it. Suddenly, he released her, and she realized she had hesitated too long.

He stepped back and she felt acutely his distancing himself from her.

"I bid ye farewell, sweet Claire. So few words, yet they take all the power of my will to say them. Leaving ye is difficult and so against my heart. I must keep reminding myself that ye were never truly mine."

It is not an easy thing to do—to blame yourself for your mistakes that cause you pain and suffering, but it goes beyond difficult when one must also shoulder the blame for decisions that inflict pain and suffering upon others.

Claire had to accept the fact that her decision to divorce Fraser was a mistake for many personal reasons: she still loved him; she'd made a life-changing decision under tremendous pressure and strain that she would not have made otherwise; she was seduced by the kindness, generosity and pretense of love that were nothing more than silver hooks of lies dangling from the silken threads of deception that Isobel and Lord Walter baited her with; and when she trusted them and turned against Fraser, she swallowed the bait and was hooked.

Fraser was gone and now she was trapped by her own gullibility. That she suffered was one thing, but to see her own stupidity as the cause of misery in her sisters' lives was an open wound that never healed.

Well, ye have what ye wanted, Claire Lennox. Ye chose Isobel and Lord Walter over Fraser, and now ye maun reap what ye have sown. But oh, she never dreamed she would pay such a great price for her foolish immaturity.

Almost immediately after the divorce was granted, Isobel and Lord Walter's first official duty was to contest Claire's right to the earldom, disputed on the grounds it could not legally descend to a female heir. It was a weak claim from the beginning, and it did not take long for the matter to be decided in Claire's favor.

It was not long until the greedy pair enlisted the help of an unscrupulous lawyer, in an attempt to have Claire declared mentally unsound, which they based upon her melancholy.

Once again, the matter was settled in Claire's favor. The Duke of Argyll addressed Isobel and Lord Walter with stern and steady frankness at the final hearing, "I ken anyone who lost a beloved family member would suffer bouts of sadness, and when ye consider this lass has lost four o' her family members in a short period o' time… Weel, I canna find fault with that, and I am concerned to hear that ye do. I find the Countess of Errick and Mains' melancholy to be normal and expected, and not an indication she is of unsound mind."

The once-happy surroundings at Lennox Castle began to change as well. Gradually, the cheerful and efficient staff began to disappear only to be replaced by aloof employees, devoid of any feeling, but with a devoted efficiency at reporting to their employers the moment anyone stepped out of line.

Laughter became a rare occurrence.

At night, Claire and her sisters would lie in bed and whisper how anyone could do anything more to render their environment less gloomy or more miserable.

It was as if the castle itself had undergone massive change, and its thick walls and huge oaken beams took on the characteristics of a prison, along with the narrow windows set high in the walls. Most of the loveliest furnishing began to disappear, as they were moved to Isobel's home, or to that of Lord Walter, in exchange for pieces of lesser quality, or for nothing at all. Soon they became accustomed to the bare places in rooms where exquisite antiques had once been.

One gloomy afternoon as Claire and Greer were on their way to their room, Greer said, "Even the paintings look frightening now, ye ken."

It was true, for even to Claire, the portraits of their ancestors, who always seemed to smile warmly upon the generations that followed them, now seemed somber and grim, as they scowled at all who passed by from the walls of the galleries.

Their first two attempts having failed, Isobel and Lord Walter began to plan other ways to gain control of Claire's title and inheritance and, utmost in their eyes was coercing her to marry Isobel's son, Giles. Claire and her sisters were placed under the supervision of a strict and unsympathetic governess, after Kathleen O'Malley was sent away.

Cora Baber was cold, reserved, and in possession of a peevish sternness and all around air of bitter discontent. She made their hours in the schoolroom miserable, and when they were punished, which was often, it was harsh. Whenever Miss Baber reported to Isobel or Lord Walter the slightest infractions of the rules, they were punished a second time, only more severely.

For some reason, Cora Baber selected Briana as her favored one to pick on, and consequently she found fault with everything Briana did. She scolded her, slapped her palms with a ruler, assigned her grueling tasks, or gave her a thorough shaking.

If Briana dared to ask a question, she would answer, "Everyone else understands, and since ye are the only one who canna pay attention, ye will have to find the answer yerself."

Because Briana was the youngest, things were especially difficult for her. Her thoughts were so much occupied with the loss of her father and brothers that she had difficulty focusing her mind on anything else. As a result, she was the recipient of daily punishment in the schoolroom because she could not concentrate. Briana, who was always the happiest child, was now known for bursting into tears at the slightest cause.

Miss Baber especially liked asking Briana a question, then answering it herself, before Briana had an opportunity to reply. She would call Briana a dunce and stupid, then she would throw the book down and tell Briana to stand in the corner because "Ye are too stupid to learn."

"Ye only make it more difficult for yourself," Kenna told her. "Canna ye see the malicious smile on Miss Baber's face whenever ye cry? Do ye not think she enjoys it when ye cry?"

"Aye, I k-ken she does," Briana said between sobs.

"And will ye be content to spend the rest of yer life pleasing the likes o' her? Is that to be yer lot in life, then?"

There were many nights when they were only allowed bread and water for dinner. Spankings were frequent and harshly administered. One day, Miss Baber said to Isobel, in front of Claire and her sisters, "One must be brutally severe at times, but that is the only way to break the obstinate will of children, ye ken."

"Oh, I agree with ye," Isobel said. "Wholeheartedly. Do feel free to discipline them in whatever manner ye choose."

Isobel did not rely on Cora Baber to provide all the misery, for she seemed to take equal pleasure in finding ways to show the girls that the Isobel they had previously known was not the real Isobel.

All the beautiful dresses she had made for the girls disappeared. The piano was sold. The art room was locked. They were no longer allowed to remove books from the library. The trips across the loch were canceled. They were not allowed to attend kirk.

When Greer commented at dinner, "I dinna like peas. They stick in my throat," Isobel smiled coldly.

"What a pity I did not know sooner," Isobel said, "for I thought ye were especially fond o' peas, and ordered cook to have plenty on hand for ye."

Poor Greer was forced to eat nothing but peas for every meal for one week. To make certain she ate all of them, Isobel said, "For each pea ye leave on yer plate, one meal will be denied of one of yer sisters."

They all suffered, but it was worse for Claire, for she felt responsible for being so gullible to believe the best of Walter and Isobel, even to the point of turning her back on her own husband. It was a rare night that she did not cry herself to sleep.

Lord Walter's favorite torment was to order them to their room for an evening or several days, depending on his mood and what the guilty person did to acquire his wrath. He also came up with the idea for cold baths during the wintertime, where they had to sit in the bath for a certain period of time, and often the water was so cold, a thin layer of ice had to be broken before they could sit down.

Eventually, all the color in their world faded away to sepia tones. For the entire winter that followed, the only cheerful sound or sight in the castle was the crackle of the burning fire and the warmth it lent to the room.

Thirteen

It was not like your great and gracious ways!
Do you, that have naught other to lament,
Never, my Love, repent
Of how, that July afternoon,
You went,
With sudden, unintelligible phrase,
And frightened eye,
Upon your journey of so many days,
Without a single kiss, or a goodbye?

Coventry Patmore (1823-1896), British poet.
The Unknown Eros "Departure" (1877)

Utrecht, Holland
Summer 1745

Fraser Graham was going home.

He did not realize how hungry he was for his family and his homeland until he saw his brother waving energetically from the boat, and felt a corresponding lump of homesickness swell in his throat.

Two years…

Two long years he had been here, without setting foot on Scottish soil; without the sight of a family face or the lilt of a dear one's voice. But that would all change now that Bran was here.

Fraser was deeply touched when Bran wrote of his plans to come to Utrecht. "I will come to visit for a week or so, then I will return home with ye," he wrote.

"I will accompany ye back to Scotland," he wrote, "for I canna wait any longer to see ye, Fraser. I also want to make certain the women in Utrecht are as beautiful as ye say."

When Fraser scanned the faces of the passengers on the boat and caught his first glimpse of Bran's face, it all became real to him: his brother was here, and he *was* going home.

Bran no more than stepped on solid ground when Fraser appeared at his side. Immediately, the brothers greeted each other with polite fondness as befitted their class, and then, in the manner the Graham brothers did since their childhood days, they tussled energetically—until Bran managed to encircle Fraser's head and lock him against his body with his arm in a tight hold.

"Ye ha' gotten weak, brother," Bran said. "I ken you will be in for it when you arrive back at Monleigh and Jamie, Niall and Callum have a go at ye. Surely ye know they will be waiting for ye."

"Aye, I ken they will, but perhaps my superior intelligence will enable me to escape that fate."

"Och...so it's a super intelligence you acquired, is it? And I was thinking ye came to study law." His eyes gleamed with mischief as he said, "Mayhap ye are better suited to wrestle our wee sister."

"Och, I let her try her hand at it when she was no more than nine or ten. When I got the best of her, she lost her temper and gave me a swift kick. It landed in a most unfortunate place."

Bran was laughing. "Oh aye, I remember that day and the sight of ye sprawled on yer back in the garden and Arabella's comment that she liked kicking better than wrestling."

"Look at ye," Bran said when he stepped back to look Fraser over. "The first lawyer in the family. Have you any inkling of how proud we are of ye?"

Fraser grinned and gave Bran's hair a bit of ruffling. "Ye are only thinking of the free legal advice."

"Aye, that, too," Bran said.

Fraser picked up Bran's portmanteau. "It is good to have ye here," he said, and the two of them started up the street, each taking the opportunity to bring the other up to date on what had transpired in their lives over the past two years.

Once they reached the house where Fraser rented two small rooms, Fraser talked about plans for dinner when Bran dropped wearily into a leather chair. "I fair to wore myself out wrestling ye, and I am grown quite gray in the head for want of sleep," he said. "I ken an hour or so of rest would make me a more jovial dinner partner."

"Then hie yourself off to my bed for a nap."

While Bran napped, Fraser packed the things in his desk. He still found it difficult to believe that after his years of study at the University of Utrecht, he would bid adieu to this ancient city. How long ago it seemed when he first arrived in the *Hart van Nederland*—the heart of the Netherlands—and saw for the first time the colorful, magical city of Utrecht, traveling as everyone did by a horse-drawn boat through the canals that linked the River Lek to the Utrecht Canal.

When he reached the bottom drawer and started to empty it, he picked up a bundle of letters. The top one was from his sister, Arabella, and the first letter he received after he arrived. He studied his sister's familiar handwriting, which he found to be similar to Claire's, although Arabella's letters had more pronounced loops.

Claire…always Claire, remaining for some time in his thoughts and mind, like the last note of a song that has ended. He thought of the broken heart that brought him here, and Claire, so beautiful, so dainty, and yet so strong, having to endure the gossip and shame of divorce, in order to be free of him.

The feel of her in his arms… God, Claire, small and sweet, whose face haunted him still. Claire, both goddess and temptress, whose beautiful nudity lying soft beneath him was a powerful balance of innocence and sensuality. Claire who said, "There is no oath so binding as to hold me to you."

More than once during his time here, he would think about her and wonder if she still considered him guilty of adultery. It still puzzled him how she could have thought him capable of such, and with such a notorious courtesan as the Countess of Stagwyth.

He remembered that day well for two reasons: Claire's decision to believe her calculating aunt over him, and how very sick he really was. He had to stop this, he thought. Put her out of your mind….

When Bran came out of the bedroom Fraser was still standing there with Arabella's letter in his hand, wrestling with his mind. He did not notice that his brother entered the room.

Bran walked over to Fraser and glanced at the letter. "It's from Arabella," he said.

His words entered Fraser's consciousness and the memory of Claire vanished. "What...? Oh...yes... Arabella...she was the first to write me, ye know."

Bran shrugged, giving his attention to the writing on the envelope. "It is more of a woman's nature to be punctual with that sort of thing. When I came into the room and saw ye, I thought at first that the letter was from Claire."

Fraser's expression stiffened. "I havena written to Claire, nor has she corresponded with me. Why would ye think she would?"

"Hold on now, I did not say I *thought* anything, except there was something about yer expression that made me think ye entertained thoughts o' her in yer mind."

Fraser's features relaxed and he put the bundle of letters in the trunk. "I ken ye to be a man of keen insight and judgment... I was thinking of her."

Fraser watched as his brother dropped into the leather chair. He was glad Bran was here. Although Fraser had made many friends in Utrecht, and had two friends from Scotland attending the university. He missed the close bond with his family. The five Graham brothers were bound tightly together by love, loyalty and family pride, and were as close to one another as any brothers could be. Arabella, by virtue of being the only sister, and the youngest of the six siblings, was the soft spot in all of their hearts.

Close in age, they grew up huddled together like the

bright red clusters of rowanberries that grew in the rocky crags, gills and becks near Monleigh Castle, high in the Highlands.

"I want to hear about the Dutch lass ye wrote me aboot. When do I get to meet her?"

"Ye willna. We have already said our goodbyes."

"The way you wrote, I thought ye were contemplating something more permanent, like marriage."

"Ye should know better than that."

"It's been long enough, Fraser. Ye need to forget Claire Lennox."

Fraser thought that sounded a lot like the same thing his brothers and sister told him when he returned to Monleigh Castle after he left Inchmurrin. He was still suffering the effects of what he knew was Isobel's attempt to poison him, and a visit from the doctor confirmed that his symptoms and Kendrew's were symptomatic of arsenic poisoning. As soon as Fraser was back on his feet, his family had wanted to know what happened, and Fraser told them, leaving nothing out. When he finished, Jamie was ready to take action. "Isobel and Lord Walter have been granted the ward of the Lennox children, and I ha' never heard of anyone, in spite of despicable acts and spending the heir's fortune, who has ever had the right of ward revoked. However, there is always a first time, but it would be a lengthy process, and Claire would more than likely reach her majority before we could get anything done legally. I am no' afraid to pay them a visit, though, and to let them know that I will no' abide mistreatment of the Lennox women."

"'Twould do no good," Fraser said.

"Why would it not?" Arabella asked.

"Isobel and Lord Walter have Claire and her sisters fooled, to the point the girls think they are wonderful, caring guardians. Claire would not stand for anyone making charges against them. I tried, and ye see what happened. She chose them over her own husband. She willna allow any outside interference."

"We dinna need their permission to interfere," Tavish said. "I say we make Claire see things as they really are, even if we have to kidnap her to do it."

Sophie, Jamie's beautiful French wife, shifted her infant son to her other shoulder and placed a hand on Tavish's arm. "No, Tavish, you cannot fight those who do wrong by doing wrong yourself. Whatever action you take must be done without bringing shame, criticism or disgrace to your clan. When you are dealing with treachery and those who excel at it, you must remember they are as slippery as a panicked trout."

Everyone smiled at her use of the trout example, because they knew it was her way of showing she was part of the family, in spite of her French birth and upbringing.

"Believe me," she said, "I know all about treachery and the minds of those who perform it without a conscience, or a care for those they destroy."

It was true, for Sophie was the granddaughter of Louis XIV, and her life had been ruled by treachery, so much so that she had risked her life to escape France and, unexpectedly, she found love in the arms of Jamie. They were a fine example of how good triumphs over evil, for to look at the Earl of Monleigh and his Countess, and the young heir, the Master of Graham, whom Sophie held in her arms, one understood that risk always involves some element of danger or failure, but the possible rewards make the risk worth taking.

"If what Fraser says is true, and Claire is of the mind that Isobel and Lord Walter are acting in good faith on their behalf, there is nothing we can do," Niall said.

"Aye," Calum said, "the best thing for Fraser is to try to forget all aboot the Countess of Errick and Mains."

"Forget Claire?" he repeated. He shook his head and gave Bram a direct look. "To say I need to forget her is like asking me to lop off my arm, or a leg. Claire was part of me. She still is."

Bran shook his head. "I dinna want to fall in love quite that much."

"What ye want doesn't have anything to do with it. Ye canna choose the depth of yer love any more than ye can choose the person ye fall in love with. I suppose there are some, like me, who have only one great love in their life, and when it's over, that is the end of love for them."

Fraser was surprised at the feeling those words evoked in him. How could he put so much pain and emotion into simple words? It would do no good to tell his brother that not even death would have separated her from him in such an acute manner. Someone like Bran, who had never been in love, would not understand the endless torment, the agony of knowing she was lost to him and yet remained warm, vital and beautifully passionate.

It was the worst kind of separation—worse even than death, for in death you know it is final, and there is nothing you can do to change it. When the one you love is vibrantly alive, and dead only to you, there is a period of desperation, when the mind plays out all manner of situations in which the rejected one can regain the love he lost. He did not know how to put this into words. Even now, the memory trapped him in a bubble of time, his apparently frozen state belying the turmoil that raced inside, and set fire to his mind.

His entire time with her seemed to play in his mind: the warm memories of their courtship; the all-too-short year they were married; the sweet passion they found together. He thought of how it all happened so quickly that he did not have time to stop the ravaging of his psyche, or his heart. What did it matter now? It was over, and when the end came, it was swift, overwhelming, and left him devastated.

He could feel Bran's gaze upon him and for an instant he felt a sort of helplessness, a state of indecisiveness, as if he did not know which way to turn, then he moved to the bed and sat down.

Perhaps Bran was right....

He had lived for too long with disbelief, confusion, anger, humiliation and despair, which was followed by a period of sadness and yearning. There were times he doubted his own sanity, and moments when he wondered if it was worth all the pain, just to stay alive. In spite of it all, and his doubt that he would ever survive it, the pain had lessened, and at some point he realized he had fully absorbed the impact of losing her, and accepted it as something as irrevocable as it was final.

The wounds had healed, but the scar would remain forever.

"Let's take a walk before dinner," Bran said. "I would like to stretch my legs."

"All right. Let us be away from here. I want to show ye Utrecht, and some of the fine, fine women we have here, and then I plan to get you drunk on beer, and who knows, I may join ye."

They both ended up quite inebriated, and on the way home, Bran decided he wanted to drink for a living. "I am *slimply slupliflied* I can drink *slo mush* and feel *schlimply slupendoos.*"

Once they were home, Fraser set to work preparing a bed for Bran, but when he turned around he saw Bran stretched out on the floor. When Fraser called his name, Bran lifted his head, gave him a sickly smile and lay back down.

"Ye big bairn," Fraser said, covering him with a downy cover and going to bed himself, leaving his brother where he had landed.

Fourteen

So sad, so fresh, the days that are no more.

Alfred Lord Tennyson (1809-1892),
British poet. *The Princess* "Tears, Idle Tears, I Know Not What They Mean" (1847)

Lennox Castle, Inchmurrin Island, 1745

The Duchess of Abbotsford and her two depressingly homely daughters finished their third cup of tea. Claire looked at her first cup, still half full. She glanced at the clock. They had been here for almost three hours, she thought, and she was not accustomed to sitting this long in one place.

Claire liked the duchess, who was truly a simple, well-meaning soul, whose days were filled with dressmakers, art lessons, tea, gardening and fussing over her children and husband. She knew the duchess had no inkling of what Claire's life was like, or how she was up before sunup, going over her accounts and meeting with members of her staff, before she made her daily tour around the island, meeting with the clansmen who were her various overseers. Two or three times a week, she made the boat trip to the mainland, to perform similar tasks. They probably had no idea she made calls upon her tenants, or went over plans for the purchase of better breeding stock, and the implementing of the latest farming techniques.

After all the boring gossip she listened to, she was thankful her ancestors had obtained patents that enabled a female to inherit the earldom. Living the life of an earl was far superior to the life of a woman married to one, she decided.

She smiled and nodded at something the duchess said. Her head was beginning to ache. She prayed the duchess would remember that she had a home and husband waiting for her.

Still, out of etiquette, Claire offered them more tea.

"I believe I will," Lady Charlotte, the eldest daughter, said. "I find it simply fascinating, Countess, that ye are able to do a man's work. Why, the numbers alone would be the end o' me."

Claire smiled. "There are days I vouch they will do the same for me. Still, it is rewarding work, and now I find I much prefer the days when I have more to do than I can accomplish in one day, to the days when I finish my work by midafternoon."

"Dinna let Claire fool ye," Kenna said. "She never finishes her work midafternoon. I canna understand where she gets her strength to handle it all. Consequently, I have decided that the men who say a woman's constitution is less than that of a man dinna ken what they are talking aboot."

Lady Charlotte suddenly seemed to be as bright as a burning candle, for her interest was certainly piqued by Kenna's remark. "I agree with ye wholeheartedly. 'Twas obviously a man who coined the phrase 'the weaker sex.' Putting up with men alone makes us stronger than they are."

Kenna picked up her tea and moved to a chair closer to Lady Charlotte, and the two of them began to expound upon the common thread of interest that ran through them.

Greer, on the other hand, was looking as out of place as Lady Charlotte's sister. Claire smiled and turned to Lady Augusta. "More tea?"

"I believe I will," Lady Augusta said, placing her rattling cup on the silver tray in front of Claire.

Claire sensed her insecurity, and knew Lady Augusta was one who would much prefer to be home spraying her roses for thirps than making social calls. In spite of all Claire did to try to put her at ease, she was still "Lady Augusta of the rattling cup."

Claire was thinking that Briana was probably the smartest one of all, for she had spent five minutes with them before she pleaded a headache and dashed from the room. In spite of her preference to do the same, Claire smiled and said, "I understand ye are a painter with exceptional artistic abilities. My sister, Greer, also loves to paint. Mayhap ye could pay us a visit sometime and you and Greer could paint together. There are some breathtaking views of Ben Lomond from the island."

Lady Augusta glanced shyly at Greer. "I have longed to have someone to paint with, and I am pleased to know ye share my interest, Lady Greer. Are ye interested in landscapes, still life, or portraiture?"

"So far I havena found a preference. I seem to paint at whim...if a scene strikes my fancy, I paint it. If I catch one of our clansmen in a pose I envision it on canvas, and I ask them to freeze themselves in that pose while I take a few sketches. In the wintertime, I find still lifes occupy my time, unless the weather permits my doing a few snow scenes."

Lady Augusta made a clicking noise with her tongue that signaled she and Greer were very much alike in their artistic taste and endeavors. She put her cup down and leaned forward. "I have some books on painting I would love to share with ye, and if ye have some I havena read, I would love to borrow them."

Greer put her cup down and said, "Oh, please come with me and I will show ye what I have painted. While ye are there, ye can see what I am working on now."

"Weel, I declare, I had no idea my daughters and yer sisters would find so much in common. I may have to speak to the duke about acquiring a boat for the girls to use whenever they want to pay ye a visit, and of course I hope they will visit us at Dinnegal Castle."

Claire and the Duchess continued to discuss the things the younger women had in common until Greer and Lady Augusta returned, then the Duchess put down her teacup.

"My, my, the afternoon has flown," the Duchess said as she arose with a rustle of silk, and gathered her shawl about her. "I canna remember when I have enjoyed myself more, or stayed this long. Do forgive our tardiness in making our departure."

Claire laughed. "When ye make the trip across the loch to pay a social call, I believe ye are entitled to a longer visit. Besides, we have all enjoyed yer company. It was an afternoon well spent."

"Why, thank ye, Lady Claire." She turned to her daughters. "Bid the Countess and her sisters goodbye," she said. "We must be on our way if we are to be home in time for dinner."

Claire took in the ample proportions of the Duchess and thought it would not do her ill to miss dinner for the next several weeks. Still, she was glad to walk them to the door, but before the butler could open the door, the Duchess had wandered off to inspect a hanging on the wall.

She turned back to Claire. "I do believe that is a French tapestry, is it not?"

"I am sure you are thinking of the *Noble Pastorale* that hangs in the great staircase, with the mille-fleurs design. It is sixteenth-century French, from the Loire Valley. There were several made to complete a series. My great grandfather was very fortunate to purchase one."

"And this one?"

Claire studied the beloved tapestry that she always felt especially close to, since her mother was born in the month of June. "That particular one is of Italian origin. It is one of the Trivulzio Tapestries produced by Benedetto da Milano. There were twelve of them, all allegorical depictions of each month. This one is called *Month of June*."

"Quite priceless, I am sure," the Duchess said.

"Quite," Claire agreed.

That was true, for Claire's father, grandfather and other Lennox earls before them were men of considerable taste and discrimination, and during their lifetimes, they built up a remarkable collection of pictures, drawings and objets d'art, especially Italian paintings of the Renaissance period, and tapestries of almost any era. Most of the paintings and tapestries were kept here, at Lennox Castle, but all the other castles in the family held a piece or two—that is until Isobel and Lord Walter arrived.

"I dinna understand why my feet hurt," Lady Charlotte said. "I have been sitting all afternoon."

"I am certain it is those new shoes. I told ye I thought they were a bit narrow for ye. Come, my dears, we really must go," the Duchess said. "Give my regards to yer aunt. I am sorry we paid our visit on a day she wasna at home. I should have enjoyed conversing with her."

Claire wondered what the Duchess would do if she told her the truth, that her aunt was, at this moment, reading a book in her bedroom because she found the Duchess too boring to waste her time upon.

The Duchess picked up Claire's hand. "I do hope ye take time to enjoy yerself, Lady Claire. Ye are still a young woman, even if ye are the Countess. Ye must no' overwork yerself. I am sure yer aunt Isobel and Lord Walter tell ye the same thing."

Claire almost snorted at that. Indeed, they were anything but concerned about Claire's happiness or her welfare. What would the kindhearted Duchess say if Claire told her her aunt Isobel and Lord Walter had betrayed her and her sisters, and that she not only suspected they had killed her brother but had attempted to do the same with Fraser. How would she like to hear that Claire now knew it was part of their plan all along to begin with kindness to gain the trust of Claire and her sisters, then go for their throats. Would the Duchess even believe her if Claire told her how she realized, all too late, the wisdom of her husband, his sound judgment and uncanny ability to recognize people for what they were, and not what they pretended to be. *Oh, Fraser, ye were right...about everything, for I see now what I was too foolish to see before—that Isobel planned everything with the Countess of Stagwyth.*

Why, for heaven's sake, did she not consider that Isobel had been the one who had sent her scampering off to whatever prearranged destination where she knew the Countess of Stagwyth had set the stage—to make something innocent on Fraser's part look as if he was up to his ears in adultery?

Claire carried the burden of knowing she had foolishly turned her back on the man she loved, and who loved her. She could not blame anyone but herself, for she was the one who drove Fraser out of her life. It did not matter that she was under stress from the deaths of her father and brothers, or that she was too young and inexperienced to know cunning when she came up against it.

What mattered now was that she and her sisters reaped the pain and suffering of Claire's mistake. But the worst of it, and the part that continued to cause her so much pain, was she still loved him and always would—not that anything could ever come of it. Fraser was a proud man and she had turned against him and thrown his love for her in his face. He would not seek vengeance any more than he would consider, for a moment, the possibility of them getting back together.

For Fraser, what was over stayed over.

Dear God, would she ever forgive herself for that ungodly decision to divorce? Yet, she could not wish it did not happen for she was convinced that the only reason Fraser did not die was because she had decided to divorce him. Isobel had no longer needed to poison him and risk the possibility of being caught when she realized the divorce would achieve her goal of getting Fraser out of Claire's life. Then she and Lord Walter could shove Giles in her face, which they did on a regular basis.

The Duchess must have seen the frown such thoughts produced on Claire's face, for she said, "You carry a burden much too heavy for any woman, much less one as young as you. I have always questioned the wisdom of allowing a title pass to a woman. Have ye thought of marrying again? 'Twould be so much easier for ye, if ye had a husband to take over the duties of managing an estate of this size. From time to time, I hear someone is interested in courting ye, but they always say ye are no interested in marriage."

Lady Charlotte put her hand on the Duchess's arm. "Mither, ye told me to remind ye not to bring up the subject o' marriage."

"That is true, my dear, and thank ye for yer reminder. I am a meddling person at heart, and I must fight it constantly. It is what my dear husband always calls my 'one fault.' Please forget anything I said."

Claire smiled. "It is forgotten."

At last, the Duchess said her final goodbye, but only after Lady Charlotte gave Claire a wink and threatened to remove her shoes.

As soon as they were gone, Claire closed the door and leaned back against it. She looked at her sisters.

"I do like them, but only in small spaces of time. Right now, all I can say is, thank God they are gone. I can discuss horse breeding or cattle breeding or crop rotation all day long. But two or three hours with a chatty group of women tires me to the bone."

The Duchess had no more than stepped through the door when Isobel came down the stairs and paused on the last step—listening to her conversation with the Duchess so she could make her appearance immediately after.

"I have been waiting for what seems like hours for that fat cow to make her departure," Isobel said. When she spoke, there was such scorn on her lips, it seemed to draw the handsomeness from her face. "Ye are far too indulgent with people like the Duchess. Ye waste hours on her to no avail. Ye should spend yer time on more worthy subjects."

"The problem with that theory is, there is no one worthy in your eyes...other than yerself, Lord Walter or yer dear son, Giles, whose illustrious name is at the top of the worthies list," Claire said as she stepped around Isobel and started up the stairs.

Isobel's hand lashed out to grab Claire by the arm, and she dug her sharp claws into Claire's skin. "I would think ye were taught to be more respectful of both yer elders and your kin." When Claire turned around, Isobel slapped her. "Giles *is* yer cousin, ye spiteful little wench."

Claire turned and pried Isobel's fingers loose. "Giles is a 'stepcousin' if ye will, since he has no Lennox blood flowing in his veins, for which I am thankful. In fact, none of ye have any Lennox blood, and I am counting the days until I must no longer suffer yer control over my life, so I might order yer despicable carcasses tossed into the loch."

"At least my first husband died. I did not have to resort to a scandalous divorce."

"Hmm, I find that interesting. Correct me if I err in my recollections, but was it not ye who was at the forefront of those who thought it best if I ended things between Fraser and myself? And did ye not bring in your harlot friend Carolina to set it all up? To remind ye further, ye are the one who suggested it. It was apparent ye had also sought counsel from yer lawyer concerning the matter well in advance of tossing it before me like a well-meated bone. How else would ye have known all the conditions, point by point?"

Isobel's delft-blue eyes grew cold and her voice crystal clear with icy warning. "I tried to caution ye before ye married him. If you had listened to me, none of this would have happened."

"No, I have a feeling I would be blissfully married to Giles, who doesn't seem to have any more feeling for me than he does for ye."

Isobel's nostrils flared and Claire knew what it took for her to hold herself in check. "Ye have no inkling as to Giles's true feelings for me. As for others, Giles is discriminating. He does not lie down with dogs. He knows he will get up with fleas. Ye would do well to consider marriage with him."

"I would sooner sup with the Devil." Claire shuddered to think of his lips on hers, but she knew she had already said too much, as the fiery burning on her cheek reminded her. Isobel was the kind who remembered every little wrong, every cross word, each slighting look, and then she would wait until the opportunity arose to seek her revenge. She would extract it piece by piece, for she was one to adhere to the law of "an eye for an eye and a tooth for a tooth."

"Giles has similar feelings about ye, but I have told him that oft it is those who are the most antagonistic toward each other who have the most passionate marriages."

Claire almost laughed outright. If Giles was passionate about anything, it was his fancy clothes. But she did not miss the way the veins stood out on Isobel's neck, or how the pale blue of her gown, accenting her eyes, gave her a glacial quality; all cold, unforgiving, and deadly.

As was her way of signaling that she was through with talking, Isobel turned around and, without another word, left.

Claire followed her with a steady eye, for she wouldn't be surprised if Isobel vanished before her eyes and suddenly reappeared someplace else, for she was beginning to realize what a wicked witch of a person Isobel really was. She wondered, why did I not see this before?

She immediately felt a stab of remorse for the way she had lashed out at Fraser each time he had tried to tell her about Isobel and Walter. He warned her when he left that things would grow worse for her, and said he regretted he would not be here to stand between her and all that she would be forced to endure.

She found it despicable that she actually laughed in his face, but she was not laughing now. Fraser had been the strong arm that held Walter and Isobel at bay, and if she had not fought him each step of the way, he might have been able to do more. She thought of darling Kendrew, and the horrible way he wasted away. Had she listened to Fraser, would Kendrew still be alive?

Claire felt the moisture seep from her eyes and she wiped them with the back of her hand. There was no way to know the answer to that, and it would do no good to torture herself with it. With a shudder, she turned away to realize the chill she felt in the room earlier was gone. It made her shiver to think Isobel had sucked that drafty chill out of the room when she departed.

Claire put her hand to her head. "I must tell my sisters that we will have no more telling of ghost stories. We have ghosts enough clinging to our coattails without fabricating more."

Her mind was still on Fraser as she climbed the stairs. If he were here now, he would protect her and her sisters from such abuse. *Oh, God, ye gave me a true man and I drove him away, and now I realize my folly. I need a hero...in the worst way.... A man with a strong arm and a guid heart...a man like the man I pushed away....*

Fifteen

No cord nor cable can so forcibly draw, or
hold so fast, as
love can do with a twined thread.

Robert Burton (1577-1640),
English scholar and churchman.
The Anatomy of Melancholy (1621)

Utrecht, Netherlands, 1745

The day of their departure, Fraser put the last of his belongings inside the trunk and closed the lid, then locked it. It was time to say goodbye to Utrecht, and he wondered if he would ever come this way again.

He smiled, remembering how Bran had been seduced by the city and its charm, and declared he truly envied Fraser's life in Utrecht. His reverie ended when, on the street below, he heard the rattle of carriage wheels on the cobblestones, and he moved to the window and parted the curtain to look out.

Their driver had arrived.

He was about to turn away when his gaze encountered the beauty of the sunrise, and the sky tinted with brilliant streaks of red. *Claire of the fiery red tresses...*

Mesmerized, he found it to be the same color of Pompeian red he always thought so aptly described Claire's hair. As he watched, the clouds seemed to take on the shape and form of a woman's long hair, as if some slight breeze had tugged the silken skeins from beneath her bonnet.

He closed his eyes and pressed his forehead against the cold glass just long enough to envision her face, turned to him, with her perfect coloring and the hazel eyes, the lips so full and red. There was an almost fragile quality about her, and yet he had never known a stronger, more determined, more stubborn human being in his life.

A smile creased the corners of his mouth at the remembrance.

He opened his eyes and felt a stab of disappointment, for the sunrise now looked quite commonplace and ordinary. He contemplated that for a moment. Why had his thoughts turned to her now? Was it simply because he was returning to Scotland for the first time since he had left there that summer two years ago?

Mayhap it was nothing more than a visit from Queen Mab last night that turned his dreams to love. No matter, he thought, and pushed thoughts of Claire aside. He gave the two rooms a last going-over and went below stairs. He met Bran returning from his walk.

"I was coming up to tell ye the driver was here."

"I saw him from the window," Fraser said, then instructed the driver to take the trunk and baggage from his room.

"And the destination?" the driver asked.

"Deliver it to the boat waiting in the canal—the one leaving for Amsterdam at eleven o'clock. See that it is properly loaded," he said, and gave the driver a generous tip. "We will meet you there in ample time."

"Very good, sir, and thank you, sir."

Fraser left his home for the last time, then he and Bran walked over the familiar cobblestone streets and across the Domplein—or Domsquare, as it was more commonly known.

Soon, he found himself in front of the old cathedral, the Dom. "Come on," he said. "You can't come to Utrecht and not see the city from the top."

They climbed to the top of one of the three towers of the great church that housed the "throne made from unicorn horns." The tower was tall and thin, and the stairs were narrow and steep, going straight up for 384 feet. They were both winded by the time they reached the top.

"It better be a spectacular view after a climb like that," Bran said.

"It is," Fraser said, then stepped through the door and looked out over the old Roman city, surrounded by a standing crown of water.

From their vantage point, they could see the coiling paths of the fourteenth-century sunken canal; the Oude Gracht—Old Canal—crowded with boats and barges and winding through the center of the city; the Nieuwe Gracht—New Canal—lined with the colorful little houses with pointed roofs that were built more than three hundred years ago for rich merchants.

Because it was a clear day, he could even point out Amsterdam, lying silent in the distance.

After the long journey back down the narrow, steep stairs, they stopped by a café along the canal for coffee. He told Bran to ignore the boys pestering him to buy their *libelles*—the pamphlets with the latest gossip. "We will buy a newspaper instead."

"Won't do me any good, unless it's in English," Bran said.

"They have them sometimes, although they aren't the latest edition. If they do not have one, ye can look at the political cartoons."

They were fortunate to buy the last English paper. They found an empty bench in the park, and Fraser handed part of the paper to Bran. After a few minutes of trying to read, Fraser's concentration began to wander and he sifted through the memories of the past three years.

He recalled the many times he had come to a place near here, while taking a break from his studies, to lie in the arms of lovely Lisanne. This time of year was always his favorite, when after lovemaking, they would lie with their bodies entwined, listening to the sounds that drifted through the open window: the singing of the birds in the trees and the chorus of frogs coming from the canal.

Lovely Lisanne, with the pale skin and pink-tipped breasts that seemed to float beneath his hands like lotus buds. Even now, the delft-blue eyes haunted him, filled with tears that fell in silence. She loved him, deeply, he knew, and it grieved him to tell her he could not love her in return.

Her last words to him came creeping back into his consciousness, and he could see her once more, standing at the door, her beautiful features subdued, her voice soft and laced with pain.

"I never knew love could hurt. To leave you now is much against my heart. It takes such strength of will."

"Lisanne..."

"No, please do not say anything more. I know you wanted to love me, just as I know you honestly tried. It grieves my soul that the heart does not always follow the dictates of the will, and no amount of desire can make it so. I wish I had the words, but I feel too much the emptiness of love. I cannot say farewell, nor can I kiss you goodbye. In time, I will love again, and perhaps I shall marry. Yet, even when I am old, I shall never lament these three years with you, nor shall I repent my love for you. You have bid me goodbye, and you will soon go. I know that time will erase for you the memory of Lisanne. How strange it is to realize that not even that has crushed all the love I carry for you in my heart. I leave you now, with all the will I can muster, although it is at the expense of my heart."

He stood and started toward her, but she held out her hand to stay him. She opened the door and turned back toward him one last time. "If ever you did hold me in your heart ever so briefly, grant me one wish. Speak not, so that I might leave with the only thing I have left...my dignity."

Then she was gone.

But oh, the memory of it would haunt him, for it did him ill to think he had so deeply wounded one whose heart was so pure. Why could he not love Lisanne, as she deserved to be loved? Would he spend his life alone, grieving for the one person he would always be denied? Would his heart always point like a compass toward Claire as the only woman for him?

How, he wondered, could he cure his heart of this love for her? How could he blot her memory from his mind?

Somewhere, a church bell chimed the half hour and Fraser took out his father's watch. He flipped open the gold lid and saw it was half past ten, just as the church bells said. The time had come to tuck the memories of Utrecht and Lisanne away, and turn his thoughts to Scotland and the future that awaited him there.

He came to his feet and rattled the paper Bran was reading. "Time to go," he said. "Ye will have to finish that on the boat, unless ye prefer to take in the sights along the canal."

Bran folded the paper and the two of them made their way back to the canal where the driver waited. For Fraser, the moment was bittersweet. He had been happy in this place, and his time here had given him a new life. His quest for knowledge was over, and the pull of his homeland was strong in his blood. He longed for his native heath and to see the Highlands rise up out of the North Sea, shrouded in mist, cragged and steep.

His heart was in the Highlands. Scotland was home; the land of his sires and the place to which his heart was bound.

Some time later he stood with his brother at the boat's railing, watching the spires of the Dom fade out of sight. Utrecht and that part of his life were closed. He was bound for Monleigh Castle, with a law degree from one of Europe's most prestigious universities, unparalleled for the study of Roman law.

"What are yer plans once we reach Scotland? Everyone is expecting ye to come to Monleigh."

"I plan to spend some time there, of course. I am most anxious to see them."

"I know ye won't stay indefinitely."

"No, I ken I will spend a month or so at Monleigh. I need to see the family again. Then I will move to Edinburgh to open my law practice."

He had a marriage and his education behind him. Ahead, lay his quest for life's fulfillment and the easing of the pain of losing Claire.

Sixteen

Memories are hunting horns whose sound dies on the wind.

Guillaume Apollinaire (1880-1918),
Italian-born French poet of Polish descent.
"Cors de Chasse" (1912)

Claire and her sisters returned from their walk, which was always the brightest point of their day. Out of doors and away from Isobel and Lord Walter's piercing eyes and domineering ways, they could laugh and sing, and be young again.

All that changed, though, the moment they set a foot inside the door of Lennox Castle. Today, when they closed the door, Briana slipped her hand in Claire's. "I dinna like living here with *them,*" she whispered. Her tone dropped even lower when she said, "I especially dinna like Lord Walter. If I think about him, I cannot go to sleep at night. Do ye think he is an evil spirit?"

Claire kissed her forehead and whispered, "No, I think he is a very unhappy person."

"And he passes it on to all of us whenever he has the opportunity," Kenna said.

"It's no' fair that others have a mither and a faither and we have neither," Briana said. "Is our family cursed?"

Claire was both saddened and surprised to hear that. "Cursed, why no, of course not. Whatever gave ye that idea? All families ha' misfortune from time to time, and I think we almost have ours behind us." Claire stroked the bright face turned up to hers. "We must all pray our birthdays come faster," she said. "Or at least mine, so I can reach my majority and we can send them on their way."

Claire saw Greer's eyes dart toward the top of the stairs. She did not need to look to know that either Isobel or Walter was there or, worse, that they both were.

"Ye are late," Isobel said. "We have been forced to hold up dinner because of yer tardiness. Save yer idle chatter for later…into the great hall with ye."

They walked in quick silence into the hall, greeted by the sight of Lord Walter, which could chill even the warmest of hearts. He seemed irritated, out of sorts—which was his usual demeanor—while he waited for them to take their customary seats, which were assigned to the girls with the understanding there were no changes to be made.

Claire looked at the plates being placed in front of them and wondered if her sisters took much notice of the unappetizing presentation of soggy cabbage and cold beef. Isobel, her face stiff and unsmiling, did not eat anything, and for a moment Claire had a terrible fear that the food served her sisters and herself had been poisoned, until Lord Walter picked up his fork and began to eat.

The girls followed his lead, each picking up her

fork. No one said a word, which somehow went with the unappetizing meal. Claire could tell her sisters were as repulsed with the offering as she, for they spent a great deal of time moving their food around on their plates, eating little. It was a miracle to her how the four of them endured such repugnance without giving in to the feeling of nausea. Claire tried to hide the disgust she felt, and was grateful the meal lasted no longer than it did.

The girls excused themselves and left, and Claire followed close behind. She had one foot on the bottom stair, when the sound of Lord Walter's steps coming rapidly behind her gave her pause.

Walter stopped a few feet from her. "I want a word with ye. In the study."

"I will see to my sisters…"

"I wish to speak to ye now, if you please." He started to turn, then looked back at her sisters still standing there. "When I give an order I expect it to be obeyed. Now, go to yer rooms."

Claire watched them scamper out of sight.

"In the study, I believe I said." He headed in that direction.

Claire followed him down the hall and stepped through the door behind him. He took a seat at her father's desk.

Claire remained standing.

"The Earl of Wick has extended us an invitation to a dance. It will not be held at Wickdon Castle, but at his home in Edinburgh, since he thought that site more hospitable to travel to than his home in Caithness. The Earl's wife, Laura Maria Cavallaro, is the daughter of a Venetian Count. After two years in

Scotland, she is quite homesick for the costume balls held during the Carnival. The Earl is giving this dance for his countess, and wants to surprise her by asking the guests wear a costume. I have replied that Isobel and I will attend, with ye and Giles, who will be yer escort."

"I do not wish to go."

"Ye have no choice in the matter. Ye are going, and ye will be with Giles."

"If I go, it will not be with him. I refuse to go with Giles."

Walter stood up and leaned across the desk, with his hands splayed in front of him. He spoke with each cold, cruel word emphasized carefully. "Ye will go. Ye will go with Isobel, Giles and myself. Ye will wear the costume I have ordered for ye from Edinburgh. Ye will laugh and dance, and convince the world that ye are happy and in love with Giles."

"Ye canna make me go."

"Oh, but ye are wrong there. Ye will go gladly, because if ye dinna, I will lock Briana in her room and she will be denied food and water for as long as it takes for ye to change yer mind. Are we clear on that point?"

Claire glared at him. "Aye."

"Good. And should ye get any ideas about telling anyone about this, I will lock all three of your sisters in their rooms, and if ye persist still…then ye will join them there."

Claire turned and started from the room, but Walter moved so swiftly around the corner of the desk that he caught her by the arm before she took two steps. He gripped her arm painfully as he jerked her around and slammed her against the paneled wall. His right hand came up to squeeze her jaw until tears gathered in her eyes from the pain.

"Do not ever turn yer back and walk out of the room until I say ye may go. Shall I give ye a sample of what will happen to ye if ye disobey me again?" He squeezed her face again until her lips were pursed, then he kissed her and thrust his tongue in her mouth.

And if that wasn't enough, he gave her breast a painful pinch.

He wrenched her arm when he yanked her away from the wall and shoved her toward the door. "That was a sample. Next time it will be worse. Ye may go now. We will leave for Edinburgh day after tomorrow, since ye and Isobel will have to have fittings done for yer costumes. Ye will have yer things packed and be ready to leave."

"What about my sisters?"

"I haven't decided about them yet. Suffice it to say, they will either accompany us, or they will remain here."

Claire did not mention anything to her sisters about what happened with Walter, or her arm and jaw, or the humiliating way he had touched her. All she said was "I will be going to Edinburgh to a ball at the home of the Earl and Countess of Wick."

"Are we coming, too?" Briana asked.

"No," Greer said. "We are too young to go to balls. Besides, I would rather stay here than go with them."

"That is good news," Briana said. "I do not want to go anywhere with him or Isobel."

Claire spent a few more minutes with her sisters, and then retired to her room. Her jaw, arm and breast were truly aching in earnest now, and she was getting a headache. She dressed for bed, washed her face, chewed on a piece of willow bark, then rinsed her mouth and went straight to bed.

Her headache was stronger now, and she attributed that to the thoughts of Isobel and Lord Walter. She knew Isobel was up to something and it did not sit well with Claire to think she had to go on about her daily life, waiting, as it were, to find her head in a noose. Her uneasiness concerning Isobel brought back old memories; only they were not seen through the eyes of the young, inexperienced girl she was when her father died.

She had trusted Isobel once, and was led to believe the worst of Fraser. It shamed her now to realize how agreeable she had been to the duplicity. The worst part of it was she not only accused him and judged him guilty, but that she refused to listen to the words he offered her in defense.

After her humiliating put-down, he never tried again. That day, that very moment and his departing words had haunted her and would continue to do so. It was not what she would have chosen, but she had been taught that in order to learn life's lessons, some things must be relived.

There is always a right way and a wrong way to resolve something, and when one makes the wrong choice, she is destined to undergo the experience repeatedly in her mind. She could not change what had happened, but she did pray that she would one day be able to expunge it from her memory.

Until that day arrived, Claire had to live with the knowledge that she had dealt most unfairly with Fraser, and because of it, the memory of the last time she saw him was a wound that never healed. The raw sound of his voice that day, the pain in his eyes…it haunted her…and probably would continue to do so until the end of her days…

"I have come against a mountain I cannot climb. I still love ye, and probably I always will. Poor Claire, ye are incapable of understanding because ye love with yer head and not yer heart. Even now, after all that has transpired between us…the deception, the false accusations…the betrayal…the words filled with venom, ye are still too dear to me, for ye reside in the very core o' my being."

Outside, a bolt of thunder rattled the shutters. She could smell the fresh scent of rain blowing across the loch, heralding the storm that was imminent. She moved to the window and saw the fast-moving clouds of a storm blowing in over the loch, thrashing and roiling, angry as the waves of frustration that pounded within her. She reached to close the shutters, and paused a moment to watch the wind whip over the loch. The waves, white-capped now, came in quick succession, slamming against the shore—ebb and flow—crashing and now receding, just as thoughts of Fraser had haunted her; thoughts of him coming and going these past years.

She watched the waves erase all the footprints along the shore, just as the images of making love with Fraser already had begun to fade, and would be gone completely in time.

The clouds darkened and rolled until they formed the likeness of his face—the hair of raven and eyes of silver-blue. The image was so sharp and clear that she could make out the straight line of his nose, the full lips she remembered so well.

Where are ye now, Fraser? Who lies beneath yer slim hips and receives the power of yer loins? Who knows the satin smoothness of yer skin, the granite hardness beneath?

I ache for ye, Fraser... I ache for ye and suffer knowing ye will never forgive me...

She could not help wondering, as she had many times previous, if she ever crossed Fraser Graham's mind, except in a bad, negative way.

She went to the big trunk at the foot of her bed and she removed a key that hung from a chain around her neck and unlocked the trunk.

Inside was an assortment of items that belonged to Fraser. She removed a long black coat and wrapped herself in it, then went to lie down on her bed. Something about his coat gave her comfort, as if she had a protector, for although Claire put up the image of a strong and forceful leader, there were times when she was terribly afraid.

Claire was strong, and she took the earldom and her responsibility as laird seriously, but it was lonesome without someone to share it with.

She grew increasingly anxious for Isobel and Lord Walter to be gone from Lennox Castle and Inchmurrin Island. There were times she thought she would reject the title, the lairdship, and board a ship for America. Then she would think of her sisters, and her father and brothers' deaths, and the clansmen who looked to her. The clans were close-knit. They took care of one another. The pride in their clan and their country was the thread that held them together. She could not turn her back on them or the blood that flowed in her veins.

It was the chief of the clan who owned the lands of the clan, and the primary responsibility of the chief was to protect the clan from enemy attack; to guide and handle disputes; to lead his people in battle. As head of the clan, the chief possessed absolute authority over the clan. Many, but not all of the clan members were related to Claire by blood, but her duty as their leader meant she treated the blood relatives and the clan outsiders the same. She had learned from her father that the clan, and loyalty to the chief, were the backbone of the clan system.

To this day, she had not forgotten, for the memory of that day, shortly before her father died, was forever burned into her mind. She had often wondered since if he'd had some premonition that in spite of having three sons, his eldest daughter might one day inherit not only the earldom, but the mantle of Chief of Clan Lennox, as well. Or was it simply a way a loving father could spend some time with the daughter everyone knew he favored.

She recalled that meeting in vivid detail, down to the clothes her father wore that day and the exact time on the beautiful Renaissance Italian clock: twenty-two past eleven in the morning. She remembered her surprise when the butler announced her father wanted to see her in his study, for she knew it was his habit to take lunch in his study at half past eleven.

It was the first time she joined her father for lunch in his almost sacred retreat.

After a lengthy discussion on the role of an Earl and Chief of Clan Lennox, he leaned back and looked her directly in the eyes as he said, "If you should fail in your responsibilities to the clan, or lose their loyalty, the entire system breaks down."

After a deep breath and a weary sigh, she rolled onto her side. She closed her eyes and whispered a prayer for guidance and the strength to face the future, whatever it held.

Seventeen

The accent of one's birthplace lingers in the mind and in the heart as it does in one's speech.

François de La Rochefoucauld (1613-1680), French writer. *Reflections, or Sentences and Moral Maxims* (1665)

How many times had he ridden down this same path, rounded the side of the mountain, and seen Monleigh Castle rising up out of the rocks, buffeted by the North Sea? Yet, it had never looked as dear and beloved as it did today.

"Welcome home, brother," Bran said.

" 'Tis a grand sight, is it not? And one I have seen in my mind's eye many times since I have been gone. 'Tis a good feeling to come home. I never realized how true this really was before now."

Arabella was the first to see them from the place in the garden where she was practicing with her bow and arrow. Bran and Fraser rode close enough for Fraser to shout, "Careful, you are aiming a bit high, lass," at the moment she released the arrow, which sailed over the target and landed in the bushes.

She stamped her foot and turned around and the frown disappeared. "Fraser!" A moment later he was off his horse and swinging the only sister in the family around in his arms.

"I have left a little sister and have found a beautiful woman in her place. 'Tis sorry I am to have missed the gradual change in ye."

She tucked her arm in his and walked along with her brothers, three black heads close together, arms around one another.

As soon as Jamie, Niall, Tavish and Calum came out, Arabella had to back away, where she stood next to Sophie, both of them with their arms crossed and a tolerant but not completely understanding expression on their faces, as they watched the six Graham men engage in mock battle with one another, until each of them had been rolled in the dirt and came up looking more like gingerbread than men.

She observed the lot of them—groaning, sweating and admiring one another's cuts.

"You look like you've been rolling in a pigsty," Sophie said.

"Aye, and ye probably smell as if ye have been in one, too," Arabella added. "One would think ye would reach maturity eventually...say, by yer ninetieth birthday. Ye have been playing these same war games since ye were bairns. Are ye no tired of it yet?"

"No," they said in unison.

"And how would ye be knowing how long we have been at this?" Tavish asked. "Ye are the youngest and could have no recollection of that."

"I'm a good listener." She had her gaze fastened on Jamie. "You are not so supple at the knee. Mayhap you are too old to be doing this and should leave it to the younger ones."

He grinned at her, then gave his wife a teasing look. "I am a wee bit out o' practice."

"Aye," Tavish said, "all that desk work, yer lordship, is turning yer backside to hog lard."

"Careful… I can still pin yer ears to the ground," Jamie said.

"Weel," Fraser said, "in that case, how about we go have ourselves a dram or two of whisky."

"There is nothing like the mention of whisky to get them moving," Arabella said to Sophie as they watched them disappear through the door.

"No, but it is certain to slow them down soon enough," Sophie said. "*Sacré bleu,* I have never seen men who could drink so much and still remain standing."

Arabella knew they would not get much sleep tonight—not with all the boisterous jokes and manly pride inflated with each glass of whisky that went down.

The next morning when Arabella came downstairs she expected to see her brothers sleeping in the hall, and she was not disappointed, but it did surprise her to see the three Scottish wolfhounds sleeping soundly and reeking of whisky. They must have spilled a lot, she thought, and then took a seat to enjoy the sight of her brothers waking, puffy-eyed and headachy.

Arabella was sitting at the long table that ran the length of the room, busily writing, as they began to wake up.

"Who are ye writing a letter to?" Calum asked.

"I am not writing a letter," she said. "I am making an accounting, and so far, I have the following:

1. Three drunk dogs
2. Six broken glasses
3. Niall's initials carved into the tabletop
4. Two black eyes and one not so black, but passing through purple at the moment, and completely swollen shut
5. Three busted lips
6. Various and assorted nicks, scrapes and cuts
7. Two shirts ripped beyond repair
8. One boot smoldering in the fireplace
9. A belt chewed in half by whichever dog was the last to pass out

"And six men who smell like they have just bathed in offal, and do not seem to mind the fact that we are leaving for Edinburgh tomorrow to attend the ball given by the Earl and Countess of Wick. Would anyone like to tell me how ye are going to go to Edinburgh and a ball with busted lips and purple eyes?"

"'Tis a costume ball," Calum said.

"Aye, 'tis at that, and now would ye mind telling me if ye are planning on wearing a pumpkin over yer head? Ye canna find a mask big enough to cover all the damage ye have done."

"We will think o' something," Jamie said. "After all, Fraser is a lawyer now, and lawyers are famous for extracting the less fortunate from their predicaments." He slapped Fraser on the back.

"I am a lawyer," Fraser said, "but I was given a degree, not a magic wand."

It was not until the night of the ball that Arabella learned how her brothers planned to work around their various swellings, cuts and bruises.

It was a blessing for Claire that she had the title of Earl, as well as the Chief of Clan Lennox, for that added another dimension to her existence. She not only had herself to think of, but her sisters, the clan, the management of the Lennox properties and the preserving of the inheritance she had been given.

Some time ago, she dedicated herself to the task, and forced herself to look forward and to push ahead with the plans and dreams her father had. She finished the construction underway on the castle. She purchased more breeding stock to improve the herds of cattle on their lands in the far northern parts of the Highlands. She kept good records, was punctual in the taking of her yearly inventory, increased the amount of land allotted to the tacksmen, and left the rent at the same nominal amount. In turn, she instructed the tacksmen to pass on the favors to their cottars, so that each would have a house, enough grass for a cow or two, and enough land to sow a boll of oats. She was careful to add that she expected it to be in places they could reach and work with their plow, and not the areas where brush and rock forced them to dig with spades. As a gesture of kindness to ease the poverty of the tenants, she freed them every year from their arrears of rent.

She poured herself into her work, for it was the only way she could hide the lonely emptiness within her. She was determined that her own misfortunes, faults and failures would not carry over into her role of

Countess of Errick and Mains, and she managed its affairs with great skill, relieving it of many debts and carrying out great improvements.

Because Lennox Castle was situated on the southernmost point of Inchmurrin Island, in the middle of Loch Lomond, it commanded a beautiful view of the loch. As the castle had been in need of many repairs when she inherited the title, she took pride in the improvements she made, both within the castle and without.

She enlarged the enclosed courtyard and built a long walkway that connected it to the castle. The gardens, which had been overgrown were planted with an impressive variety of vegetables and herbs, and the trees in the small orchard produced an abundance of fruit, most of which Claire insisted on drying. To anyone's eyes, she took on responsibilities that packed an incredible amount of work onto her slim and narrow shoulders.

When she wasn't attending to affairs of the clan, she served as both sister and mother to her three sisters, became the family historian, local politician, and an expert horsewoman and archer. But she scandalized her youngest sister when Briana woke up one morning and looked out over the loch and saw Claire's flaming hair in the water. That sent Briana running down the hall to Kenna's room to tell her their sister was doing "the wickedest thing. She is in the loch!"

Kenna only smiled and said, "Then she must be swimming," and went back to sleep.

Briana gave Kenna's arm a shake. "I didna ken she knew how to swim."

"Weel, ye ken now," Kenna said.

"May I swim, then?"

"No, ye don't know how to swim."

Briana shook her arm again. "Do ye think Claire will teach me?"

"Why don't you ask Claire?"

By the end of the summer, all four of the Ladies Lennox were regularly swimming in the early hours of the morning.

Claire found she liked having so much to do, for hard work hid the emptiness inside, and kept alive the incentive to do more, and ignore the cost it extracted from her person.

The primary benefit was when she went to bed at night, she was too tired to look back on the past, or to think about the future. Her life and her reward was her work and the things she accomplished.

The millstone around her neck continued to be Isobel and Lord Walter, and now she had the ball she did not want to attend to look forward to.

Eighteen

I am as comfortless as a pilgrim with peas in his shoes—and as cold as Charity, Chastity or any other Virtue.

Lord Byron (1788-1824), English poet.
Letter, November 16, 1814, to Annabella Milbanke—later Lady Byron (published in *Byron's Letters and Journals*, vol. 4, ed. by Leslie A. Marchand, 1975)

They left before daybreak for Stirling, and although it was too dark to see, Claire did not need the light of the sun to know they passed through the beloved green-and-purple countryside she had known since she was born.

The sun was well up by the time they passed the impregnable stronghold, Stirling Castle, sitting as it had for centuries atop a steep, stony hill of volcanic rock. She thought of many of her ancestors who took up residence there for protection, and the battles fought below the castle; the first the Battle of Stirling Bridge, where William Wallace defeated the English; the second, the Battle of Bannockburn, where Robert the Bruce and the Scottish army routed the forces of King Edward II.

Today it stood silent and solemn as they passed beneath it and headed out of town on the ancient Roman road that ran from Stirling to Edinburgh. A few times they veered off the main track to ride along rather dubious bridle tracks through low and marshy terrain that ran down to the Forth, and on toward their destination through fields of heather and bracken.

By the time they arrived in Edinburgh, Claire found bogs, heather and bracken far superior company to that of Lord Walter and Isobel. Now she had meeting up with Giles to look forward to.

Prestonfield House, where they would stay, was remarkably close to the heart of Edinburgh, yet it had very much the feel of a country house, lying as it did in the lee of the volcanic mass of Arthur's Seat, surrounded by lovely parklike grounds. As they approached the white-fronted house, they passed a herd of Highland cattle.

Lord Walter, who had been rattling on about how Prestonfield was built in 1687 for Sir James Dick, the Provost of Edinburgh, by the king's architect, Sir William Bruce, was suddenly drowned out by the raucous complaint of a large group of peacocks displaying brilliant plumage. Claire ducked her head lest he see how it did please her to see his preaching drowned out by the cry of peacocks.

A few seconds later, she had to put her hand over her mouth to cover her laughter, for what the peacocks were screaming sounded like *Help... Help...*

When they stopped at last they were greeted by liveried footmen who escorted them inside to the entrance hall, where a ceiling with a very large cupid towered over them. Everywhere she saw splendid gilding, opulent velvets and Italian brocades, mingled with an exceptionally fine collection of art and antiques, many of them Italian, which probably helped the Countess to feel connected to her homeland.

Fortunately, the Earl of Wick's wife, Countess Laura Maria Cavallaro, had placed Claire in one of the finer bedrooms, as due her status of Countess of Errick and Mains, while the disgruntled Isobel and Lord Walter were given lesser quarters along with Giles, who seemed too bored with everything to care.

The next day, Claire and Isobel ventured forth into Edinburgh to be fitted for their costumes, which by Lord Walter's orders, had already been started, and only needed a final fitting. Claire wondered if Lord Walter was trying to tempt Giles by choosing for her to go as Lysistrata, from an outrageous Greek comedy about war and peace written by Aristophanes. It was reportedly a bawdy play, at least that was the reason her father gave for not allowing her to read it.

A few nights later, on the night of the ball, Claire stood patiently considering herself in the full-length mirror. Two maids fussed over dressing her in the shimmering, gossamer folds of a saffron-colored silk gown, beautifully embroidered.

She was allowed to sit afterward while they piled the masses of her red hair up in the classic Greek fashion of the era and dressed it with ropes of pearls and golden ornaments. Her cheeks were painted, and seven golden bracelets clinked on her arm. She held out her feet to study the saffron silk evening slippers.

She felt like a doll, with nothing to do but sit around

beautifully dressed and coiffed, looking quite ravishing in a dress she thought was too sheer, with her feet in dainty saffron evening slippers.

Half an hour later, Isobel, dressed as Zenobia, Queen of Palmyra, came for her, and the two of them proceeded downstairs where Lord Walter and Giles awaited them in a large supper tent erected in the garden. The Earl and Countess of Wick, dressed in Renaissance splendor as Beatrix and Dante, were seated on a low dais to greet their guests as they arrived.

Claire felt as if she had stepped inside a de Medici villa when she entered the tent, which was completely floored with Italian tiles and warmed by the golden glow of candlelit sconces and candelabra. Roman tapestries hung on the walls, interspersed with fine marble statues and fluted columns. In the center of the room, towering almost thirteen feet tall, stood an antique Italian gazebo, made of Vicenza stone. Beautifully carved Italian urns, filled with flowers were everywhere.

And on the other side of the tent, she caught a glimpse of the side of a man's head, and for a moment she thought it was Fraser Graham.

She dismissed it as wishful thinking and gave her attention back to the boring account Giles was giving of his latest grouse hunt, but when he had proudly shown off his birds he found he had killed ptarmigan instead.

Giles did not seem to have the nasty side his mother possessed, but that could have been because of his tendency to dismiss Claire altogether. In fact, she noticed that he seemed to dismiss *all* women with the same bored indifference. He did get a nice gleam in his eye whenever he stopped to speak to another man, however. Claire began to put six and six together. Oh, wonderful, she thought, would it not be perfect to be married to a man who had a preference for other men? *Weel, Claire, it might be preferable to having to suffer through making love with someone ye canna stand.* It doesn't matter, she thought, for she would not marry Giles, and she began to think of ways she could prevent that.

The dancing started off with dancers from Sicily and Sardinia performing their folk dances in native costume. When it was over, Giles escorted her to join the highly popular country dancing, where they joined groups of eight or ten people and danced to the lively strains of reels and strathspeys, accompanied by piano, flute, accordion and fiddle.

He was a good dancer, and she complimented him on his graceful movements. "Where did ye learn to dance so well?" she asked.

"William, Baron McCandless, taught me."

"Oh, he is a dancing instructor?"

"No, he is a baron who likes to dance as much as I do."

Claire concentrated less on conversation and more on dancing after that, which seemed to be what Giles preferred, anyway.

In spite of his weasel face and darting eyes that always made her uncomfortable, she had to admit that Giles could have been worse. His biggest problem was his customary rude and disrespectful behavior, which was not so prevalent tonight. Claire did not know if the change was his doing, or because Lord Walter had given him some kind of ultimatum, but she suspected the latter.

The strains of the contredanse, a playful dance that started with a thump on the floor by one of the musicians, startled everyone into laughter. Soon Claire was stomping to the rhythm of the dance, laughing and thumping her heels to the warm, dark sound of the flute that swirled in a rhythmic pulse around her, and she responded with a burst of energy that seemed to make her feet fly. That is, until she looked up and saw a man standing among those not dancing. He was watching her and all the laughter she felt inside vanished.

When the dance ended, she sent Giles for something to drink, and she ventured a quick glance around the room, but did not see the man again. She tried to think what it was that she found so startling. After all, he was wearing a mask, so she could not see much of his face. Yet, there was something....

She felt uneasy, and certainly not in the mood to dance anymore.

"I knew ye would not care for whisky, so I brought ye a drink made from Sicilian lemons. The ladies around the table who were drinking it said they found it most pleasing." He handed the cup to her.

"Thank ye, Giles." She drank a few sips. It was quite good. "I find it verra delicious."

Giles was looking around the room. "What? Oh, I am pleased to hear ye find it satisfactory."

"Giles, please do not feel ye must stay here with me. I do not wish to dance again, but do not want to prevent ye from doing so. I would like to visit with the Countess of Wick, and a few others, and then I shall retire."

"You are certain ye do not want to dance again?"

"Yes, I am not accustomed to so much dancing in one evening. I find I am tired."

Giles seemed delighted to excuse himself and Claire noticed he was soon talking to a tall young man about his own age. She was beginning to think Giles did not care for women in the normal manner of most men.

The cry of a peacock made her think of the charming garden and she decided to leave the tent for a while, so she could sit upon one of the lovely Italian benches. She waited until another dance started then slipped quietly from the tent, to make her way to a bench without a back that was sequestered behind a rowan tree.

She seated herself and removed her mask. She took a deep breath. The air was clear and fresh, and scented with lilacs. She could still hear the strains of music coming from the tent, which was a muckle more to her liking than being inside. With a sigh that hovered somewhere between weariness and relief, she leaned back and looked at the stars overhead, thankful that she was alone in the garden.

Nineteen

The best way will be to avoid each other without appearing to do so—or if we jostle, at any rate not to bite.

Lord Byron (1788-1824), English poet.
Letter, April 25, 1814, referring to his affair with Lady Caroline Lamb (published in *Byron's Letters and Journals*, vol. 4, ed. by Leslie A. Marchand, 1975)

Behind her, the leaves on the rowan tree rustled, and before she could turn, the man she had seen earlier seated himself on the bench next to her, but from the opposite side, so that they faced each other.

"I did not mean to startle you," he said.

Oh, God, that voice…

Fraser…

No, it canna be, she thought. It is only my imagination.

Was she destined to see every man as Fraser for the rest of her life? She turned her head away and concentrated on the fountain, in the center of which was a statue of Neptune holding a trident, with one foot resting upon a dolphin. She put her hand on her skirt and made a move to rise, when his hand came out and caught her by the arm. "Stay," he said in that soft, seductive voice she remembered so well. "Please, if only for a moment."

Lord, it was Fraser's voice...but it couldn't be Fraser's voice, for Fraser would not seek her out or speak to her. She looked at him and noticed his bruised cheek and the cut on his chin. She wished the mask was gone, so she could be certain if it was or was not Fraser, for even now, a part of her could not believe Fraser was here, in this garden, with her by choice. She wished the light in the garden was better, so she could see the color of his eyes.

At last, when she could stand the torment no longer, she whispered, "Is it ye...is it truly ye?"

"Aye, Claire, 'tis Fraser, stepping out of the past and into the present."

She picked at her skirt. "I heard ye were in Utrecht, studying law."

He seemed amused to hear she knew where he had been and what he was doing there, for she saw that all-too-familiar sparkle in his eyes. "Aye, I was in Utrecht. I have only arrived back in Scotland a few days ago."

"And ye are happy to be back home, or did ye fall in love with Utrecht?" As soon as she said it, she wished she had used another phrase.

"I try not to fall in love with anything anymore, but it has been a long time since I walked on Scottish soil, so aye, I am verra glad to be home."

"Ye were gone awhile, but time did not pass any faster in Scotland while ye were gone."

"I was not prepared to see ye here tonight. When I

saw ye dancing with Giles…for a moment I doubted what my eyes were seeing."

"I was as stunned by the sight of ye as well, although I must admit this first meeting after so long is nothing like I would have expected."

"Ye have thought about it, then?"

"Not in the sense that I expected it to happen, for I knew that ye would go to great lengths to avoid me, if ye did see me."

"Ye seem to be more confident about the way it would have been than I. Why would ye think I would avoid seeing ye again, Claire?"

"I have not forgotten yer last words to me, Fraser Graham. Do not tell me ye have."

"No…weel, I may not ken my exact words, but I believe I said something about hoping our paths never crossed again."

"Close," she said, "but I can get closer. In fact, I remember exactly, for what ye said was much longer than that, and far more biting. What ye said was, '*I hope that I never see yer sweet face again. How much better it would be if our paths never cross, but should it happen, I pray to God that the face I wear convinces ye that not a fig of affection for ye remains.*'"

"Ye always did have an extraordinary memory…at least where my shortcomings were concerned."

She smiled at him without really being aware that she did, because it was always so natural to smile around him, and he had a way of making her smile with almost anything he said. "Mayhap ye gave me a lot o' practice." She fell silent and neither of them said anything.

After a period of time, she asked, "Is that what it was? A shortcoming?"

He did not answer straightaway, yet she did not have the impression he was searching for the answer.

"They were words of suffering born of pain, but time is the great equalizer, is it not?"

"So you are fully recovered and truly have what you prayed for…not a fig of affection remaining for me."

"Ye are spooning words into my mouth afore I open it, lass."

Her heart began to pound. Could it be that he had not forgotten her as easily as she imagined? No, she scolded herself. *Do not build yer castles at high tide. Do not read more into this than is there. Do not let him suspect how ye feel. Do not let him ken how ye regret putting him oot o' yer life, or how ye wish ye could live that part o' yer life all over again.*

It was time to change the subject before she made a fool of herself, or started crying. Or both. She looked him directly in the eye because she wanted him to see the words she spoke came from her heart, and not her head, as he often accused her of doing. " 'Tis truly nice to see ye have survived me, Fraser, for I have oft thought about those last days, and the horrible…" She felt on the verge of tears, and she knew she could not go on with what she wanted to say. "Have ye an office here in Edinburgh, where ye practice yer law?"

He was looking at her strangely, as if he was trying to see through the words she said, to get to the back of her mind, where the words she wanted to say resided. "No, but I plan to open one here relatively soon. I plan to look for a suitable office while I am here."

"I am so verra proud o' ye for doing what ye did. I

ken it made it easier for ye, to get yer life back together after ye left Inchmurrin."

"When the dream ended prematurely, I had to find something to fill the void." And she detected a sadness there, in spite of what he did to hide it.

" 'Tis difficult to imagine ye with a brass plaque on yer door, with yer name engraved in fancy script... Fraser Graham, Lawyer. I do hope it is a nice, shiny plaque, and do make certain it is big enough to see from the street."

He laughed. "Ye make it sound far grander than it is, Claire. Have ye not heard what most people think o' lawyers?"

"I dinna suppose I have," she said.

"Weel, it goes like this—a lawyer is a man who arranges an appointment with a man he doesna ken, to sign a deed he hasna seen, in order to buy property he doesna want, with money he hasna got."

She laughed. "Ye jest, Fraser Graham, for 'tis a fine, fine thing ye have done, and I see nothing bad aboot declaring to all and sundry that ye are a learned man, and a kind and good-hearted lawyer for hire. And an honest one, at that!"

"I wish I ha' yer confidence, but I shall do my best."

"And what sort of law shall ye be doing? Divorces?"

His mouth curled upward in amusement. "No. I shall endeavor to try to stay as far away from those as possible."

"Ah, weel," she said, without so much as a smile, "that should not be difficult for ye then, for at least ye have had some practice at it."

He laughed outright. "Ye always had a good memory for the things I would just as soon ye forgot, lass. However, at the university I found my interests lay more in the direction of representing those facing trial on criminal charges."

"That is what ye will practice…saving poor souls from the gallows?"

"Hopefully, but I could resort to scraping by on deeds, family settlements, perpetuities and conveyances like a great many lawyers are forced to do."

"Ye willna have to do that, Fraser, for ye will be the best lawyer in Edinburgh. Mark my wird on that. Where are ye living now? Are ye visiting with yer family?"

"Aye, I have been there since I returned. 'Tis good to spend time with my family."

"How are Sophie and Arabella? And young Master of Graham? I never see any o' them, but then I never really go anywhere."

"Perhaps you will get to see for yerself. They are all here tonight."

"Arabella and Sophie as well?"

"Oh, aye. Do ye think Arabella would let us come to something like this withoot her? Or that Jamie would leave Sophie?"

"Sophie wouldna let him." Claire laughed softly, remembering how authoritative Arabella could be around her brothers. "As for Arabella, she had a knack for wheedling things oot o' the lot of ye. What is her costume, so I can look for her?"

"She is Margaret, wife of Robert the Bruce."

"A good choice," she said. "Margaret was a wise woman, and verra strong."

"Tell me who ye are, in your beguiling yellow gown."

"I am Lysistrata."

"Aah, Lysistrata. Ye are referring to the one by Aristophanes, no?"

"Aye, Aristophanes's bawdy comedy."

He smiled. "Ye have read it then?"

"No, my father would not allow it, but he did tell me a wee bit aboot it, ye ken, and how the wives of the men fighting in the Peloponnesian War decided to withhold their favors from their husbands until they agreed to lay down their swords."

"That is a good version of it for a man to speak of his daughter. I didna ken he would tell ye the whole of it, for it is quite descriptive of the physical aspects of what happens between a man and a woman."

"How descriptive?"

Fraser didn't say anything.

"Och! Why bring it up if you willna speak of it to me again? What is the harm in telling me of it? We were married, after all, so it isna as though I no have any inkling about what happens in the marriage bed."

"Weel, to quote the master Aristophanes himself, or at least a reasonable translation of the original Greek: 'All we have to do is idly sit indoors with smooth roses powdered on our cheeks, our bodies burning naked through the folds of shining Amorgos' silk, and meet the men with our dear Venus plats plucked trim and neat, their stirring love will rise up furiously, they'll beg our knees to open. That's our time! We'll disregard their knocking, beat them off—and they will soon be rabid for a Peace!'"

It was one of the rare times in Claire's life when she could think of nothing to say.

"I apologize. I have shocked ye."

"No, to the contrary…that is, I am not shocked. It is more that I am a wee bit miffed that I havena read it. I wish my father had not removed it from the library. I shall have to think upon a way to obtain another copy…discreetly, of course."

"Of course," he said, making a valiant effort to hide his amusement.

"Go ahead and laugh. I ken ye are dying to do so."

"Aye, it is difficult to refrain from it."

She lifted her head slightly to look him over, searching for a clue as to his disguise, but his dress could have belonged to a number of historical figures. Not that it mattered, because her mind kept straying to the things she remembered so well: the silkiness of his hair, the shine of his eyes, the velvet of his skin and the sensitivity of his lips, and the feel of them upon hers.

Her gaze rested on his hands…those hands she remembered so well, touching her with devoted gentleness, caressing her until she thought she was going daft with wanting; hands that protected her, teased her, hands that held her close. She closed her eyes against the memory.

"Is anything wrong?" he asked.

If ye only knew… She shook her head, for she dared not speak—not yet—for she needed to get her thoughts off the softer things, the memories. "And ye," she said after a few seconds, while she prayed her voice did not break, or worse that the tears she felt inside revealed themselves. "In truth, I have tried to guess yer disguise, but I canna think o' anyone I could identify by a cut chin and bruised cheek."

His hair fell across his forehead. He reached up and

pushed it back, and removed his mask before he turned his face toward her. "Still no clues?" he asked.

She shook her head. "No, still no clue. But the cuts look verra real," she said, and without thinking she lifted her hand to touch one.

"They are real," she barely had time to say before he caught her hand in his.

"I am sorry. I did no mean to touch ye. 'Twas inconsiderate and out of place for me to do so." She made a move to stand, but he held her hand.

"I am not offended," he said. "Ye need not apologize."

It pained her to realize that while she had changed, he was still the same—the same wonderful Fraser—when she hoped he had picked up some habit or mannerism that she found detestable, or that he had lost all of his hair, or his teeth, or had grown long in the tooth, or suffered from a protuberance of the stomach. Anything to make him less desirable than she remembered him, but in truth, he was bonnier now than before. Alas, if anything, time apart had served him well, for he had the polish and maturity of a man of the world.

He released her hand. "As I said, Arabella is Bruce's wife, Margaret. Jamie is Robert the Bruce, and the rest of us are some of the gentry who fought wi' Bruce at Banncockburn."

"Ah, and so yer bruises represent the fact that ye fought beside yer king at Bannockburn."

"No, they reflect the fact that my brothers and I had a tussle when I arrived home from Holland."

Fraser gave her that mischievous look that so effectively reduced her will to the consistency of boiled oats. It still had the same effect on her, and she had to make a conscious effort to make herself look at the face she still held so dear. Desire for him rose within her and she prayed he could not sense it.

"And yer brothers? Are they as bruised and cut as ye?"

The mischievous look bloomed into a smile and from there into a laugh. "Eh? Are they as bruised and cut as myself? Oh, aye, 'tis true that they are in as bad a shape, and 'tis true that some o' them are worsted."

For a brief moment, it was as if the years, the divorce and all the pain between them suddenly vanished.

"Ye have a gleam in yer eye, Fraser Graham, and I ken it is a spark o' mischief I have seen afore now. In truth, ye seem to be speaking in riddles."

She leaned closer to look at the bruise on his cheek. "One o' yer brothers did this?"

"Aye."

"It doesna seem like a tussle would do something like this."

"Mayhap it was more like a fight, then."

"A fight with yer brothers. Ye should be ashamed."

" 'Twas a welcome-home fight."

"And all o' them partook?"

"Aye, ye dinna think one o' them would consider being left oot of a good fight, do ye?"

This playful banter was something she missed so much, and being with him like this now brought back the warm affection they felt for each other, which kept them close between the moments of deep love and intense passion. "Which one o' ye looks the worsted?"

Fraser burst out laughing. " 'Tis true," he said, " 'tis the Earl o' Monleigh himself."

She was laughing now. "I should love to see them.

The music from the tent died away, and she knew it would be time to lounge in the garden while the dinner was laid out. It would not do for Lord Walter, Isobel or even Giles to see her here with Fraser.

When she saw the first couple stroll into the garden she sprang to her feet and said, "It was good to see ye, Fraser Graham, and I wish ye the best of good fortune with yer legal practice in Edinburgh."

Fraser came around the bench and stood close to her, blocking her way. His gaze rested on her mouth, then lower to look her over. "'Tis good to see ye, Claire, and to see ye look well."

She thought of what it would be like to feel those arms around her again, to know the lips that teased hers once more, softly, gently, until the intense yearning to mate with him became unbearable.

"I am glad we were able to converse with each other in a respectful manner," she said. "Now I willna wrestle with so many devils the next time I come to Edinburgh, for fear I might see ye."

"You should know me well enough to understand I would never treat you with disrespect."

"That was then, Fraser. Times change. People change. I thought the worst o' ye. I accused you o' terrible deeds. I hurt ye, and for that I have always been verra sorry. Not that any of that matters at the present time, you ken, for even if we had stayed together, we probably would have grown distrustful of each other by now."

"Ye are too hard with yerself, lass. The important thing is ye recognize yer mistakes and learn from them."

"But I always seem to make the same mistakes over and over. Why can't I learn it the first time?"

His smile brought a gleam to settle in the depths of his eyes. "Repetition teaches the donkey."

She turned away and swallowed back the tears that rode in on a flood of memories. She had forgotten how charming he was, and how he always had the gilded gift of humor. She wished she had not come here tonight, for it seemed to undo all the work that masked the pain she felt inside. Now she was as raw inside as if the wound was brand-new.

It would do no good to dwell on the past or what might have been. Her obligation to her clan and family came before her own personal happiness, or lack of it. This was a dangerous time for her and she needed to keep her mind focused and her eyes and ears observant. She was walking on the thin and narrow edge of a bottomless pit. One false move, one step taken without paying attention would mean her end.

She was not fool enough to think Isobel and Lord Walter would wait forever. Even now, she knew they planned some sort of wickedness. To know, and not know, kept her in torment. Her spirit was burdened, yet both heart and mind were determined to stand firm and staunch against whatever devious or deceptive action they might take to gain control of her.

She had nowhere to turn. If she accused them she had no proof, therefore no one would believe her. Part of her cried out to confide in Fraser, for she yearned for someone with whom she could share her burden. She needed a man experienced in such, a man to confer with, to seek advice from, and partake of his wisdom.

"Ye have grown quiet. Did I say something to offend ye?"

Ye could never do that, Fraser. She shook her head. "No."

"What bothers ye, Claire? A trouble shared is a trouble halved."

"Humph!" She made a hopeless sound of doubt. "There are riddles that make no sense, and questions that have no answer, and my woes have no solution, save time."

"Much has changed between us, but I would like to think one quality still remains. Surely ye know I would help ye, if ye had a need. I am no longer yer husband, but I am still someone ye can trust. Ye canna go through life with all yer hopes dashed."

"Thank ye, Fraser. 'Tis nice to know." Claire knew it was impossible to go through life without trust. The problem lay with the fact that she was afraid to reach for it. Was it real? Or was it a rose that hid the poison?

There were times when she truly hated being a woman, hobbled and shackled to the old ways. Within her, the chords of rebellion trembled and her very soul shook with vibrations of resistance. God had given her the fighting spirit of a man, and the body of a woman. It was her nature not to acquiesce or tremble and quake, but to resist and fight back with all she possessed, but instead of a Highlander's broadsword, she was handed a paper dirk.

She was doubly cursed by the title and lairdship she inherited, and the fact that she was born a woman. She had neither a man's authority, power or strength, nor his sword arm. Being born a woman came with its long list of restrictions. Even a queen's power was diminished by the men who surrounded her and fought to be the strength behind the power of her title. A man might be born a king, but a queen had to prove herself. It was the men who wore the patriarchal robes.

For once, she would like to state her views and put forth her ideas without having them immediately discounted because she was a female. It was unfortunate that authority, power and recognition required testicles.

Aye, she was a powerful woman who was respected and looked up to as the chief, but that was not given to her along with her title, but by her will, dedication and hard work. The ground she walked upon was uneasy. Her walk was a lonely one, filled with fear, uncertainty and dread, where she kept both her mind and her gaze focused on what lay ahead, because she was too afraid to look behind her to see the fiend that followed so close behind.

After waiting a few moments, he said, "I will walk you back inside."

"No, it is best if ye do not. I cannot be seen with ye, Fraser. Lord Walter..." Her voice broke. "I am sorry," she said, "for everything." She could not finish, and before she made a fool of herself, she turned and hurried back into the house.

Once inside, she decided to go back to her room. She knew Isobel and Lord Walter would be angry, but she had dealt with their anger before. Facing them at their worst was nothing compared to being so close to, and yet so far away from, Fraser.

Once she was back in her room, she exchanged her clothes for a gown and climbed into bed. She closed her eyes and saw the bonny banks of Loch Lomond and Inchmurrin Island, and on the southernmost tip of the island, Lennox Castle, sitting as it had for centuries. She imagined riding in the Vale of the Leven, and crossing the burn Leven that slipped quietly into the loch. She wanted to wake up and see old Ben Lomond poking his head into the clouds, and walk through the fine woods and fields with her sisters, her dogs and Dermot MacFarlane at her side, where wildflowers and ferns grew, where she could sit on the stone fence, overrun with wild roses and honeysuckle.

It was there that she felt closest to her father and her brothers buried just beyond the castle. It was there that she found her strength and her courage. She imagined how it would look now, in the darkness, with Ben Lomond's vast height only a black silhouette, while beneath the smooth surface of the loch, the waters slept, still and dark, and deep.

She tried to sleep, but thoughts of Fraser superseded everything else. Seeing him tonight made her realize she needed someone she could confide in, someone she could rely on: a man with courage and strength. Not some legendary knight out of an epic to slay all her dragons, but a real man of integrity she could believe in—a man with wisdom born of experience, who possessed strength of mind and body, a man of honor, without fear. A man like the man she had once married—married and chased away.

She rolled to her side and buried her face in the pillow. "Oh, Fraser, why are ye so far away from me now when I need ye to stand beside me?"

The answer she knew was twisted still the sinews of her heart: he was yours and you turned him away.

Aye, he had been hers, and she knew that losing

him was her entire fault. She should have had more faith, she thought. "I should have trusted ye," she said. "I realize that now, but will it change anything? Are ye as lost to me as yesterday?"

A stabbing pain shot through her head. The draperies at the window billowed from a puff of whispered breath, and she could swear she heard a whisper…words, dry and thin, carried like leaves driven by the wind…

We will see…

Twenty

Tell me not here, it needs not saying,
What tune the enchantress plays
In aftermaths of soft September
Or under blanching mays,
For she and I were long acquainted
And I knew all her ways.

E. Housman (1859-1936),
British poet and scholar

Over the next few months, Fraser prided himself on the way he was able to overcome the effect of seeing Claire and the impact their meeting had upon him.

When he had caught his first glimpse of her he felt himself sinking beneath the shock of it, and the subsequent flood of old memories and desire. He had not planned to say more than hello, and how have you been, but when he sat down beside her, the curtain that separated them drew back. That he would enjoy talking with her was another surprise, along with the thoughts of her that remained with him, long after that night was past.

As time progressed, he put things back in their

proper perspective by allowing the reasons why they divorced to supersede the reasons why he fell in love with and married her. It was all there—the accusations, the pain of her distrust, the wounds left by the ease with which she turned him away—tucked neatly away where he could return to it when he pleased, and out of the way so he did not trip over it in the day-to-day management of his life.

Fraser was in his room, packing the last of the belongings he would take to Edinburgh, when Jamie entered and handed him a packet of papers.

"Are ye certain you want to leave today?" he asked. "'Tis quite a storm out there—lightning that leaps from peak to peak, and thunder so strong it rattles the crags."

"Aye, I heard the wind roaring all night. It is still early yet, and I am hoping the rain will empty her clouds and allow the sun to come out. Rain before seven..."

"Dry before eleven," Jamie finished. "But what if it doesna stop?"

"Then I shall arrive with a nasty disposition, cursing the slow pace of my horse, the stiff joints, our ancestors' decision to build Monleigh Castle so far from Edinburgh, and the celestial oversight that I was not born a king."

Jamie walked over to the bed and picked up a small miniature of Claire Lennox. He held it out to Fraser. "Are ye going to pack this?"

"No...I was, but I decided it best to leave it here."

"Why?"

Fraser fixed his gaze on the miniature, but instead of seeing it, he saw images of Claire—in her bath, in her bonnet for kirk, working in her study, on the loch in her boat, lying naked in their bed, her body damp and glowing in the aftermath of their lovemaking. He looked quickly away. "I am not sure. 'Tis either resisting temptation, or having no temptation to resist. Take your pick."

"Why did ye have it out if you didna plan to take it?"

"It was a weak moment, nothing more."

Jamie studied the miniature. "It is probably just as well. She was much younger in this painting, and while she was a beauty even then, maturity has given her a more womanly quality that make a man's thoughts gallop bedward. It's a face few men could forget."

"I have managed to forget it," Fraser said. When he saw the dubious way his brother was looking at him, he added, "Most o' the time."

Jamie laughed and handed the miniature back to Fraser, who set it aside. "Are ye saying it did nothing to ye when ye saw her at Lord Wick's party?"

"Drop it, Jamie. I am over her."

"Eh, are ye now? I ken that is easier said than believed. Ye spent a wee too much time with her in the garden for her to be nothing more than a stranger to ye."

"It was completely benign, believe me. We talked as two educated, well-bred and civil human beings."

"Och laddie, you are waxing philosophical, and a bit too lavishly. If ye want to be believed, Fraser, ye had better eschew painting it with such brilliant colors. It would sound better to say ye felt a twinge or two of the old attraction, or that you despised her still, but perhaps with less venom."

Fraser was about to put the trews he folded into the portmanteau he was packing, but he paused midway and asked, "Why should I say something like that?"

"Plausibility, brother. Plausibility... Most people know the truth, anyway, or they think they do. All they want to hear is something reasonable enough to believe. In other words, who is going to take one look at Claire and believe there breathes a man who could feel not a dram of emotion."

"All right, I was not completely unaffected by her, but I have no desire to waltz back into her life, ye ken."

"And how does she feel?"

Fraser threw the trews into the portmanteau and slammed down the lid. "I do not know how she feels. And I didna ask her. If ye want to know, why don't ye ask her yerself?"

Jamie was laughing. "Hout! I probably will, when I see her again."

Fraser drew his eyebrows together in a menacing look meant to warn his brother away from the dangerous territory he was venturing toward. " 'Tis none o' yer affair, Jamie. Leave it be. There can never be anything between Claire and me."

Jamie nodded. "I apologize if I have put ye out of sorts."

Fraser sighed as he gave Jamie a half-apologetic look. "I was already a wee bit cranky. Arabella said I woke up that way."

"Maybe you need to get drunk."

"Humph! I have considered it a time or two already."

"If the rain doesna stop, come doon and have a drink with me."

"Aye, if the rain doesna stop, I will," Fraser said, "although it will clear off by midday and I will be on my way to Edinburgh."

It rained all day.

Jamie and Fraser were drunk by ten o'clock—not incoherently drunk, but at the midpoint.

Arabella came into the room and found Fraser and Jamie totally inebriated. "Too much liquor will kill ye, slowly, but for certain."

"That is all right," Jamie said, while closing one eye in order to focus the other. "We are not in a hurry, lass."

"Tch-tch…Jamie, just look at ye, and ye, Fraser Graham, planning to leave for Edinburgh, and here ye are, neither of ye able to get those silly grins off yer faces, and obviously drunk. Sophie will have a few words to say aboot that, I ken."

"A man can drink withoot being drunk," Fraser said.

"Och, that is true, sure enough, but it is not verra true of the two of ye, sitting there at the height of idiotic innocence, reeking o' too much ale," she said. "Now, off with ye to sleep it off afore ye are too drunk to climb the stairs."

Fraser made it up the stairs in fine fashion and opened the door to his room by himself. He even remembered to close the door and take his clothes off. After that, everything got a bit fuzzy and he fell into bed, naked as a Highlander's bum, and fell asleep.

He stirred in his sleep and came against the warm flesh of Claire sleeping beside him. The sound of his heartbeat pounded in his ears, and sent the blood pumping wildly to his head and further south. *Claire…sweet…love…*

He was drowning in the sweet, musky scent of her. He kissed her face and she turned her mouth to his, open, wet and welcoming. His hand began to wander, over the firm braes of her breasts. She was open to him…willing…warm…wet…waiting…and all his.

Oh, God, Claire…

He moved over her and positioned himself, but before he could enter her, Claire's hands came around him to cup his arse as she pulled him closer and he slipped within the warm cove between her legs.

I love ye….

Fraser was fondling Claire when Calum came into his room to wake him the next morning.

" 'Tis not like ye to oversleep," Calum said. "Did ye pass a bad night after consuming too much ale?" When Fraser did not reply, Calum went on. "Ye dinna look so weel, Fraser. Are ye certain ye feel like leaving for Edinburgh today?"

Fraser sat up and looked at the place in the bed beside him, not rumpled and not slept in, either. He ran his hands through his hair. Losh! It was only a dream. Too real, he thought. It was too real to be a dream.

"Ye are not going back to sleep?" Calum asked.

Fraser let out a breath and ran his hand through his hair. "No, I willna."

"I will see ye below stairs, then."

"Aye, as soon as I have dressed."

Fraser leaned back. He wasn't ready to get up just yet. He had passed many nights filled with dreams of Claire since their divorce, but never one that was as vivid or as powerful as last night. Even now he felt groggy, not from the ale but from the unbalanced feeling... He was caught in that gray area between a dream and wakefulness, and no longer felt a part of either.

He tried to remember the details—each part of making love to her—the feel of her skin, the scent of her hair, the warm haven of her mouth, but he could not recapture the feel of emptying himself, or the way she tightened around him when she cried out his name. He knew it happened; he remembered that much, yet the exactness, the duplication of the feel of it escaped him. It was like staring at a shadow and trying to envision a real person.

They were connected, but they would never be the same.

The dream left him feeling as if only a part of himself existed, as if the only way he could become whole again, was to experience that which he only had a shadowy recollection of.... He wanted to...no, he knew he had to make love to her again.

Claire. Always and forever, Claire.

She was the beginning and ending of all things for him. She was in the scent of heather in the air he breathed; the blue in the skies overhead; the kiss of sun upon his skin. His life began when he met her, and it ended when she turned him away. She was his first love, and his last.

There would never be anyone for him but her.

Calum paused at the door. "It isna just the ale, is it? It's Claire. Ye canna let her go. I worry for ye, Fraser. We all do. It has been long enough. Why don't ye let her go?"

"Because I canna."

"Then go to her and try to reconcile things between

ye. She seemed receptive enough to ye in Edinburgh. Perhaps she feels differently now. It is worth a try. God knows, anything is worth a try. Why dinna ye go to Inchmurrin and talk with her?"

"I canna. I canna forget her, and I canna go back. There is an immunity that comes with grief. It is like the measles. Once you have had it, you canna have it again."

"After watching you go through this, I hope to God I never fall in love."

Fraser gave his brother a smile that hovered somewhere between teasing and sadness. "Therein lies the crux. To live withoot a lass in yer life is no life, and if ye fall in love yer happiness is set upon the cast of dice."

Calum puffed out his chest in an exaggerated way. "I ken I will be the one to break hearts instead."

Fraser laughed. "Even then, there is no guarantee that some lass willna come along and turn yer life tapselteerie."

"I think I will go below stairs and drown my disappointment in breaking my fast. Are ye going to join us?"

"Aye, as soon as I get my breeks on."

After Calum left, Fraser tossed back the covers and stretched. He dropped his feet over the side of the bed, where he remained, naked as a tree in winter. The sun was warming a square of the floor with the promise of a beautiful day, and he stretched his feet out and plopped them in the middle of the warm spot. He wiggled his toes.

Aye, Claire was gone....

And yet he lived....

He had much to be thankful for, and he was a man who counted his blessings. He had a large, loving family and a rich heritage. His health was excellent. He was financially secure. He was moving to Edinburgh and would open his law office.

He was happy and life was good.

Twenty-One

He is a fool who thinks by force or skill
To turn the current of a woman's will.

Samuel Tuke (1620?-1674),
English royalist and playwright.
The Adventures of Five Hours (1663)

Things did not bode well for Claire.

Tired of waiting for Isobel to succeed, Lord Walter contrived to bring her under his control. He informed Isobel that he was taking charge.

"What do ye have in mind?" she asked.

"She must be isolated. She draws strength from this place, as well as her sisters."

Isobel's face registered her surprise. "Isolated? I dinna ken what ye mean by that."

"I shall take her north, to my family's castle in the Highlands."

An uneasy silence engulfed the room. Isobel looked anxious and glanced warily around. "You mean to take her to Kalder Castle?"

"Aye. I have given it much thought and deem it the

perfect place to put her in a more agreeable frame of mind."

"But it is in near ruin...and completely isolated on that promontory jutting into the sea. There are no servants there, nor any neighbors within miles." Isobel tried to keep the uneasiness from her voice. She hoped above hope that Walter did not intend for her to accompany him, for it was a horrible place and one she feared. To merely say the name Kalder Castle filled her with fright. It was aptly named, for it was dark and sinister, and a place where horrible things had occurred. It was a cursed place and haunted. No one would go near it.

"I have sent word to Angus Sinclair that I will have need of his services while I am there. He will gather that which we will have need of and meet me there."

"So ye plan to go alone?" she asked, praying it was so.

"Alone? No, not alone, for I shall have your lovely niece to keep me company."

"Ye do not plan to..."

"Ye are losing sight o' the purpose here, Isobel. It isna seduction. If I wanted to take advantage of her body—which holds no appeal for me, by the way—I would not need to go to such lengths. I could have taken her here, anytime I pleased."

"She will not go."

A sinister smile stretched like an evil snake across his face. "Och! Ye are wrong there. She will go and gladly, for if she refuses, her sisters go into the turret and they will not come down again."

"Ye mean to harm them?"

"That is up to her."

"But…what have ye in mind?"

"I must decide between starvation, or a diet of nothing but salted pork."

Isobel shuddered. She remembered the story of the unfortunate Earl of Ness, who was imprisoned at Kalder Castle by Walter's grandfather. The Earl was given nothing but salted beef, not even water. He died, screaming and raving, insane from lack of water. It was said he tried to eat his own hands before death claimed him. The castle was abandoned a generation later because of the earl's ghost, which still suffered his torment in the dungeon during the day but was allowed to haunt the castle at night, where he wandered eternally in search of water.

"When do ye leave?" Isobel asked.

"I will put the question to her tonight, and let her choose—Kalder Castle, or death to her sisters."

One of the servants, the grim and formidable Mrs. Macklin, brought word to Claire.

"My lady, Lord Walter awaits ye in his study and advises ye not to be tardy."

As soon as the Grim Reaper—the girls name for Mrs. Macklin—left, Claire's sisters gathered around her.

"Do ye have any idea what he wants with ye?" Kenna asked.

" 'Tis nothing good, I ken," Greer said.

Briana threw her arms around Claire. "Dinna go, Claire. Dinna go. I am afeard for ye."

At the sound of the desperation in her sister's voice, Claire looked down at Briana's upturned face and stroked the rosy ringlets hanging loose around her delicate neck. Her eyes held an abundance of love, mixed with fear.

Although Claire herself was worried about the reason Lord Walter had sent for her—for these kind of summons were never pleasant—she did not want to cause alarm in her youngest sister, for Briana was filled with terror at the very thought of encountering Lord Walter. Whenever she recognized his step in the house, she was desperate to find a place to hide or seclude herself until the sound of his steps passed.

Claire took Briana's face and framed it in her hands. "Ye must act like the lady ye are, Briana. Ye are almost grown, and ye must act the part. Do you understand what it means to be grown-up?"

"Aye," she said, "it means ye will be alone."

Claire hugged her close, regretting one so young had to have such a bleak outlook on life. Claire spoke to her in a calm voice. "Ye ken I must go, Briana, else it will bode ill for all of us, ye ken."

"Shall we accompany ye?" Kenna asked.

"No. 'Twould only serve to make Lord Walter angry. Dinna worrit. I doubt he is going to quash me over the head with a club or hurl me into the fire." When Claire saw that her words did nothing to ease the apprehension in Briana, she continued, "What say ye if I bring ye back an oatcake and some almond milk?"

"I only want ye to come back, Claire," Briana said, clinging fiercely to Claire, as if afraid to let her go.

"Now, let me go, so I willna be late. I shall return soon," Claire said.

"No, ye willna…ye willna…."

After Claire left, her sisters went to the window and sat there looking out at the loch, as they often did for comfort, for it was one of the few things in their lives that remained constant.

All of a sudden, Kenna jumped up.

"What is it?" Greer asked.

Kenna turned to her sisters. "I will be back in a little while."

"Where are ye going?" Greer asked.

"Shh." Kenna put her fingers to her lips. "I want to find out what Lord Walter wants with Claire."

"I want to come," Briana said.

"No, stay here with Greer. 'Tis best that I go alone. That way, if I get caught, only one of us will be punished."

"Are ye going through the secret passage?" Greer asked.

Kenna nodded. "Aye, and wise Claire was when she told us not to let Isobel or Lord Walter know it existed."

Before she left, Kenna instructed her sisters not to tell anyone where she went. "If they ask, say you havena seen me, ye ken?"

"Aye, we willna say anything," Briana said.

Kenna nodded and turned to light a candle, and carried it from the room.

She no more than left when Greer said, "Wait here. I will be right back."

"Where are ye going?"

"I want to find oot where Isobel is. Mayhap I can hear something like Kenna hopes to."

"I want to come."

"Ye must stay here, in case Kenna comes back before me. Otherwise, she may leave and we will never know where Claire is."

Greer opened the door and peered into the hall, and finding it clear, she stepped out and closed the door behind her.

At the far end of the hallway, Kenna pushed a wooden panel and stepped into a black void. The room was dark. The candle did not put out a great light, but it was enough for Kenna to see her way up a narrow stone spiral staircase. It opened to a small room on the second floor, right behind the study. She made her way toward an ornate metal grate and peered into the study.

Claire was standing in front of the desk, with Lord Walter seated in their father's chair behind it. He removed a feather quill from the ink jar and drew the plume through his fingers.

Near the grate, a large wooden panel was set into the stone. When Kenna pushed on the panel, a painting in the study tilted back so she could hear the conversation in the study.

"The time has come for a change. We will be leaving Inchmurrin tonight," Lord Walter said.

"How long will we be gone?" Claire asked.

"That is up to ye. It could be weeks, or it could be for the rest of your life. Once we are there, ye willna leave until ye agree to marry Giles."

"And my sisters?"

"They will remain here with Isobel. Nothing will happen to them...at least not for the time being."

"Where do ye take me?"

"Full of questions, are ye not?"

"I feel it is the least I deserve."

"I am taking ye to my grandfather's castle."

"Where?"

"In the Highlands. Ask no more questions about where ye are going. I have said all I am going to say on the matter."

"How much time do I have?"

"For what?"

"To pack and say goodbye to my sisters."

"Isobel has seen that some of your clothing has been packed. As for your sisters, ye have seen the last o' them. If ye wanted to bid them adieu, ye should have said goodbye before ye left."

Overhead, Kenna put her hands over her mouth to stifle her gasp. Her mind raced as she tried to decide what she was going to do with the information she had gathered.

She pushed the panel back in place and returned the way she had come. When she entered the room, she was greeted by Briana's lovely voice.

"'Tis a grave situation we are in. Why do ye sing at a time like this, Briana?"

"I am singing so I will no' be afraid."

"Ye have naught to fear, at least for now. 'Tis Claire who is in danger."

"What did ye find out?" Briana asked. "Does it bode ill for Claire?"

"Aye, it..." She paused and looked around the room. "Where is Greer?"

"She left."

"She left? What do ye mean she left? To go where?"

"She went to spy on Isobel, to see if she could find oot anything."

"She should have remained here, like I asked her to do."

"Ye ken Greer doesna always do what she is told. And neither do ye."

"Weel, for that matter, Lady Briana, neither do ye."

"Aye, 'tis true enough, but tell me, what did ye find oot?"

"I heard Lord Walter tell Claire that he was—"

The door opened and Greer slipped into the room.

"Hurry," Kenna said. "I was about to tell Briana what I found oot."

"Oh, good," Greer said. "I am most anxious to know what ye heard."

Kenna started her story again, and finished it this time.

"What can we do?" Briana asked. "I think we should go after her."

"We canna," Kenna said. "What would we do when we caught up with them? We are powerless. We dinna ken where this castle of Lord Walter's is."

Tears began to slide silently down Briana's cheeks. "We canna sit here and do nothing. We must help her. We must."

"Aye," Kenna said. "We will, but first I must think of a way. If only we knew where Lord Walter was taking her."

"I know where he is taking her," Greer said. "Or at least I ken the name o' the castle."

A puzzled frown settled on Kenna's brow. "What do ye mean he is taking her to a castle, and ye have the name of it? How do ye ken these things, Greer, when Lord Walter did not mention them to Claire?"

Greer shrugged and folded her arms across her

waist. "I wanted to help, so after ye left, I went to find Isobel. She was in the solar, so I went into the oubliette that adjoins it. It wasna long until Lord Walter came to tell her he was leaving and taking Claire with him. Then I heard Isobel ask him, 'Are ye certain Kalder is the right place to take her? It is verra far and terribly isolated.'

"Then Lord Walter said, 'Aye, and that is the reason I chose it.' Isobel then expressed her doubts about this Kalder Castle because, according to her, it was partially destroyed. Lord Walter said that was what made it the perfect choice, for who would think to look for them there."

"Kalder..." Kenna said thoughtfully. "It isna a Celtic name nor a Gaelic one. It must have come from the Saxons or the Normans, although it sounds more Norman, and if that be true, then it would be in the far northern part of the Highlands, more than likely. Not that we should worry overmuch about that now, for I ken we should be able to track it doon withoot much difficulty."

"Aye, but how do ye ken we go aboot it?" Greer asked. "What can the three of us do? We are powerless, even if we do find oot where this Kalder Castle is located."

Kenna saw the glum expressions on the faces of her sisters, and that seemed to give her an added dose of optimism. "Aye, 'tis true we canna handle something like this by ourselves. It is as father said, 'A monk canna shave his own head.'"

"What has that go to do with anything?" Greer asked.

"Weel, if a monk canna shave his own head, then

he must find someone else to do it for him, ye ken? Dinna fret and fash yerself. 'Tis plain as the snow on Ben Lomond that we canna do this alone. I plan to get help."

"Will ye seek help from the clan, then?" Greer asked.

"No, this isna the fifteenth century when the clans settled all grievances. How could we move so many men withoot arousing suspicion?"

"Then who shall we ask to help us?" Briana asked.

"I shall leave immediately for Edinburgh," Kenna replied.

"Edinburgh?" Greer and Briana asked in unison.

"Aye, 'tis where Fraser Graham is practicing law."

Greer's face registered surprise. "Fraser Graham? Are ye daft, Kenna? Ye canna ask Fraser," Greer said. "Claire would die if ye did."

"Claire may die if I dinna. Any port is welcome in a storm. Fraser is the only man I know that I trust enough to ask," Kenna said.

"Why dinna ye tell some of the men and let them help."

"Ye ken how the clansmen are. They would immediately arm themselves and ride off as if they were going to war. We need someone calm and levelheaded. Otherwise Claire will never come home again."

"Do ye ken Fraser will even want to help?" Briana asked. "After the way Claire divorced him, I couldna blame him if he wanted nothing more to do with any of us ever again."

"Fraser will help. I am certain of it, but I canna tarry overlong talking aboot it. I must leave for Edinburgh immediately."

"Ye canna go to Edinburgh alone," Briana said. "It isna safe for a woman to travel alone."

"I will wear a pair of Kendrew's trews and put my hair inside one of his bonnets. Everyone says I ride as well as a man. With Kendrew's cape on, no one will think I am a woman."

"Ye mean to ride astride?" Greer asked.

"Aye."

"Oh, I wish I were going," she said, "for I have longed to ride that way."

"Next time," Kenna said. "Come, sisters, and help me dress."

Twenty-Two

Like one, that on a lonesome road
Doth walk in fear and dread,
And having once turned round walks on,
And turns no more his head;
Because he knows, a frightful fiend
Doth close behind him tread.

Samuel Taylor Coleridge (1772-1834),
British poet.
Lyrical Ballads "The Rime of the Ancient
Mariner" (1798)

Claire opened her mouth to speak, but someone must have been waiting behind the door, for she heard a noise behind her. She started to turn, when something swooped down and over her head, and the world went dark.

She was thrown to the floor, and the air was knocked from her lungs.

"Make certain the bindings are secure," Lord Walter said. "We dinna want her wiggling loose."

"Aye, she willna get loose, your lordship, I can promise ye that."

She did not recognize the voice of the other man who yanked her arms behind her. She was wrapped in something—a plaid more than likely—and her body was tied and bound, snug as a moth in a cocoon.

It was an odd sensation to feel her body hoisted upward, and then the jarring motions of movement as she was carried where she knew not. She only knew Lord Walter was at the bottom of it, and wondered what he had in mind. She prayed her final destination was not going to be the bottom of the loch.

She winced with pain when she was lowered, and then dropped roughly to the ground or something hard, at least. She landed shoulder first and cried out at the excruciating pain.

Soft voices were speaking Gaelic, but they were spoken too softly for her to have any understanding of whom the voices belonged to. The sound of someone walking across rocky terrain overrode the voices completely, and then the crunching steps stopped.

It was eerily quiet, and she found it did strange things to her mind to lie helplessly out in the open, unable to see who or what was about. Never had she felt so vulnerable.

"Take her."

Airborne again, she heard the splash of water, and then the sensation of being lowered to a surface that gently rocked from side to side. The next thing she heard was the sound of the water in the loch slapping against the side of a boat. She was leaving Inchmurrin.

"No, ye willna…ye willna…."

Briana's words came back to haunt her, and she tried to think if there was something she could have done, even if she had known, as Briana seemed to, that she would not return to the company of her sisters. Would her absence be permanent?

Homesickness settled like a heavy stone within her and weighted her spirits down. Would she ever again see the beloved tower of Lennox Castle again, or feel the loving embrace of her sisters? The burn of tears stung her nose, but she forced them back by remembering the things her father taught her. *I am the Earl of Lennox. I am the laird of my clan and the head of my family. The memory of my father still rules my spirit, and I am the thread that follows the needle. They willna make me cry. I do not break, nor will I allow my faith to falter because some men are ruled by the dark side of life. I may be only a woman in some eyes, but they err who think that brands me weak.*

I am not a weakling. I will defend...

I will defend...the motto of Clan Lennox. The very thought of it caused the blood to surge within her. She was only one link in the chain, but she was determined not to be the weakest one.

Lord Walter underestimated her if he thought he could force her to sign away her heritage. Did he not know that the old Celtic earls of Lennox were once the ancient Celtic Mormaers of Levenax, or that they commanded the Vale of Leven, the River Leven, and the great lake the ancients called Lochleven, now called Loch Lomond? Did he not know that their blood had soaked the land there for centuries, since they first fought the Danes hundreds of years ago? Did he truly think that she, knowing all these things and more, would give him what he wanted?

She would rather die along with her sisters and see

the title revert to the crown than fall into the hands of Isobel and Lord Walter, because she knew that once he had the Lennox title and wealth in his hands she and her sisters would all meet with death.

In a way, Claire was glad this had happened, for she felt it was the prod she needed to fight back. As plainly as if he were sitting beside her, Claire heard her father's voice speak the familiar Gaelic words he taught all of his children: "*Cuimhnichibh air na daoine bho'n d'thainig sibh.*"

Remember the people whom you come from....

With a rejuvenated heart, she felt a sense of peace—not that it would be easy, but she was of sound mind and stout heart, and would follow the right path no matter what. With that thought to comfort her, she drifted off to sleep.

Later, when she awoke, she knew by the cooler temperature that it was dark. She longed to stretch her muscles, for her body was stiff and numb from being in one position for so long.

Footsteps grew louder. Someone approached, then paused. Her bindings were loosened and the hood pulled back. She could only see the dark silhouette of a man—not Lord Walter, but one of his ilk. A hand slipped behind her head. A voice she did not recall hearing before said, "Drink." A cup was pressed to her lips and clanked against her teeth.

She was thirsty and drank greedily, even though the water had a bitter taste that overrode the taste of metal. When the cup was emptied, she was gagged and the hood was pulled back over her head. She was bound once more, but she did not have the sensation of it being as tightly done, or as painful this time. Nor did she care, for she felt drowsy and warm, as if she were floating.

"Load her in the cart." She identified the voice as familiar, but her brain was too fuzzy to do more. She closed her eyes, and was mercifully out cold by the time she was roughly tossed in the back of a small cart.

She had no way of knowing how much time had transpired between the time she closed her eyes and when she awoke with a nauseous lurch of her stomach. She realized she was dangling, head down, over the back of someone, as if she had no more worth or weight than a common sack of barley.

She was jarred and jostled, and carried she knew not where. She only knew that no attention was given to the discomfort it caused her, or the grinding pain as her ribs thumped against a hard-boned shoulder with each jolting step. If not for the gag that bound her, she would have cried out in pain.

The scent of the sea penetrated the hood even before she heard the mournful cry of seabirds and the gentle lapping of waves against the shore.

"Give her something to drink." She recognized the voice and knew Lord Walter's accompanying her meant only one thing: she was being kidnapped, probably to some unknown and isolated place where he could take his time trying to bend her to his will, using whatever means he chose.

Pity he did not remove her gag, else she would have told him it was a waste of time, for she was not the naive girl she once was when she refused to believe Fraser when he tried to warn her about Isobel and Lord Walter. *Ye were right, Fraser, and it is sorry I am I turned against ye and did not believe what ye said.*

Their brief words came back to haunt her:

"'Tis the Lennox wealth they are after, Claire. Can ye not see that, lass? Do ye not understand that they had a hand in the death of yer father and yer brothers? When you begin to see the truth in that, then I ken ye will see why it is important for them to ruin things between ye and me. Once I am gone, ye will be free to marry Giles. Surely ye see that Giles is too weak to withstand Lord Walter and Isobel's plotting."

"What are you saying, Fraser? That they will murder ye?"

"Aye, I ken they will, just like they did Kendrew."

"Kendrew was ill, with the fever."

"Kendrew was poisoned."

"You lie!"

He looked at her sadly. "How many deaths will it take, Claire? How many loved ones will you bury afore ye see the truth?"

The memory vanished then, for someone called out, *"Greas ort!"*

Hurry up...

It was Lord Walter's voice, she realized, and Claire gave a start at the sound of his voice telling his men to move quickly. Evidently he was losing patience, which could bode ill for her.

Someone yanked the hood back. She blinked against the blinding brightness of the sun. The gag was ripped from her mouth, and because it had dried, it tore some of the skin of her lower lip, and she made a slight grimace against the pain. When a cup clanked against her teeth, she turned her head.

"No, I don't want more...please..."

Someone grabbed her by the hair. Her scalp burned

when her head was wrenched back. She looked into the peculiarly arched nostrils of Lord Walter. "Drink it down to the last drop, or I will send one of these miserable lads back to bring your sisters so that they might share your fate."

The cup was rammed against her mouth and water sloshed over the rim. She was so exhausted and thirsty by this point she decided sleep was preferable to the treatment she had endured thus far, and she drank the contents of the cup, not knowing if it was another sleeping draft, or poison.

The last thing she remembered for some time was the sound of Lord Walter's voice. "Put her on board."

A boat, she thought. It was the last coherent thought she remembered.

She had no inkling of the passage of time, only the vague recollection of the cup being put to her mouth at least two more times. Slowly, she was becoming aware of her surroundings—the feel of sea air on her face, the stiffness of her limbs, the headache that pounded like an angry surf against her temples, and the wretched taste of the sleeping draft in her mouth.

It was at this point when she realized both the hood and the gag had been removed. She took a quick glance around the boat and spotted the silhouettes of two men standing at the wheel. She did not see Lord Walter, and surmised he might have gone below.

She lay unmoving and silent, and stared at the full moon and stars overhead, not wanting to draw any attention to the fact she was awake, for fear they would force the draft down her again. Her stomach grew mutinous from both hunger and the effects of the sleeping potion she knew she had been given.

She was weak from hunger, yet the thought of food nauseated her. She licked her lips and felt the crust of blood where the gag had torn her skin. She closed her eyes. Perhaps sleep was the best way after all.

She awoke some time later when someone put a hand on her breast and began to squeeze. She was too groggy and weak to display much of a reaction, but she did attempt to roll over, when the sound of Lord Walter's voice cut through the air.

"I'll no' warn ye again. If you so much as look at her wrong, I'll cut yer throat."

Again? Claire shuddered to think that someone had touched her while she slept. She was thankful that Lord Walter had not sunk quite that low—at least not yet.

She did not know how much time had transpired before someone put a hand to her shoulder and began to shake her roughly. She barely opened her eyes when she felt a hand snake around her waist. Her wrist was caught in a painfully tight grip and she was yanked upright, into a sitting position.

She did not know the man, although she had some recollection of having heard the voice shortly after she was abducted. She thought no more upon it, for all the laudanum she had been given was having an adverse effect upon her. Wave after wave of nausea churned her stomach. She was going to be sick. She no more than thought it, when her head was shoved forward to the railing and she heaved violently into the sea.

When the nausea subsided, she was pulled back and a cup came toward her. She turned her head and said weakly, "No more. Please, I canna…"

"Stop yer blithering. 'Tis almond milk. 'Twill ease yer stomach."

Her head was yanked around and she gazed down into the cup. The scent of almonds wafted upward and she inhaled the familiar scent. It was at this point that she realized her hands were no longer bound. Her hands were shaking badly as she brought the cup to her lips, and she had only the faintest recognition of the deep bruises and crusted blood that covered her wrists before she took her first hesitant sips.

When she finished, she handed the cup back to the same sharp-nosed man who gave it to her. His hand slithered around the cup and curled tightly over her fingers. She tried to withdraw her hand, but he held her fingers trapped firmly against the cup, and in her weakened state, she had precious little strength to display.

She looked him in the eye and said, "Release my hand..."

"What's yer hurry, lass? We've a way to go yet, and time to become better acquainted, ye ken?" He pulled a small bottle out of his pocket. *"A bheil thu g iarraidh uisge-beatha?"*

Her stomach revolted at the thought of it. She shook her head. "No, no whisky."

"One little drink... What's the harm? 'Twill warm ye."

"No," she said, only this time, more firmly.

The moon was bright enough that she could easily see the lustful leer, and the way he licked his lips in an indecent manner when he forced the bottle against her lips.

Disgusted as well as repulsed, she turned her head away. Never had she been so humiliated, and never had anyone dared look at her in such a lascivious way. Had she not been in this situation with Lord Walter, he would not have dared such disrespect.

From the corner of her eye, she saw a blur of movement, and then everything passed quickly after that. Lord Walter suddenly appeared, and Claire could only watch what happened next with horrible disbelief.

With a flick of his wrist, and a flash of moonlight on metal, he sliced the man's throat.

Blood spurted from the artery. Claire screamed, "Dear Mother of God, ye have killed him."

Calm and poised, without so much as a ripple of remorse, Lord Walter released the man with a shove. Claire watched his limp body disappear over the side with a splash.

He gave a quick glance in Claire's direction before he leaned over the side of the boat and rinsed the knife in the water. He wiped the blade against his breeches as he said, "Just so ye know. This is not a game we are playing. And my patience does have its limits."

She was numbed by what she had witnessed. Aye, she had seen death before, but never had she seen someone brutally murdered before her eyes.

"Well, have ye nothing to say, Countess?"

No, she thought, how could I? She was horror-struck. The viciousness of what she had witnessed continued to play over and over in her mind. In response, Claire was unable to do more than slowly shake her head.

With his thin lips pressed tightly together, he watched her through narrowed eyes, the knife still held at his side, as if it was his way of reminding her that he could just as easily slit her throat.

The role of an angry god suited him, and he played

it well, for there was little doubt in her mind that her life was in the balance and subject to his whim. She could picture him sitting on Mount Olympus, playing a game with the lives of humans.

"Shall we kill her? Or shall we let her live?"

"Let her live, so that we might amuse ourselves with her."

"An excellent idea. Toy with the minx."

"As long as she pleases us."

Claire remained silent, although a churlish reply waited on the tip of her tongue. The urge to hurl defiance was strong, but it was also premature. She had not yet assessed her circumstances. She had nothing, save her words, with which to defend herself and barter for her freedom. Words were the weapons of captives. To respond now would be flagrantly stupid, for anything she could say would be as superfluous as lighting a candle in the sun.

For the time being, she must look upon him as a formidable foe; one who controlled her life and held her future in the palm of his hand. She would do well to be miserly with her words, as the frugal man is with his money. She would be sparing, and use each word wisely, as long as she was confident; they would buy her time and her eventual freedom.

For the time being, at least, she yielded to his dominance, for clearly he was in the controlling position in this situation.

Apparently, he waited for her rebuttal. When one was not forthcoming, Lord Walter turned sharply and walked away. The danger, for now at least, had passed, but his seething hostility was still evident, riding just below the short supply of patience.

Twenty-Three

Then must you speak
Of one that lov'd not wisely, but too well;
Of one not easily jealous, but, being wrought,
Perplexed in the extreme; of one whose hand,
Like the base Indian, threw a pearl away
Richer than all his tribe.

William Shakespeare (1564-1616),
English poet and playwright.
Othello (1602-1604), act 5, scene 2

The morning sun rose golden and dazzling, touching the deep blue of the rising swells with the faint blush of rubies. Claire did not move but focused her gaze on the sunrise, now nothing more than a pale pink tint on the horizon, and her thoughts on something more pleasant than her present circumstances. She found if she concentrated her thoughts on the years she and Fraser were together, it made things bearable.

Soon the memory of another sunrise slipped into her unconsciousness as she remembered a night when she and Fraser were returning from a dance at a neighbor's house across the loch and, on their way home, Fraser made love to her in the boat.

She could feel the warmth of his breath on her skin, and she heard the way he breathed the words into her hair. "Claire, to think that ye are mine pleasures me, but to know that I shall grow old with ye…it fills my heart fair to burstin'. I watched ye dancin' tonight, and a fire burned inside me. I wanted ye all evening, and I kept thinking how soft ye were, and how warm, and how wet ye are when I touch ye. I will never get enough of ye, Claire Lennox."

There was something about his kiss that night that she never forgot—a combination of fiery passion, urgent need, and yet a soulful tenderness that wrenched her heart. If she ever doubted his love for her, that kiss would have removed all doubt. She never knew she could react so strongly to a kiss, and the next thing she knew, he shifted their position and turned her to lie beneath him, without breaking the kiss. She recalled the way he groaned, and she closed her eyes. She could feel it now—Fraser pressing himself against her softness, and her feeling his penis grow strong and hard in response. She dug her hands into his hair, and pulled the leather thong to set it free. She went crazy that night, and she had to hold on to him tightly to keep from crying out when he drove her past herself.

When he drew back, she clutched at him. "Dinna go," she whispered. "I need ye, Fraser. I need ye."

"Aye, and ye shall have me, as soon as I get my breeks opened."

She whimpered in frustration, and sighed when she felt his weight against her again; his hand going under her skirts. Her arms hugged him close as she opened her legs to him, and when his hand found what it searched for, she felt like a flower opening.

Her hands slipped down to the smooth skin of his buttocks, so she could hold him against her and feel the power of his thrusting loins. She loved him so much, even this beautiful mating did not seem enough. She wanted to be consumed by him, to be joined in a way that could never be separate from him. "I love ye, Fraser," she whimpered, her breath coming in short pants.

She pushed his shirt back and kissed his nipples until they were hard, and he crushed her against his chest.

"By the legs of St. Andrew," he said, and she felt the surge of his warmth.

They made no move to sit up, content to lie in each other's arms, rocked by the ripples in the loch, him with his arm around her, and her lying in the cove of his arm with her head on his shoulder.

"Were ye embarrassed to make love in a boat, under the stars?" he asked.

"Aye, I was at first, but then, after ye came into me, it was like we were moving as one with the boat."

"I ken it added another element that heightened our pleasure."

"If it was any higher, I think my heart would have stopped beating."

He leaned forward and kissed her forehead. "I go to heaven with ye in my arms."

"What about the rest of it?" she whispered in his ear, and bit the lobe. "How do ye feel then, Fraser Graham?"

"When I touch ye where ye are all warm and slippery, and ease myself into the cleft between yer legs, I go crazy with wanting ye, and the insanity builds and builds until I think I will die from it. When I think I can bear it no more, all the pent-up love I feel for ye washes inside ye, and I ken I am a part of ye, as ye are a part o' me. I would die for ye, Claire, and I vowed the first time I made love to ye that I wouldna ever break yer heart. I will love ye and protect ye until the moment my maker lays his hands upon me." He rose up on one elbow, and she remembered the exact play of the moonlight on the handsome planes of his face. "Dinna hurt me, Claire. I love ye too much to bear it."

"I willna, Fraser. I belong to ye now."

They lay in each other's arms, neither of them aware that they had fallen asleep.

"Look, here be a lad and a lassie laid doon in the boat," said a strange voice.

"Hoot! Ubh, ubh! Cò ris tha 'n saoghal a' tighinn?"

What is the world coming to?

Claire was wondering the same thing, as she opened one eye just enough to see the sun was definitely up, and they were still in the boat. Ye gods, had they truly drifted in the loch all night? How would she live this embarrassment down? How thankful she was that she did recognize the voice, and she most certainly did not want to make his acquaintance. She wished the boat could have drifted right out of the loch and into the sea.

How could they have fallen asleep?

Well, never mind that, she thought. What is done is done. She closed her eye and hoped Fraser would send them on their merry way.

About that time, another voice spoke up, once again in Gaelic.

"Feumaidh Beurla a bhith air fear dhiubh."

One of them must be English? She was wondering who this voice belonged to, when Fraser burst forth with a hearty laugh.

"Madainn mhath dhuibh." Good morning, Fraser said to them in Gaelic, which she supposed would put their minds at ease about either of them being English.

Claire stole a glance and saw two old men with a few fish. They nodded at her and she nodded back, while trying to make certain her dress was fastened and her limbs covered. She did not want to think about her hair.

"Cad is ainm duit?"

Oh, they canna be asking our names, she thought. Surely, Fraser willna give them our names.

"Fraser Graham, and this is my wife, Claire Lennox."

The men were looking at her and Claire gave them a weak smile.

"The Countess?"

"Aye, one in the same. I take it ye are no' Clan Lennox."

"MacGregor's."

"Aye, weel good men all o' ye."

Claire slid down into the boat and gave Fraser a sharp jab with her elbow, but the three of them went on talking.

The sun climbed higher in the sky. She was getting hot. Her arms were starting to blush pink.

Just then, she caught part of something Fraser said…"dipping in the loch." Was he daft? She nudged him again, harder this time.

"Aye, a pennywecht o' love is worth a pound o' law," Fraser said, and she wanted to choke him. And he said women were overly fond of blithering?

She was about to poke him again when the men finally said goodbye and left.

She looked up and saw Fraser grinning down at her.

Claire sat up and looked around. "Lord love the loch! We are almost up to Ben Lomond. I canna believe we drifted this far."

"I ken we helped it along a bit with all that rocking motion."

She picked up the oars and shoved them toward him. "Since ye are so full o' vinegar, ye can row us home."

He did, and he sang two verses of "The Twa Magicans" all the way back.

"The lady sits at her own front door
as straight as the willow wand,
And by there came a lusty smith
with his hammer in his hand.
He couped [tumbled] her on a grassy bank,
the lassie for to please,
But aye she sighed an' sweetly cried,
but wouldna' pairt her knees."

When they were almost back to Lennox Castle, Claire, growing weary of hearing the same two verses repeated, finally asked, "Are two verses all you know?"

"Aye."

"Good," she said.

The look on his face was made for laughing, and

she could not pretend she was angry when mirth danced throughout. Their gazes locked and they fell upon each other weak from laughter.

She was haunted by memories, for that was all she had to cling to. Claire looked toward the shoreline and felt herself suspended in time; somewhere between the past and the present. She usually never allowed herself to think back upon the year she and Fraser were married, but there were times when she could not hold the memories at bay.

She was glad today was one of those times, and that she had the warm memory of a happier time to keep her company. It had been so very long since she had laughed, and the sound of Fraser's wonderful laugh that day…it still echoed through the chambers of her heart.

There were so many things she wanted to say to him, and yet she carried precious little hope that she would ever walk away from her present circumstances alive. She would never give in to Lord Walter's demands, and he would not accept anything less.

Things seemed to be coming to her in twos today, for there were two things she wished she could be granted before her life ended:

She wanted to tell her sisters goodbye.

She wished she could see Fraser one last time, to tell him she was sorry. Not because she thought it would change anything and make him love her again. She knew it was too late for that. She simply wanted to empty her heart and clear the torment of remorse away.

Claire did not realize she was crying until she felt

a tear splash on her hand. Why does one do and say things they will live to regret? she wondered. Why did she turn away from Fraser during the troubled times when she needed him beside her—when she knew in her heart she loved him still? She was sorry for so many things, but none wounded her as deeply as knowing she'd hurt him. Losing him, as much as she loved him, did not hurt her as much as the thought that she had caused him pain.

The sleek keel of the sailboat sliced through the water toward the bold promontory of jutting rock that rose majestically out of the depths of what had to be the North Sea. Below the promontory, where the landmass met the sea, huge boulders looked as if they had been violently ripped away and thrown into the sea.

It was a peninsular neck of land, joined to the mainland by a narrow stretch of land that appeared to be around three hundred feet in length with a deep ditch called a fosse, or goe, that ran behind the castle all the way to the isthmus. She thought she was looking at the coast of Scotland, but she had no way of knowing. It could be Ireland, or even the land of the Norsemen, for it was a place she had never before seen.

"Where are we?"

"Kalder Castle… Caithness."

"Kalder…" Claire had heard of it, of course, for it had a long history of unfortunate events attached to it. Even the name Kalder—an old Icelandic word—meant "deadly cold."

Deadly…not exactly the word she was longing to be reminded of, but she was, at least, relieved to know they were still in Scotland.

She was suddenly reminded that she might not ever leave Kalder Castle, that it was very likely she would end her days locked in the dungeon and abandoned to die of starvation.

She studied the main block of the castle, which rose five floors. The boat drew closer to the pend, and the porticullis was raised, which allowed them to drop sail and glide under the arch beneath the castle that would soon be her prison.

Never had she felt so alone, or more bereft. She would never have the chance to tell Fraser how sorry she was, or that there had never been a day since he left that she had not regretted what she had done.

Twenty-Four

Only stay quiet while my mind remembers
The beauty of fire from the beauty of embers.

John Masefield (1878-1967),
British poet and playwright.
The Collected Poems of John Masefield
"On Growing Old" (1923)

Claire's defiance lasted three weeks before Lord Walter issued her an ultimatum.

"I have sent word to Giles to join us here. Ye have until the day he arrives to change yer mind. If ye do not marry him by the second day after his arrival, ye will be removed to the dungeon and there ye will stay, Countess, until ye die or marry."

"I will not hand my inheritance over to ye."

"Do not be so noble. Shall I remind ye that after your death one of yer sisters will inherit the title. Perhaps she will be more disposed toward marriage with Giles. Hear me well. I will not stop. Moreover, if I must throw each of yer sisters in the dungeon to suffer yer fate I will not hesitate to do so. I will warn ye now, do not think ye can outsmart me. It is impossible."

True to Lord Walter's word, he took Claire to the dungeon three days after Giles arrived. She was taken down the narrow, damp steps that led to the portcullis beneath the main building, where the North Sea surged against the rock the castle was built upon. They were almost to the portcullis when he made a sharp turn, and she saw the prison cell. It was, as most dungeons are, small, cold and damp, with only one tiny window some twenty feet above the dungeon floor. It had literally been hewn from the rock. There was no wooden door, but one made of iron bars that let in the cold and moisture from the sea.

He left, without making any mention of food or water, taking the lamp with him, although he did gift her with the punishing sound of the iron door closing forever on the life she had known.

It was late afternoon, and the cell was now almost completely dark. He did leave her with a thin blanket, and a suggestion that she sleep on the musty straw piled in the corner. She was truly and completely alone, with nothing for company but the relentless sound of the sea hurling itself against the rocks.

She paced the small perimeter of her cell. The damp chill was already beginning to penetrate her very bones, and she drew the blanket over her and found it made precious little difference. She studied the damp walls, the tracks of moisture running down. Were these the tears of those abandoned souls who, like her, were condemned to such a horrid fate?

She had nothing to look at but the four dripping walls and the pictures of her sisters and Lennox Castle sitting on the shores of Loch Lomond that she called up from her mind. When the sun went down, everything was black as pitch. She could hear the scurrying of night creatures, and the never-ending sound of the sea. All else was silence.

She walked and walked, and cried until her eyes were swollen and the tears would no longer come. She was exhausted and afraid to sit down for fear some rat, or worse, would come into her cell through the iron bars. Not long before daybreak, she moved to the iron gate and leaned her head against the cold bars. What had she and her family done to deserve this end? What would happen to her sisters and the members of the clan now that she was left to rot in this remote place?

She was given a meager amount of food the first week, although she barely touched it. She was like a caged animal as she paced back and forth, searching for some way out, while knowing all along that escape, save through death, was impossible. She realized she should have tried an escape long before now. They sailed fairly close to shore, and she could have jumped over the side. Swimming to shore would have been no problem for her, and once there, she would have had at least a chance of escape.

At some point during that first week in the dungeon, she began to keep account of the days by marking the stones with a rock. She knew that once the food stopped and she was given only water, there would be neither reason nor strength to make the mark. If there was a good side to all of this, she would not spend years incarcerated. She knew not how long she could survive without water, although she supposed it would not be more than two or three days.

The second week, she heard the sound of the rusty key turning in the lock, followed by the creaking of the hinges as the gate opened. Lord Walter came into the cell to give her what he called her last meal, before he informed her that for the rest of the week, she would only be given water every other day.

"The third week, the water will stop. You will receive nothing to eat or drink after that. Does marriage to Giles really seem a fate more grim than the one I have just offered ye?"

"Ye misjudge me, Lord Walter. Ye confuse my young age with stupidity. Do ye truly think I believe anything ye say? I am my father's daughter. I am capable of looking beyond what ye present as the final stopping point, but I ken marriage to Giles would only be the beginning, and I would soon meet with an accident or, like my poor brother, be slowly poisoned to death. Once I am gone, ye will see that my sisters suffer a similar fate and then ye and Isobel will have yer hands on the Lennox wealth—that is, if Giles cooperates. If not, then I ken my dear cousin will join the rest o' us in the grave."

On the morning beginning the third week, Lord Walter paid her another visit and handed her what he called "Your last cup of water."

Claire took the water and watched how the Belgian lace beneath his velvet doublet fell to his knuckles. His hands were pale, long and thin, and a shiny new gold ring encircled the middle finger. His finery, she knew, was bought with Lennox coin. "Ye have wasted no time in spending money that isna yours. I may not live to see it, but be forewarned, ye willna get away with this. And when yer punishment comes, I hope it is sufficient to equal all the misery, suffering and pain ye have dealt my family."

"Yer bold insolence will be yer ruin, and it is wasted on me. I prefer my women weak and compliant. Drink up, for 'tis the last water ye will receive, unless ye change yer mind," he said.

Claire drank thirstily and handed him the cup. "Lord Walter, I grow weary of yer oily tongue. I will thank ye kindly to hie yerself away from my presence, and then ye may go to the devil who fathered ye."

He backhanded her and she was knocked backward, where she struck her head on the stones. Dazed, she dropped to her knees. He put his foot on her shoulder and shoved her backward, so that she fell to the floor. She could feel the trickle of blood from where his ring cut her lip. "And so, God has recorded yet another cruelty ye shall be punished for."

She could see a million threats in his cold eyes. Yet, he surprised her when he threw the cup against the stones in the wall, where it clattered and fell to the floor. This time, he called out to a guard to open the iron gate.

Keys rattled and the lock was turned. With a scraping sound, the gate was opened. Before he stepped through, Lord Walter said, "Yer death is o' yer own doing and the sin rests upon yer own head. 'Tis a cross ye must bear alone. I accept no responsibility. I offered ye a way out."

"Aye, and I ken God will be meekly abiding by yer declaration. Yer days are numbered, Lord Walter, and I wouldna want to be in yer shoes. And now, I will be offering ye to remove yer despicable presence from my sight and let me meet my maker in peace, so that I may give a personal accounting to Him of yer many misdeeds."

After he was gone, she looked at the bright shaft of sunlight streaming through the opening high overhead. She could hear the cry of seabirds and the pounding of the waves against the boulders below. The smell of the sea was fresh, and although the air was mild, Claire shivered from weakness.

Her life was a gift from God, and it would end by reuniting her with her creator. She picked up a chalky rock and went to the pile of straw in the corner. She dropped to her knees and drew a cross on the stone, going over the lines again and again, until it was a few inches wide.

Beneath it she wrote the words *ne oublie.*

There, on her knees, in front of her makeshift altar, she prayed for deliverance. If that was not forthcoming, she prayed that God would see to her sisters, and that Fraser would somehow know she truly never stopped loving him.

"I ask ye to let him know that the words on my tongue were never in my heart. And if it be possible, I pray there will be forgiveness from him for the wrong I did him. I ask for forgiveness for being too young, too inexperienced, and terribly foolish for trusting Isobel. I pray my death will cancel my guilt."

Her last prayer was for the end to come quickly.

Claire wanted to face death bravely, but fear gathered like dark clouds, rumbling and churning within her. She did not want to die like this—alone and isolated in her imprisonment. Her prayers were a comfort, and she had no qualms about her afterlife and the peace she would find. To die as ten thousand of Scotland's finest and brave men did on the battlefield at Flodden Field was as powerfully moving as it was tragic. To die as she would die, lying on a bed of straw in a place occupied only by the creatures that crawled here was ignoble and lonely. Such a death came at the end of hope.

She reached inside her bodice and pulled out a thin gold chain threaded through a golden band. She removed the ring and looked at the engraving inside, where the Lennox clan motto, I'll Defend, was engraved.

It had been her mother's wedding ring, and when Claire and Fraser married, it became her wedding ring. Fraser had added his own word to the inscription... *thee.* He followed that with the Graham clan motto, *Ne Oublie,* do not forget. Completed, the inscription read I Will Defend Thee, Ne Oublie.

She put the ring on her finger. Because of the weight she'd lost, the ring was too loose, so she wound a damp piece of straw around the shank of the ring so that it fit more tightly. She curled her fingers into a fist and she lay down on the straw, pulling the thin blanket over her. She did not take her eyes from the cross, but continued to stare at it the rest of the day, while she prayed continually.

When the sun reached its zenith and began its descent in the blue Scots sky, Claire closed her eyes and dreamed...as always, of Fraser.

Twenty-Five

The hour is come, but not the man.

Sir Walter Scott (1771-1832), Scottish novelist.
The Heart of Midlothian (1818)

Jamie dismounted and walked up the slope of the hill where Fraser stood near the edge of the trees. "It is there," Fraser said, "just as we hoped it would be."

Jamie looked toward the castle hugging the cliff on the edge of the North Sea. "Aye, it looks like it was described, and the location is the right distance from Wick. It has to be Kalder."

"If we only had some idea how many men he has," Fraser said.

"Let's see if we canna get a wee bit closer, so we can get some idea what we are up against," Jamie said.

"We will need to wait until after the gloaming, for the distance between here and the castle is mostly free of trees and offers us no place to hide."

When darkness finally closed in, they motioned to the men, twenty-five of the Grahams' best and most-seasoned to move forward. With Fraser and Jamie heading, they moved ahead until they were close enough for Jamie and Fraser to secret themselves among the boulders where they had a good view of the castle.

It was the perfect vantage point, for they were higher than Kalder Castle, which afforded them a good view of the keep and the bridge over the inlet where the sea curved around the back of the castle.

There did not appear to be a great many men present, but they knew there was always the possibility that a larger number than what they were seeing were inside in the barracks. "If only we could see the barracks, but it must be on the level beneath the one we see," Jamie said.

Suddenly Fraser realized something. "We can see the stables," he said.

"Aye, but what… Of course! If we can see how many horses they have, we should have a good idea how many men are present."

After two hours lying on their stomachs, trying to see and count by the light of the torches gleaming from the castle walls, Jamie said, "I feel comfortable with the last number we calculated."

"Forty-seven?" Fraser asked.

"Aye, and twenty-five o' our men, added to the element o' surprise, and I feel confident we will rout the bastards and find yer lass."

"That is the part what worries me," Fraser said, "for there is no doubt in my mind that Lord Walter wouldn't kill her the moment he realizes they are under attack."

"We need to make certain ye are one o' the first ones within the castle walls so ye can find her before he realizes we are here."

With that, they moved back to their men and outlined the plan, and then they began to move toward the castle.

As they approached the bridge, they looped around to the left side, where a thin strip of land could be walked over, so the bridge could be avoided. The wind was up and blowing in over the sea. When combined with the cold spray that rose up when the waves crashed against the cliff it rendered the air perishingly cold.

By the time they navigated their way and were within the walls of the castle, the keep was almost deserted. "I think the main body is having dinner, which is a stroke o' luck for us," Jamie said, and he waved at Niall and Calum to bring the men forward.

Tavish, who had scouted ahead of them, returned. "There are only four men I could see on the outside. Two near the stables, and one standing guard by the main door to the castle. I have a pretty good idea that the dungeon must be on the lower level, where it can be accessed from above as well as from the sea. There is one guard standing by the stairs that go down toward the porticullis. It is my guess that it also leads to the dungeon, which is where he is probably holding her."

Jamie nodded. "All right, when we move in, we will take care of the guards in the courtyard, while the main body o' men will enter the main part o' the castle. While this is happening, Fraser will go down those steps and pray all the way that is where the dungeon is, and that Claire is there."

Jamie moved back to his men and lay the plan before them, and then he moved back to where Fraser waited.

"Tavish, Calum, Niall and I will enter with ye. Ye can take the guard by the steps that lead beneath the castle, while we take care of the others. The rest o' the men will enter the castle."

Without a sound, they moved in. Without looking back to see where his brothers were, Fraser crept behind the stables and closer to the guard standing by the iron gate in front of the steps that led downward.

He picked up a pebble and tossed it against the castle wall. When the guard looked to the left where the sound came from, Fraser slipped behind him and quietly cut his throat.

He found the key to the gate on the dead man, and just as he stood and slipped it into the gate, a great shout arose behind him, which was followed by the sound of swordplay.

He opened the gate and started his descent, when one of Lord Walter's men suddenly appeared out of nowhere, his sword drawn.

Fraser, by virtue of being on the steps below the man, was at a definite disadvantage, but after several minutes of swordplay, his adversary made a bad decision to lunge and Fraser's sword caught him in the chest.

Fraser grabbed a torch from the wall and took the steps at a fast pace, then saw just ahead what had to be the dungeon.

Above him, the sound of battle rang out and he knew the main body of Grahams had encountered Lord Walter's armed guard. He withdrew the ring of keys he had taken from the guard above, and found the key that fit the dungeon door.

He was praying mightily that he would find her here, and alive.

* * *

Claire was awakened by the sound of battle above her, and she lay there listening to the clang of swords and loud shouting, interspersed with the occasional whinny of a horse.

She had no idea who was fighting Lord Walter's men but felt it must be some neighboring duke or earl, for she was certain no one knew of her whereabouts. For that reason she had ruled out the chance of rescue from the very beginning.

She heard the gate being opened and she turned her head.

Twenty-Six

The right man comes at the right time.

Italian proverb

He saw her as soon as he stepped into the dungeon, lying on a pile of straw in the corner of her tiny cell. There was precious little light, but nevertheless, it was enough light for Fraser to recognize the long skeins of fiery red hair that curled about the small form in the corner. Her back was toward him, and bits of straw were tangled in her hair, but it was Claire.

"Claire...lass..." He saw the cross she had chalked on the stones of her prison, and then he saw the words Do Not Forget—the Graham clan motto. He was choked with emotion, both for her faith and in knowing that even when she was faced with the end, she thought of him.

Aye, he would never forget. Fury, white-hot and intense, welled within him. He was sorry he took the time to have papers for Lord Walter's arrest drawn up, because he would like nothing better than to give him a sword, and then kill his miserable hide in a fair fight.

Fraser came farther into the cell and paused long

enough to shove his torch in the iron receptacle, and then he leaned his sword against the wall. He kneeled next to her, not realizing the wealth of emotion he still had for her until he placed his hand on her shoulder and felt nothing but bone. He turned her toward him and gave her a shake as he called out her name once more. "Claire…lass…"

She did not stir. He pushed the matted and tangled hair back from her face, and saw the sunken places beneath her cheekbones. Even in the stingy light, he recognized the unhealthy pallor of her skin, and the purplish-yellow tint of a bruise across her cheek, and he knew instantly where it had come from.

He was praying intensely, *Dinna let her be dead….*

"Claire…"

Her eyelids fluttered and his heart soared. Thanks be to God, she wasna dead. He noticed she kept her left hand tucked beneath her, and when he pulled it from under her body, he saw the gold wedding band he had placed on her finger when they married. He tried to open her fist, and she stirred, then said, "No… dinna…"

He pried her fingers apart and the ring slipped down her bone-thin finger, almost falling into the straw, but he caught it in time. He saw the bit of straw she wound around the band so she could keep it on her finger, and understood why she kept her hand fisted. He held the ring up and turned it as he looked inside and found the inscription he sought. I Will Defend Thee, *Ne Oublie.*

He threw back his head and fought the anguish that made him want to let forth with an agonized cry, but not wanting to frighten her, he simply said, "Why, Claire…why?" Why had she denied him the right to stand beside her, to protect her, to love and honor her as his wife?

Why had it come to this? When he realized how close he had come to losing her... Had it not been for her sister's determination to learn where Walter was taking her, and Kenna's brave ride through the night, dressed in the clothes of her dead brother...

Emotion clogged his throat and brought tears to his eyes. Claire...to see her thus.

Her eyes fluttered then closed. He called her name again, and saw her brows rise, as if she was trying to open her eyes and found the task too difficult. He gathered her in his arms and drew her close, then with a gentle shake, he said, "Claire, open your eyes. 'Tis Fraser, lass. I have come to take ye home."

The brows lifted again, only this time he found himself gazing into the same beautiful hazel eyes he feared he might never see again. He saw the despair and the resignation to her fate in their depths, and he was determined to replace that with a desire to fight and to live. He had lost her once, and God be with him, he would not lose her again.

To find her alive, when he half expected to arrive too late staggered him, and left him bereft of words. He was both overjoyed and overwhelmed with every tender feeling, every emotion he ever felt for her. He buried his face in her hair and whispered her name over and over, like a litany....

Claire...Claire...Claire...

He heard the sound of footsteps coming down the stairs, and he reached for his sword.

"Fraser, where are ye?"

Calum... He laid his sword down.

He saw the parched lips move in a wordless attempt, and he turned and called out to his brother, "Calum! In here."

The tread of boots, the ring of spurs, announced Calum's arrival. When he stepped through the open doorway, Fraser said, "I need drinking water... quickly."

When he looked back at her, he saw she had moved her hand enough that she could clutch his sleeve in her small fist, as if she wanted to be certain he was real, and if so, to hold on to him so he could not leave.

"I have come to take ye home, lass. My brothers are here with me. They are rounding up Lord Walter and his men. He will ne'er bother ye or yer sisters again."

Calum returned with the water and hovered nearby while Fraser gave her small sips. "She is bone where there ought to be flesh. See if ye can find a kitchen and something for her to eat, and send someone to scout the inside of the castle. I need to know if there is a bedchamber in the wing that is still intact."

"Would it be better to take her to an inn?"

"Aye, mayhap it would, but she is in no condition to make any more of a journey than to the nearest bed. The bastard has starved her nigh to death."

"Ye came."

"Aye, Claire, I ken I would walk barefoot through the fires of hell for ye if ye have need o' me."

She clutched his sleeve more tightly and managed a weak smile before she closed her eyes, and it brought tears to his eyes when he tried to move, and saw that even in sleep, she would not relinquish her tight grip upon his sleeve.

"I thought mayhap it would do her good to drink

this," Calum said when he returned with a cup of warm broth. "Seems Jamie caught Lord Walter when he was about to sit down to a hearty soup of barley and beef."

"And the bedchamber?"

"Niall is making the rounds now. If ye dinna need anything else, I will go back to help them secure the castle." Calum paused with a quick glance at Claire. "Do ye need any help carrying her inside?"

"No, thank ye, I can manage from here on oot."

Calum smiled. "Looks like she has a fair grip on ye."

"She has always had that," he said, "only she did not know it."

"Aye, I ken she wants to make certain ye dinna slip away. Puir lass," Calum said, and with a wink and a quick salute, he was off to find his brothers.

Fraser raised Claire to a half-sitting position. "Claire, I have some broth for ye." He held the cup to her mouth, but it took some coaxing to get her to take that first sip. "Try to drink it slowly. And drink it all. You need to regain some of your strength, ye ken."

She nodded and took another swallow. After that, she took a swallow each time he brought the cup to her lips.

She seemed better by the time she finished the last drop, and he felt a surge of happiness when she said, "How did ye find me?"

"It is a long story. I will tell ye after I get ye safely oot o' here."

Twenty-Seven

An orange on the table,
Your dress on the rug,
And you in my bed,
Sweet present of the present,
Cool of night,
Warmth of my life.

Jacques Prévert (1900-1977), French poet.
Paroles, "Alicanté"

They remained at Kalder Castle for several days, to give Claire time to regain her strength. Fraser used this time to answer Claire's questions and to give the real credit for her rescue to her sisters, especially Kenna's daring ride to Edinburgh, wearing Kendrew's clothes.

She told him about the changes in their lives after their divorce and he chastised her for not asking for his help. By the night before they were set to leave, they had discussed everything save the one thing that hung in Claire's mind.

How did Fraser feel about her?

They finished dinner a few minutes before, and Fraser walked Claire to her room. When they stopped outside her door, he asked her, "What are ye going to do, after ye return to Inchmurrin?"

"Throw Isobel's arse into the loch, if she isna already gone."

He laughed. "I ken she willna be there. I told ye I took care o' that before I left. By now the sheriff has arrested her and she awaits her fate in jail."

"I hope my sisters are all right."

"Jamie sent word to Aggie and Dermot afore he left Monleigh Castle, so they should be enjoying a reunion with yer sisters aboot now."

Fraser was standing with one arm propped against the wall, the rest of his body leaning on it. When they lapsed into silence she took advantage of the lull to study his profile. Like his brothers, Fraser was a good man, with a strong sense of family pride. He was honest and forthright, and she knew that his name would one day be written in the history books, for there was no doubt in her mind that Fraser would be anything but one of the best lawyers Scotland had ever known.

"What are ye thinking?"

"That ye will be a great and verra famous lawyer. What are ye thinking?"

"That ye are showing promise, and one day, yer clan will speak o' the Countess o' Errick and Mains with pride in their voices."

"Ye are making light o' me," she said.

He turned and took her in his arms. "Claire Lennox, there is not one little red hair on yer head that I take lightly, ye ken? Why do I have to keep making that point clear to ye?"

She wrinkled up her nose. "Mayhap I simply like hearing ye repeat it."

He pulled her tightly into his embrace. "I swore to myself that I wouldna do this, but I seem to have a weakness for a lass with violently red hair and a saucy nature."

"Violently red? Did ye say my hair is violently red?"

"Claire, will ye be quiet long enough for me to kiss ye?"

She snapped her mouth closed and relished in the most beautiful sound in the entire world—Fraser Graham's laugh. She should have known better. She was, after all, a smart woman, so she attributed it to her lack of experience and her inadequacy when it came to such things as having the ability to discern the sensuality behind Fraser's slow, lazy smile.

He took both her hands in his and drew them to his lips and kissed them softly—first one palm, then the other. Naturally, it had the appropriate devastating effect, and everything internal collapsed faster than a house made of playing cards. Inside, she felt positively molten.

He pushed her sleeves up, allowing his fingers to caress the sensitive skin of her wrists, where her pulse beat the strongest. "In spite o' everything, I still miss ye."

Claire's heart pounded and she opened her mouth to speak, and sneezed instead. Another sneeze followed that one.

"A healthy sneeze for one so small."

"Size can be deceptive, and some small things can be verra exciting."

"Careful," he said.

Tears banked in her eyes. "Oh, Fraser, I am so verra

sorry for everything horrible I did to ye, and I hope ye can forgive me for it."

Her next words died in her throat when Fraser's lips covered hers tenderly. With slow languor, he trailed kisses over her skin, drawing her out of herself and into him.

When she leaned into his kiss and their bodies aligned, Fraser opened the door to her room and led her inside. He leaned against the door and drew her to him.

She saw the way his gaze drifted from her face to the bed. Her heart began to pound. If he was contemplating the bed, he just might be tempted beyond himself to make love to her.

So, why was he standing there as if he were a decoration—which he was, of course, because she wanted him to decorate the space on the bed, with her next to him.

She lifted her face to his. He kissed her lightly, then took her hand. "I have a better idea."

He led her to the bed and lay down beside her. He rolled on his side so that he was lying half across her, with his top leg nestled between hers. While he kissed her, his hand deftly unfastened several buttons to allow his hand to slide inside, where he caressed her breast, then took the nipple between his fingers, before he replaced them with his mouth, alternately sucking and pulling it between his teeth.

She felt the contracting response between her legs and they moved apart at the slightest pressure from his legs. His hand ran over her skirt and pulled it upward, higher, and higher yet.

She gasped when he slipped his fingers inside her.

He kissed her long and hard, while his hand drove her on and on toward the edge. "I want to look at ye," he said, and pulled her skirt higher.

She was breathing heavily, yet languid and relaxed beneath his warm gaze. She was lost in her own world of mounting pleasure, when Fraser whispered, "Raise yer hips."

She did as he asked, and realized he was removing her drawers, so that nothing touched the lower half of her body, save his gaze. She felt his mouth kissing her and her legs moved farther apart in an unconscious movement. She heard a groan, half recognizing it came from her. Time and again he kissed her, deeply and tantalizing, until she writhed and begged him to keep going, only to say the next moment, "I canna stand it, Fraser. Stop."

He raised himself up on one arm, while the heel of his palm continued to torture her, then it moved away. "Ye are so beautiful here, where everything comes together in the colors of a rainbow."

She seemed to lose herself after that, as time became like beads strung on a chain, stacking against one another. She tried to grasp the moment as dizzy seconds passed, but although she reached for it, she couldn't quite sort who she was, and where she was, and whom she was with, and what it all meant in relation to the sun, the earth and two people in search of answers. Only jagged moments sliced into her consciousness, and visions of Fraser's dark, beautiful hair, a glimpse of candlelight, the thunderous sound of a powerful wave crashing headlong against the rugged crags of mountains rising out of the sea.

I love ye, Fraser. I love ye.... I love ye.... I love ye....

And I dinna ken why I canna say that to yer face. Surely ye must ken how I feel. Canna ye see it in my eyes? Canna ye hear it in my voice? Canna ye tell me ye love me? I am so close to ye, and yet so far away.

He remained where he was, with his hand behind her neck, and she thought that any moment now, he was going to kiss her again, but when a rather inordinate amount of time passed, she sighed and closed her eyes.

She heard him chuckle. He lifted her hand and kissed it. "The choice is yers, Claire. Do I go or stay?"

He seemed to be in possession of an inordinate amount of patience, but at last he said, "Claire, do ye have a preference? Is yer silence a yea or a nay? Or are ye afraid to make a decision? I never figured ye for a weakling."

"Oh, Fraser, I am so verra afraid to ever make another decision. I have made too many bad ones. Sometimes I feel like I must be going crazy."

His features softened. "No, Claire, ye are not going crazy. Never ye." His arm went around her, and she flopped against him as if she were stuffed with cornstalks.

He stroked her arm, and neither of them said anything for a while. She inhaled and released a deep breath. Having him here beside her lifted all the weight she felt bearing down upon her. "I am glad ye are here, Fraser."

She pegged her feelings as a mixture of admiration and gratitude, so she was unaware, at first, of exactly what was going on between them. It wasn't until she looked into the blue depths of his eyes that she felt the zing of a current of emotional transference between them, and she identified it by its name: awareness.

The teasing banter, the jovial play on words vanished, and taking its place was a fully charged thunderbolt of intense desire. She was melting from the look in his eyes. She did not know where they were going from here, but she knew where they would end up, and she wanted it, had wanted it for so very long. There were no obstacles, or fears, or thoughts of a failed marriage in their past. There was only now. He had come without her asking, at a moment when she needed him most. She loved him so much, her heart hurt.

"Claire…"

The husky raggedness of his voice as he whispered her name sent ripples of exquisite pleasure washing over her. The next thing she knew, he shifted his position so he was leaning over her, his face mere inches above her own. He covered her face with kisses, time and again, as if he had been commanded to leave no place un-kissed.

She was melting again and was barely conscious of him pulling it away. A ripple of excitement followed the chills. Her heart was pounding hard; she wondered if it would stop from pure exhaustion. As if he knew, his hand came to rest on the place between her breasts, where her heart beat the strongest.

"Does yer heart beat for me, Claire? Do ye feel the same excitement I feel when I touch ye?"

"It always did, and it does now," she said. She groaned when he lay his head between her breasts and listened a moment, before he shifted slightly and began to kiss her breasts, her belly, and lower. His hands were spread across her waist, his thumbs circling and teasing her skin to acute sensitivity, then moving lower to trace the sunken valley beneath the bones of her hips.

She shuddered and sucked in her breath. What he was doing? It was agony. It was ecstasy. She could not remember him taking so much time, and paying so much attention to each little part of her, touching, kissing, loving, until she thought she could spend the rest of her life lying beneath his spell.

After a while she began to think he did it on purpose, that he knew he was driving her wild with wanting him, and yet he continued, touching just the right spot and moving so agonizingly slow that she wanted to scream from the torment and the pleasure of anticipation.

He was so thorough and calculating that she almost smiled, thinking he was a lawyer, and he had to be certain he had everything right before he proceeded to the next point. She never remembered that he kissed her feet before, and never, did she think, did he do so to the back of her knees. Was there a place on her anywhere that he missed? She was doubtful, and vowed even if there was, she was not going to tell him. So ready she was now for the mating, she was growing impatient. Faith, if she had the equipment he had, she would have flipped him on his back and had her way with him, but such was not her role.

She could inspire poetry, but she couldn't write it.

Claire was at a point she had never reached before, and she wanted him with an intensity that almost frightened her, so strong it was. "Please, Fraser, I want ye."

"I ken ye do, love, but ye must be patient. We dinna want to leave anything oot."

He began to kiss a trail from her throat, over her breasts, her belly, and then he was only inches from the juncture of her thighs. Instinctively, she tried to draw her legs together.

"Oh, no, ye arena going to miss the best part," he said, burying his face against her.

"Oh..." She could not go on. Her stomach knotted and something inside her felt as if pressure was building and building, and she writhed beneath him, trapped in the exquisiteness of it, until she heard him groan and something inside her shattered.

She dug her fingers into his hair. "No more...I canna breathe...."

"We arena even halfway there yet."

"I willna live that long, Fraser. Ye are going to kill me."

"No, but I will in a moment," he said, and he lifted his body ever so slightly and brought his face up to hers, and took her lips in a deep, plunging kiss that perfectly mimicked the movement of his hips when he thrust himself into her.

She clutched his shoulders. It had been so long, the feeling was foreign to her now, and she was so tight. But after a few thrusts, everything seemed to work perfectly together, like a mechanism so intricately designed and built with precision until the parts functioned together as a whole.

Whatever you called it, he was a master at the execution, and he had her moaning and whispering his name and shamelessly telling him not to stop. And then suddenly, she could not speak anymore, and her body followed the urging of his, until they moved as one.

Her hands stroked the satin smoothness of his back, and down over the hard musculature of his buttocks, so well sculpted and surging with power. The body was truly a marvelous thing, and the capabilities of it were limitless. She found pleasure both in what he was doing, and what they did together, as well as the little excursions of exploration she made on her own.

And then she was hit with a powerful wave of feeling that made her toes dig into the bed. It was much stronger and more powerful than the shattering-glass feeling she felt earlier. This was a deep and intense wrenching of feeling, where her body felt as if it was pushing away from itself. She wanted to encompass him and draw him into her, and keep him there, for she knew this was the moment of complete and perfect union, when they were truly joined and committed, in agreement, each giving and receiving the pleasure and the joy.

Her wild and frantic breathing finally began to taper off. Her body gleamed with sweat. She was too weak to move, but Fraser's arm lay along the side of her cheek, and she turned her head to kiss the soft skin there.

She should not have done this. She was wrong to couple with him, because she had found the answer to the question she had been too afraid to put to herself. She still loved him; in truth, she had never stopped loving him. Only now, after the loving, she knew her love had reached a depth and breadth she had never known.

How, she wondered, could she pick up and go on without him in her life? He would go back to Edinburgh and the law practice he spent years educating himself for, and she would return to Loch Lomond and her beloved Inchmurrin Island. Everything would be the same; only for her, nothing would ever be the same again.

He lowered his head, and drew circles on her cheek with his nose. "If ye were no' such a scrawny lass, I would make love to ye again."

"Mayhap I could be more passive this time…to conserve my energy, ye ken."

He threw back his head and laughed. "Claire… Claire…I have missed ye and yer funny ways. No one has ever made me laugh the way ye do."

Her heart wrenched. She ached to hear him say he loved her; that he wanted them to try to find the magic they had before. She knew he cared for her still, for Fraser was not the kind of man who made love indiscriminately. There had to be feeling in it for him.

Epilogue

MIRANDA: *I am your wife, if you will marry me;*
If not, I'll die your maid: to be your fellow
You may deny me; but I'll be your servant
Whether you will or no.
FERDINAND: *My mistress, dearest;*
And thus I humble ever.
MIRANDA: *My husband then?*
FERDINAND: *Ay, with a heart as willing*
As bondage e'er of freedom: here's my hand.
MIRANDA: *And mine, with my heart in't.*

William Shakespeare (1564-1616), English
poet and playwright.
The Tempest (1611), act 3, scene 1

Fraser was never certain if it was merely lust, or the knowledge that this might well be the last time he ever made love to her, that drove him to see, taste and feel every possible part and place of her.

He wanted to see her the way God made her, and he eased the rest of her dress from her. Her skin was as white and gleaming as a pearl, and the glossy curtain of her hair spread like a scarlet cape. She was every beautiful woman written into a poem, each exquisite form captured by an artist's eye, and yet no mortal could have painted her more beautiful than she was to him at this moment.

He kissed her and kept on kissing her, with his hands torturing her breasts and his hips joined in perfect movement against hers. He loved her more now than he had before, when he thought it impossible to go beyond the love he felt in his heart. His lips yearned to whisper about his tender feelings for her, and the depth and breadth of his feeling, and the agony of loving someone so much, and yet being afraid to open your heart to show them what lay within.

So he tried to show her without words, as if she could absorb the meaning of each touch, every move, the disconnected staccato of each breath.

He kissed his way down between her breasts and across her stomach, until he found the place he sought between her legs. "Sleek as an otter, slick as gloss, as slippery as a snowy track. Ye are the satin petal of a flower, the silk on a butterfly wing. Ye are so perfectly formed, Claire, that each time I look at ye, I feel as though some of my life is sucked oot o' me."

He lowered his full weight upon her and sheathed himself with a powerful thrust, as far as he could go inside her. "No matter what," he said, "ye will remember this day for the rest o' yer life."

He came at her again and again, in a fierce hammering, driving to the hilt each time, as if each movement, every stroke was a message to be deciphered, and a way to show his power and supremacy over her. They were joined by the sweat of their bodies, and she saw his dark hair was wet with sweat, his body and face gleaming from exertion. Her legs ached, and she could feel the mark of bruises to come, but he showed no sign of stopping, nor proof that he was tired at all.

Again and again, with smooth repetition, as if he was asking the same question over and over, and throwing the answer back at her when it was not the one he wanted. The pain she felt crossed a threshold and pleasure slipped into place. "Oh..." The words jammed in her throat dissolved into short, gasping pants as she moved to his rhythm, wanting him faster, harder, deeper, until she could feel the joining of their souls.

"Aye," he said, "ye will not forget this day's work, lass, and stay with ye it will, for I will not stop until I ken ye are completely mine."

He lifted her legs over his shoulders, so he could go beyond the point he had reached before. His mouth covered hers, not with the gentle, coaxing kisses as before, but with a kiss that was demanding and urgent. Her lips felt as if they might split, and she bit his lip and, a moment later, tasted his blood.

She was wild beneath him. Her hands raked and clawed his back, then lower, where she clawed the hard curve of his buttocks. Once or twice she felt his bite on her neck, and his teeth pulling her earlobe until it stretched with...was it pleasure or pain? She could not tell anymore. The lines were blurring, and all the colors of the world were running together, until there were no lines, no beginning and no end.

She heard him moan and cry out a curse, and she fought him, fearing he wanted to draw her completely into him, and feeling the need to do the same to him. "Dinna stop, Fraser, dinna ever stop."

She would have thought further upon it, but the fierceness, the hard edge to him now made her lift her hips and not receive him gently, but to meet him equally, thrust for thrust, until her whole body knotted and coiled into itself, and she cried out with spasm after clutching spasm, wanting him to stop, needing him to continue, and wishing this moment could go on forever.

He called out in Gaelic, and she vaguely recognized the sound of her name, and then she lost herself in him and knew by giving him what he wanted, she got back the same. She heard his groan, then felt the weight of him collapse fully upon her.

She was not sure if she passed out or went to sleep, but at some point she was barely cognizant of his weight rolling away from her, and his arm drawing her close against him, as if he needed to separate from her in gradual intervals.

When he kissed the top of her head, she sighed and curled closer against him, with one arm tucked under her chin and the other lying across his chest, her fingers moving in slow, careless circles and a lopsided oval that slipped in from time to time.

Her eyes opened to see if he was awake, and she was greeted by the deep blue of his teasing eyes. A faint smile curled lazily to lift the corners of his mouth. There was a question there, she knew, but she was not going to make the first move.

"Was this a contest?" she finally asked, wanting to force him to be the one to speak of it. "More important, was there a winner, or did it end in a draw?"

"You tell me."

He knew the game too well, and he was well schooled on his defenses. She decided it would do no good to push, so she let it go, as one would cut the line and watch the fish too big to land swim slowly out to sea.

He did not say anything, but he did stretch out and fold his arms beneath his head, flaunting his wares as if he were daring her to ignore that which he knew some women would scratch her eyes out to have. He pulled her against him and cradled her close. Yet he said not a word.

Hurt feelings welled within her, and she felt slighted by his callous disregard that made her feel like a common camp follower, who gave her body for use, and not lovemaking, and when it had been used well and then ignored, she dressed quietly and slipped away.

She decided to get up and made a move to do so, but he stayed her with a detaining hand.

"Why would ye wish to leave me?" he asked, slipping his arms around her. "The lying together afterward is the best part, ye ken. I am sorry if I was too rough with ye, Claire."

"I got in my fair share of it," she replied. "How is your lip?"

He touched his lip gingerly. Already a lump had appeared. "It announced its existence some time ago. I ken it will be around long enough for us to become well acquainted."

"Weel, 'tis yer own fault, ye ken."

"I wouldna change anything about it. I like it when ye draw the battle lines and refuse to retreat."

"Come here," he said. "Bide with me for a while."

He tugged on her arm and she dug in her heels, so to speak, still smarting from her hurt feelings.

He shook his head and caught her up in his arms and pulled her back to lie beside him. He caught her chin and lifted her face to receive his kiss, but she pulled back. "I canna make love again, Fraser."

"I didna ask ye to, Claire." His lips were warm and soft, and so very gentle she wanted to cry. He cuddled her against him, talking to her in that soothing tone that vibrated through her, while his hands showed her a gentle touch could be as arousing as its stronger, more forceful brother.

She buried her face in the crook of his shoulder and slipped her hand around his neck. So many things she wanted to say to him, and would have, if he had only given her some glimmer of hope. But he had not, and she let her pride get in the way.

It was sad to realize that this separation was more painful than the first, because this time she felt the bite of finality, and knew this would be the last time she would ever be with him like this.

It was over. The end had come.

The rush of passion in their blood had slowed to a creep, and the sensation of being near each other did not send ripples of desire pricking at their nerves, or cause the quickening of each indrawn breath. Her heart was sick, her body weary, and the wheels of her mind turned ever so slow.

All things hastened toward their end. To draw the final moment out would be the worst thing to do. When the time for ending arrived, it was best if done quickly.

There came a time when the candle must be

doused, and the fire put out; a day when the last rose of summer resides in the garden alone, and the waves rolling toward the sandy shore will erase the footprints left there.

Her heart was breaking and she feared she would start to cry. She did not want him to see her like this, or to know the depth of her love and feeling for him. "We have an early day tomorrow. I need to sleep, and so do ye."

"Are ye telling me I need to leave ye now?"

"Aye."

"Why so cold a tone, when ye were so verra warm a moment ago?"

Tears slid across her cheeks, and she almost hated him for doing this to her. "I am no made o' stone, Fraser. I have a heart, and it can be broken, the same as yers. There are many wounds I carry, and it is time I saw to the healing o' them. I will always be grateful for what ye have done, and will never think unkindly o' ye. But I canna lie her beside ye any longer."

"Why?"

She was crying in earnest now. "Why are ye doing this? Are ye trying to punish me for the hurt I caused ye? Would it please ye and salvage yer wounds if I gave ye my wrist and asked ye to draw blood? What do ye want from me? Tell me and I will gladly give it to ye, and then we can have done with the suffering and the torture. End it. I beg ye. Tell me what ye want."

"Is it so verra difficult to figure oot? Can ye not see I want nothing more from ye than I ever wanted? I want yer love, Claire, and yer heart, and yer promise to love me until ye die, and beyond that even, if it be possible."

She began to pound him with her fists. "Then why didna ye tell me afore now? Why did ye torment me and leave me hanging?"

"Because I had to know how ye felt, Claire. Ye are not the only one who carries scars, ye ken?"

A calm settled over her and she relaxed against him. "What happens now?"

"Weel, I ken we will leave in the morning."

"And?"

"We will travel toward Inchmurrin, with one stop in Wick before we continue on."

"Wick? What is in Wick?"

"A minister, I hope."

"A minister? Fraser, are ye planning that we should marry again?"

"Aye, and this time it is for good, for I willna be giving ye a second divorce, Claire, so ye better be making up yer mind afore we reach Wick."

"Oh, Fraser, my mind was made up when I heard ye call oot my name in the dungeon."

Two classic holiday stories from
New York Times bestselling author

DEBBIE MACOMBER

THE CHRISTMAS BASKET

More than ten years ago, high school sweethearts Noelle McDowell and Thomas Sutton planned to elope–until he jilted her. This Christmas, Noelle is home to celebrate the holidays, and to see if the decades-old rivalry between their mothers stands in the way of a second chance together.

THE SNOW BRIDE

It's a month before Christmas and Jenna Campbell's flying to Alaska to marry a man she met on the Internet–until her seatmate takes it upon himself to change her plans. Now she's stranded in tiny Snowbound, Alaska, alone with Reid Jamison, and then there's a blizzard.... Maybe she'll be a Christmas bride after all!

No one tells a Christmas story like Debbie Macomber!

Available the first week of November 2004 wherever paperbacks are sold!

www.MIRABooks.com

MDM2110

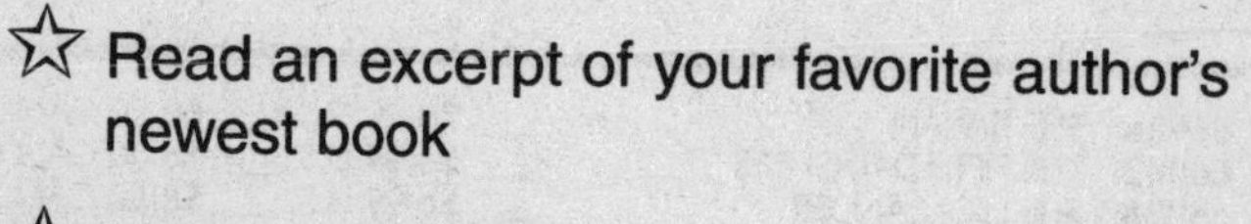